A PROMISED PLACE

-- A NOVEL --

Written by: J. Marie

A PROMISED PLACE by J. Marie
Copyright 2019, J. Marie

www.jmariebooks.com

Cover art by Kelley Nemitz & Katie Eney 2019

1969, January

So - here I am, Lord. I turn once again to you because where else can I turn? I am at the end of myself and my ability to cope. I simply cannot turn off the questions that torment me.

I ask myself, how did I get here? What happened? At which point should I have turned right instead of left? Was there a point in my life that I could have changed the story?

Because this right here? As hard as I try to see it differently, this feels like The End.

CHAPTER 1

2017, March

The post- 7pm Los Altos sun was taking its time setting over the California hills that evening. It hung in the sky for long, delicious minutes as it resisted the inevitable sacrifice it would soon make to the waters of the Pacific just beyond the rolling hills and trees of the Portola Valley.

Lauryn watched her husband as he paced back and forth through lazy streaks of sunshine that shimmered across their deck. It was another work call. She could tell by the way he tensed up with anticipation as he read the number and then headed outside, ditching her and their dinner without a second glance.

As she added her dinner plate to the dishwasher and covered his uneaten dinner with plastic wrap, she glanced outside again. Still deep in conversation, he now stood with his back towards her and ran his hands through his dark hair with reflexive habit. A few months ago, he'd mentioned to her that he was thinking of cutting his hair short again, but Lauryn had convinced him not to. She loved his hair long, almost touching his shoulders.

There were lots of things about Elliott that she loved, and her thoughts wandered along unabated as she wiped the rim of her water glass. She loved his laugh, deep and mellow, and the way she fit "just right" when he hugged her, near his chin and against his heart. As she watched him hang up his call and turn towards the house with a small, self-satisfied smile, her heart melted, and she thought of a few others. Yeah, his hair was just one of many reasons she loved her husband.

He opened the glass door that led from the deck into the kitchen, crossed the space between them in a few purposeful strides and stopped once he reached her by the kitchen counter, all without saying a word.

"What?" She finally asked him. Still silent, he took the dish towel out of her hands and pulled her gently towards the living room couch, "What, Elliott?" Lauryn laughed as she stumbled over his feet and plopped down unceremoniously onto the soft cushions as he landed next to her.

"Oh, it's nothing much." He said in a low, teasing voice, "Just something I have to tell you."

With his comment, Elliott wound his arm around her shoulders and snuggled her deeper into the plush velvet. Laughing as the movement of his arm pulled her long hair haphazardly across her face, he continued, "So what do you say, Mrs. Grant? Are you ready to leave behind all this California sunshine and head north again?"

Lauryn swept the loose waves of blonde hair out of her eyes and tried to sit up straighter. In her confusion and hesitant disbelief, she wasn't sure she'd heard him correctly. Could it be real this time?

"Get outta here-" She said, her voice tense with excitement as she pushed him away so she could look him in the eyes, "Don't tease now. Are you serious about it this time?"

Lauryn's fingers gripped at his forearm which was tightly ribbed and tan from the hours of bike rides in the California hills, while her eyes searched his eyes earnestly, doubtfully. After all, they'd been here before.

Over the past few years, he had other offers to sell the business; but each time, he'd dropped out before they got to the finish line. She'd always hoped if, or when, he ever sold his company maybe they could move back home. Could this finally be their chance?

Their life growing up in Minnesota, before they were married a few years ago and decided to make California their home, was beginning to feel like a fuzzy, distant memory. Because their families still lived in Minnesota, they tried to make it back there for major events and holidays. But, each time they boarded the plane after those visits, bound for California again, their new "home," Lauryn would take hold of Elliott's hand, squeeze it tightly, and will herself to remember that wherever he was, that was where she was happiest. He was her home.

She had lived without his physical presence in her life for those five long years when he came out to California first for college and then stayed for his career. Now, life without him? Well, it was incomprehensible. She would always want to be with him, even if it meant living in a city that never felt the magic of snow at Christmas.

"Yes, I am serious, Lauryn. It's why I've been so preoccupied lately and that phone call I just took was our attorney telling me they agreed to our terms. This time it's going to happen. In fact, it's a done deal. We sign the papers this Friday."

The rich brown flecks in his gold-green eyes seemed to sparkle in the setting sunlight that filtered through the window and he casually smoothed some of the stray hairs that still grazed her cheek.

"I love you so much," He said, "And this is the right offer, it's the right time. I know you don't think I want this, but I do," He kissed her softly on the mouth before he sighed with an intoxicating contentment and said, "I *want* to sell it."

Lauryn realized that she was holding her breath, having waited for years for him to reach this decision and to say this. And, while it was a happy day to know they would be free to move now, it was an incredibly sad day as well. He was finally letting go of his video gaming company, EL Go. The company - which he had started in his bedroom as a teenager - was so much more than a way to make money; it was his baby.

"After all these years," Lauryn was dropping deeper into his gaze, thinking about all the time he'd spent building his business, "It's been such a ride and I'm so proud of you. Congratulations, Mr. Tech Titan." Breaking the gaze, she leaned towards him with a mischievous grin and kissed him, enjoying the slow tingle across her lips at the touch of his mustache and neatly trimmed beard.

Then, she sat back suddenly and searched his eyes again, a million questions and what-ifs exploded in her mind all at once.

"You know, this all sounds good - that you found the right buyer and all that - but, won't it drive you crazy without all the creativity and the constant activity? I mean, your employees are our friends. It's all you've known for so many years."

"I know, but it's not like it's a shock to everyone at EL Go. They're all aware that I've been in talks," He assured her, "And, I think everyone will be supportive because the employees go along with the deal and they will get better benefits than I was able to give."

"But, do they think you will go along with them to the new company?" Lauryn asked.

"No, I've been upfront that the best deal would be one where I'm out, like a clean break. I've told them it's not in me to keep doing this for someone else. I think they understand."

"So, how much time will you give to the transition?"

"Six months on the outside. We'll get through these two new game releases and then they will go it on their own. I know they will be great."

"And, then what will you do?" She couldn't picture Elliott without a cell phone in his hand, making decisions, up all night dreaming up new games and solving company problems.

"Are you trying to ask me what I'm going to do all day? What, do you think I'm going to just lay around here and be lazy?" He poked her ribs with his elbow.

Laughing, he continued slowly, his face turning serious, "No. In fact, I have another career in mind. I'm thinking of applying for a job with this woman I know. She's got this great home renovation company. She's super-smart and super-hot ... and I think she likes me. Pretty sure I've got the job locked down already." He smiled wider as he spoke and moved closer as he glanced towards her mouth.

"Oh?" Lauryn pushed back against his chest, "And, what makes you think you're qualified for that job? You can't even hammer a nail in straight. If it's the same woman I know, I think she hires carpenters, not software gurus."

Lauryn laughed skeptically at the thought of him working alongside her on the job site. Renovating these houses was a big deal and frequently she felt way over her head and was searching for a full-time carpenter right now. She needed help all right, but she couldn't see how Elliott, who had proven himself to be the exact opposite of "handy around the house," could be of any help to her in that regard.

"Ha, you might be right," He conceded meekly, "But I happen to know she also needs someone to help with videography and social media - someone who can up her game a little. You know, she needs to stay relevant. She needs someone with skills." Elliott raised his eyebrows suggestively and pulled her closer again.

"Are you telling me that my videos are boring?" Stiffening in his arms, Lauryn's brow turned down into a frown as she thought about the home renovation company that she had started two years ago.

It had all started with a tip from one of Elliott's co-workers about an older home that needed quite a bit of work but had great potential. After a few days, Lauryn had finally convinced Elliott that they should buy the house, give up their lease on their apartment and live in it while she worked through the renovations. After negotiating with him that they would fix the second story first before they moved in - so he could have a clean place to sleep and work - they made the deal and started the job.

Lauryn found that living in a house while renovating it is as difficult as everyone says it is, but the moments of frustration were always surpassed by the moments of elation as she uncovered the craftsmanship throughout the old house, and along the way she found history of previous owners which made the project even more magical for her.

It was this first project that became the inspiration for naming her company My House, and the video logs of her work during the project were the inspiration for her web page and YouTube channel.

After the renovation was complete and the home sold within a week of listing it, they moved out and she moved on to a second project. And, although they chose not to live in the second project home and instead moved into their condo, her business My House was born, and she tried to recreate the same feeling, the same energy, with each renovation.

A fresh approach and unique designs were key to her target customers who were typically younger, many of them first-time home buyers. Most were drawn to her work through social media, Pinterest and word of mouth and the hard work seemed to be paying off. Referrals for potential flip homes were coming in weekly, many of them from other locations around the country, three were even from Minnesota.

Now that Elliott's plan to sell his business was certain, she wondered belatedly, what would be the impact on her business? She sat up straighter, her full attention on her business and the next steps that would have to take place. Suddenly overwhelmed by how different her life could look a month from now, Lauryn found herself going numb in her mind.

"You've talked about selling for so long that it's almost like I didn't think it would happen," she said. "I don't know what it means for My House."

"Well, that's up to you. It's the kind of business you can do anywhere, right? Here, or in Minnesota, or wherever you want. And, seriously, I would enjoy working with you on My House for a while. Until I figure out what my next move is."

"But, what about that?" She turned towards him anxiously, "Your next move, I mean. Don't get me wrong, I would love having you follow me around with a camera all day, but that's temporary. Where do you want to live? Where do you need to live to find your next move?"

"Lauryn," Elliott's voice was soothing and calm, "I just need to be with you. The sale for EL Go is structured over a few years, so it will take care of us financially. Plus, I have the sideline investments. We will be fine. So, if you want to stay here, I want to stay here. If you want to move back to Minnesota, I want to move back to Minnesota." He paused a moment, then continued slowly, holding her gaze for emphasis as he took her fingers in his hand and rubbed the backs of them softly, "It's up to you, Mrs. Grant."

Lauryn thought for a moment, the pictures of the three homes in Minnesota flashing through her mind, and soon she was seeing visions of their future. And, her visions didn't look at all like California.

"Well, then, I think I'd like a white Christmas this year." She smiled at him and pulling her fingers from his hands, she reached around his neck and threaded them through his hair as she kissed him. Happily, she remembered again all the reasons she loved him, and named them in her head as she drifted along.

After a moment, the thought interrupted the reverie like a slow-moving current, not always front and center, but nevertheless, always there. Lauryn pulled away from his kiss and looked deep into her husband's eyes, hoping to find his full support for the other hopes she had for their future.

"Elliott, I'm thinking this type of change might be good for us in other ways too maybe-" She began cautiously.

He must have known from her tone of voice what she meant; she didn't have to say the words explicitly. Elliott's eyes shadowed and his mouth took on that downward turn she was familiar with when she raised the subject.

But she just couldn't help it. How could they discuss their future together without discussing a baby?

She did it even though the subject was fraught with pain – memories of celebratory announcements, dreams of baby showers and nurseries – all of these, ending in pain. And lonely, doubt-wracked disappointment. Carrying three babies, their life force each beating inside her, and then losing each precious one.

"Lauryn, please let's not start that again." He dropped his arms and Lauryn noticed his shoulders slumped inward as if he was protecting himself.

"I know, I know. All I'm saying is that maybe it will be good? You know, something might happen, and it will be good next time."

Elliott sighed deeply as he pulled away from her and with his elbows on his knees, he rubbed his eyes with long fingers and then looked at her again, smiling a weak, thin smile.

"Yeah, hon, maybe next time it will be good." He turned his face away then and while he gazed out the window at the setting California sun, he disappeared. As she watched him, quietly absorbing all that was going on inside him, Lauryn wished she hadn't brought it up at all.

Later that evening, still basking in the glow of their telephone calls back to Minnesota to tell their families the exciting news of the sale of EL Go, Elliott stood at his sink brushing his teeth, as he watched Lauryn wash her face at her sink next to his. Her hair was pulled back from her face with a terry cloth headband and she was dressed for bed in a faded gray t-shirt top which looked a size too small and white pajama pants with thin red stripes which looked a size too large. But still, he found himself catching his breath whenever he looked at her, really looked at her.

He had loved his wife since they were kids. He knew the light spattering of freckles across her nose and cheeks and the arch of her pretty eyebrows like the back of his hand, but he didn't realize what this love truly was, he didn't realize the depth of it, until they were adults. That was when God had finally blessed him with the "grand revelation" and if he had waited to say something to her, this life together, as a married couple, might never have happened at all.

Elliott's memory of that idyllic summer weekend was vivid, full sensory and 3D – it was the weekend of Lauryn's brother Daniel and his wife Madison's wedding. Often in the years since, snippets of it still flashed through his mind – the way Lauryn's long, curly hair was gathered to the side the night of the groom's dinner, the way she seemed to float in that dark blue dress the day of the wedding and how it made her eyes seem even deeper blue, the perfume she wore – just all of it, clear and unforgettable.

It was that weekend where Elliott figured it all out and then was compelled to tell Lauryn how he truly felt about her – before he lost her to another guy she'd been seriously dating. In hindsight, Elliott couldn't say he was completely shocked, but he knew he would be eternally blessed, when she told him she felt the same about him.

So many mind-blowing, truly life-changing, things were revealed that weekend. Not only did he figure out what he felt for Lauryn and what she felt for him, but even more importantly, Elliott figured out what he felt about his Savior. *That* life-changing revelation was inspired by his mother who, at that time, was probably the least likely person on the planet to hold any sway over Elliott and the path his life would take.

His mother Rebecca was addicted to drugs and alcohol. He could say the words now, but for many years, he could not form the syllables and speak them out loud. With his mother, his early childhood was fraught with neglect. Moving from one sketchy, unsafe place to another, drugs, alcohol and abusive people became as commonplace in his childhood as cereal and television.

Although he'd never told anyone this, her addiction, and her lifestyle, was so bad that there were many times he found himself envisioning his mom in a casket. Sometimes he would wake up dreaming about it, because that was how severe it was, that's how far gone she was. Elliott rationalized that if he went to worst-case scenario, he could somehow prepare himself for losing her for good. It was like, Okay, next time she's not coming back. Ever again.

His father had never been part of the picture, so when his mother was faced with an extended incarceration for a repeat drug and alcohol offense when he was thirteen, Elliott had been forced to move to his grandparents' farm outside Lake Belle, Minnesota, where he met Lauryn and her family. And, he never lived with his mother again.

But then, when she found herself in the depths of hell on earth, his mother finally found a treatment center that worked for her. This one focused on whole person healing - mind, body and spirit - through Jesus Christ. Hearing her speak her testimony that Sunday morning after Daniel's wedding shook something in Elliott and from that point forward, he was mired less and less in the tortured history between the two of them and flourished more and more in his relationship with Jesus Christ.

Now more than three years later, while they still struggled to understand and accept each other because they had missed out on so many formative years together, Elliott was learning to truly accept his mother's sobriety was authentic. All because he was witnessing her faith in God - her reliance on God - was authentic.

Elliott found that his mother's transformation deepened his own faith in radical ways. For him, it was like all the stars suddenly aligned and his mind was blown away by the depth of it. He thrived in a different stream now and he lived life more fully, more confident in his faith and with a different purpose somehow.

And, along with all that, his life with Lauryn finally became whole. Living their lives as a couple, after spending so many years together as best friends, was a real mind-bender for most of their family and acquaintances. But, for Lauryn and him, it was all by instinct – like breathing - naturally leading to their marriage. And, now, here they were three years later.

As he watched his wife in the mirror and the many memories of his life with her seeped through him, he smiled from somewhere deep inside, still unable to grasp all that he felt.

He loved her beyond words. She was his partner in every way.

"What?" She smiled back at him in the mirror as she patted the water off her fresh face with a hand towel, "You've got that look on your face again."

He laughed at her blunt statement as he rinsed his mouth and replaced his toothbrush on the holder. Thank you, God, for my wife, he thought. Was that "the look" she was talking about? He realized that he must wear that look a lot.

"And, what look is that?" He regarded her in the mirror, loving the way her blue eyes twinkled when she smiled. With Lauryn, a smile was genuine; it always traveled up from her mouth and ended in her eyes.

"I don't know," She answered, "Kind of like - bemused, I'd say."

"Oh, okay. Well, interesting word choice. I'd call it my I'm-in-love-with-my-wife look, but you can call it bemused if you like." He smiled as he hung the towel on the hook next to his sink and leaned back against the counter, pulling her gently towards him until she was wrapped in his arms.

"I love you, Lauryn. I'm just standing here thinking tonight how much God has blessed me. More than I could ever have imagined. You, the business, mom's recovery, just everything." Elliott pulled lightly at the headband that held back Lauryn's blonde hair until it released the waves to play through his fingers and he looked into his wife's bottomless blue eyes that still carried a hint of hesitant sadness after their conversation earlier that evening, "And, I know he will bless us with a baby too. We just have to trust his timing."

She leaned into him then and laid her head on his chest, sighing heavily while she nodded. A sudden sense of protection overwhelmed him as he glanced up towards the ceiling debating with himself over their continued expectations that God was going to bless them with a baby. She was so insistent on that being the only satisfactory outcome but all he was certain about was that he didn't want anything to hurt her ever again.

These miscarriages over the past two years had been severe hits to their armor. Each one had taken a tougher toll than the last. But, even knowing this, it was like he couldn't protect her from it happening again. In the end, he felt powerless to stop what he knew may lay ahead.

"Yeah, I know. His timing." She whispered it faintly into his chest, almost as if she was repeating it to herself in her mind, but he heard every word.

CHAPTER 2

2017, May

"Hey, Lauryn, so I'm not sure, but I think we have a problem with the hot water heater!" Elliott called from the shower as Lauryn finished drilling in the last of the screws needed to hang the blinds in their bedroom. This old rental house was pulling out all its punches, their first night here and already she had to fix a leak in the kitchen sink, the back-door lock had to be replaced and now the water heater was trashed?

"Oh, no. Did you get done with your shower before we lost all the hot water?" Lauryn yelled back, thinking to herself as she wiped her dusty hands on the legs of her jeans, I hope I can get it figured out so I can take a hot shower tonight.

"Yeah, just barely. I can help you look at it, just give me a sec." Elliott replied from the shower, but Lauryn was already down the wide, oak-planked stairway and headed for the basement door in the kitchen.

The rental house was all part of the plan; it was a temporary place to stay while Lauryn started a new project and they looked for a more permanent house they could purchase near their hometown, Lake Belle, where her parents and his mom and grandparents lived.

The past two months were a flurry of activity with the sale of EL Go, moving out of their condo in California and relocating to

Minnesota. Elliott had been kept busier than originally expected with the company transition and because she was between projects, many of the moving details had been left up to Lauryn.

She chose the rental house because of its central location between three potential project homes she had in mind. Each of these houses had their own merits, but none of them had the "history hooks" the houses in California had. Those had all been solid winners – like the stone and stucco Colonial whose original builder had also built ships and used nautical influences throughout his house or the gorgeous American Craftsman that had survived the 1906 San Francisco earthquake whose owners had preserved original photographs and journals from that time.

Lauryn felt that the history hooks she had found in most of her home renovation or house flip projects had been important to the "story" she would build in her video logs of the projects. The hook was key to the success of the renovation, in her mind. So, not finding any obvious ones in the three contenders this time had her slightly uneasy. And, while Elliott had encouraged her to just jump in and purchase one of them, for some reason, she was unable to commit.

"Can I get you anything to fix it? A wrench or something?" Elliott spoke from behind her shoulder, dressed in a light green t-shirt and navy Nike basketball shorts with his hair still dripping, startling her out of her thoughts.

"No thanks, I brought my bag with me. This connection was loose," Lauryn pointed to the connection on the pipe leading out of the water heater and the water that had sprayed over the floor. "But it will need to regenerate now though so it will take a while before we will have hot water again."

"Oh, sheesh, sorry I took the last of it, hon." Elliott smiled ruefully at her, "I was so itchy from working up in the attic near that insulation, I couldn't stand it. I got all that stuff up there though, let's just not forget it when we leave, ok?" He paused for a moment, "Or -maybe we can forget about it? I'm sick of moving it." He finished with a laugh, thinking of the boxes of old books and mismatched odds and ends they'd lugged along back to Minnesota with them.

"Don't you dare throw that stuff! I know somewhere in there I have some of our high school photos and I still haven't found that set of precision drill bits that I bought last year. I think they're in one of those boxes."

"Well, now I know what to get you for Christmas." Elliott laughed as he started mopping the pooled water into the sump pump hole in the basement floor.

"Ha, ha. I will find them. I know I will." Lauryn replied as she climbed the wooden steps towards the kitchen to wash her hands. With a sigh, she turned from the sink, wiped her hands on a towel and surveyed the stacks of unpacked boxes in the kitchen and living room.

After two long days where Lauryn drove her work truck across half the country and Elliott drove their Jeep, they arrived back in Minnesota last night, tired but happy to be reunited with family again in Lake Belle. They spent an hour or so with her parents basking in the joy of homecoming before they crashed in her old bedroom, so tired they felt punch-drunk, and laughed themselves to sleep.

The arrival of the moving van this morning though brought a new energy and now it was early evening and the family of helpers had all gone home over an hour ago already. Give her a few days to ruminate on the high ceilings and the original oak woodwork in this old house and she could get this place looking fine, she thought with a tired smile.

"-yeah, we should be around tomorrow afternoon. Did Grandma give you the address? Ok, we'll see you then." Coming up the basement steps, Elliott swiped to end the conversation on his cell phone as he jiggled the loose handle of the basement door in a vain attempt to fasten it. Finally giving up, he jammed the door shut by leaning his shoulder into it then glanced her way with a doubtful look.

"I know, I know," Lauryn chuckled, "But, before you say it, let me just remind you that this place is temporary. And I just couldn't see us wasting money on expensive rent in a new construction. Not when we found a place with this kind of character." Lauryn rolled her eyes over the time-worn maple kitchen cabinets on one wall that were original to the house and had been supplemented over the years with a second wall of cabinets painted in a curious shade of cerulean green. Now, she pondered inwardly at the sight of the faded yellow walls in the kitchen in dire need of a fresh coat, what color should one choose to complement cerulean green cabinets?

"Oh, is that what you call it? Character?" Elliott laughed doubtfully as he reached into the refrigerator for a bottled water and uncapped it while leaning back against the counter, "By the way, that was my mom on the phone. She's coming over tomorrow after church."

"Well, that will be nice." Lauryn offered slowly while watching his expression, "Won't it?"

"Yeah, I guess. If I'm honest though, I am a little nervous about how this will go. Me being back here - with her clean - and all that." He shifted uncomfortably, staring downwards at the kitchen floor, his thick, dark lashes seeming to rest against his tan cheeks.

"You mean because living in California put a safe distance between you two?"

"Yeah. I guess I didn't realize it until we're back here, but that's kind of how it feels. Now I have to deal with her back in my life full time-"

"As your mother, who will want to stop over and get to know you again." Lauryn finished his thought where he left off.

"Mhmm. But we've come a long way in the past three years. I can see how we've both changed. It should be fine. Right?" He lifted his head towards his wife, drew his dark, wavy hair back with his hands nervously and Lauryn melted at the vulnerability evident in his voice and in the green-gold eyes that she loved so much.

"Elliott," Lauryn stepped closer to him, wound her arms around his waist and gazed up into his troubled eyes, "Your mom is amazing and you're amazing. This will be more than fine. This will be great."

Later that evening, Lauryn finally allowed herself to sit down for a moment at the kitchen table to check messages when an Instagram private message caught her eye with the attached image of a late 1890's two-story American Craftsman home. The photo was captioned "A House with a Past" which of course was all it took to grab her undivided attention.

"Oh my gosh, Elliott!" Lauryn exclaimed, her heart racing as she finished the brief message, "Elliott, where are you?"

She called upstairs first and then realized that Elliott had finished hooking up his computer equipment and was now outside throwing the packing material in the moving dumpster. As she rushed outside to tell him the exciting news about the house, she was already trying to rein in her excitement. Things often go wrong with these deals, the two parties cannot come to a mutual agreement on price, the house may have structural damage or need new wiring, etc etc. But, still, her optimistic side argued against the practical side, you know this house is perfect! Just look at that front porch!

"I found it! I found the house! And, guess where it is?" Lauryn gushed excitedly as Elliott joined her on the deck.

"In California?" He joked, and then laughed at the frustrated expression that crossed her face.

"No! Ha, ha. It's in River's Bend, that's only about 20 minutes from here and the location is the bomb, there is a river going through the middle of town, I've been through there, lots of shops and a few restaurants-" She paused her run-on sentence to catch her breath and looked at him, her eyes dancing, "I want to go see it and the sooner the better. Like tomorrow after your mom leaves. We could just do a drive-by. Are you with me?"

"Well, let me see it before I commit." He reached for her phone, although he knew already that if Lauryn was committed, they were both committed. He scrolled through the few photos she'd found of it and had to agree, the house seemed to fit her lane perfectly.

"What 'past' does this house have?" He asked, noticing the subject line on the message.

"Well, the seller is telling me that the house was built by the town's doctor in 1898 and since they didn't have a hospital in town at the time, he would treat some patients at the house. But the best part is that he used to deliver the babies of unwed mothers there, quite controversial in a small town at the time, I guess. Some of the mothers even stayed there for months afterward until they got on their feet. From the sounds of it, he was quite a radical."

"Wow, it sounds like a lot of your research is already done for you. Who's the seller?"

"A great, great granddaughter to the original owner, it's been owned by the same family the whole time, although it's been a two-unit rental property for many years now. She lost her parents in an accident a few years ago and this house was part of her inheritance, but she has a job out of the country and wants to let go of it. She follows me on social media and YouTube and said she reached out because she loves the history angle of the flips we've done."

"That's great, sounds like just the house for you. How much does she want for it?"

"I don't know, I haven't asked yet. But I see that it was listed for sale last year and then taken off the market. So, I'm not sure what it will take to buy it."

"Or, *if* you want to buy it, Lauryn. You need to see it first." Elliott cautioned.

"Yes, of course. But I have a feeling about this one and I'm rarely wrong about these things, you know." With her comment floating in the air, Lauryn turned on her heel and headed inside for a shower.

Thank you, God. Something to dig into again, something to keep my mind busy. She realized that she had missed the challenges of a house project with all its overwhelming details and mountains of work to be done. Man, she hoped this one panned out.

As she scaled the steps headed towards the second-floor bathroom, she hoped her simple fix on that water heater was successful because she needed a hot shower in the worst way.

The next morning on the drive back to their house after attending the Sunday service at her home church in Lake Belle, Lauryn found herself staring out the window at the passing scenery as Elliott took a call from one of his friends in California. As she listened to him recount their drive across the country and the move, she eventually tuned him out and noticed that she felt herself drifting into the funk that she often felt lately.

Minnesota. This place had a rhythm that resonated with her. The people, the culture and the landscape - all mixed together effortlessly into a pleasant blend of something indescribable to her. It was more than safe and comfortable, but those words probably best described it for her.

Lauryn watched out her window as sloping green hills, rowed with foot-high corn crops and quaint farmhouses gave way to lazy river bottoms with thick stands of trees. It was all here, unchanged – this place she had missed for so long – now, it was right in front of her.

She was finally here again, surrounded by the comforts of the place where she grew up and with a family she loved. She had Elliott, her best friend and her husband. He was freed up from his crazy work life, finally able to enjoy the benefits of all the years he'd tirelessly devoted to his company. They were financially secure. She had a new project house to be excited about.

She should be completely, thoroughly, ecstatically content, right?

Then why did she feel so disillusioned, as if God had let her down somehow? It was like the time when she was a little girl – her mom had promised she would get a treat if she "behaved herself" in the grocery store, but when the time came to check out, her mom handed her an apple, not a candy bar.

As she mulled it over in her mind, Lauryn realized it had something to do with the sermon – this funk – this feeling she was having. The pastor spoke about trusting God for everything. *Every last thing.* And he wove at least eight Bible verses into his talking points. A few years ago, Lauryn would have listened raptly to him, written the verses down in her notebook and prayed about them that evening and into the week that followed, finding solace, finding certainty in it all.

Now, she realized that she didn't even bring her Bible with her to church anymore. She slid a glance across the seat at Elliott's Bible tucked next to his leg in the Jeep and then furtively averted her eyes to the passing scenery again. Elliott was stepping up in his faith and she really did find it inspiring to witness how integral his faith had become to his identity. Elliott's faith in God made him whole-hearted, incredibly generous and forgiving.

Often, she had witnessed firsthand how finding faith in God could totally change a person. Her mother-in-law Rebecca's life of sobriety and the deepening relationship Rebecca had with Elliott was just one testament to the power of faith that she could point to as evidence.

Sure. She had many examples of people who had found a deeper faith in God.

But what happened to a person if they lost that faith? What if the promises you thought God made to you, those promises that answered the dreams that originated in the most precious, intimate parts of your heart, the ones that mattered the most to you. What if he never delivered on those promises? What if you couldn't prove that He was really listening? The quiet voice whispered the questions in her mind, eventually trailing off so silently that she wasn't sure she'd even heard the voice.

Abruptly sitting up straighter in her seat, Lauryn decided she didn't like this funk. Not at all.

She tore her eyes away from the passing scenery and turned in her seat to face her husband, all the while, doing her best to put on a brave smile and join him in the conversation he was having over the Bluetooth in the Jeep.

This funk that she was feeling? This feeling must end.

"I love it! This place has so much character!" Rebecca exclaimed brightly after exchanging hugs and kisses with Lauryn and Elliott when she arrived at their house that afternoon, her arms loaded with two bags of groceries.

"That's what I told your son, but I don't think I've convinced him yet," Lauryn laughed. "And, what's with the new 'do? I love it!" Lauryn exclaimed, surveying Rebecca's sassy, short-cropped haircut which replaced the long, straight blonde tresses she'd worn ever since Lauryn had known her.

Lauryn had always thought Rebecca was hauntingly beautiful, even during the worst years of her addiction. Now that she had put on some much-needed weight and her face had a healthy, natural glow to it, Rebecca seemed like a completely different person than the woman she'd seen drift in and out of Elliott's life while he was growing up.

"Oh, thanks! Well, it's just one of many changes this year, I guess." Lauryn knew about Rebecca's recent job promotion where she now co-managed a woman's shelter for domestic assault victims, but her comment begged the question, what other changes? But, before Lauryn could follow up, Elliott spoke.

"What's with the bags, Mom? Did you stop off to do some grocery shopping on the way over here?"

"Yeah, I thought you probably hadn't been to the store yet. Hope you're not too disappointed though, I bought you a bottle of fizzy white grape juice instead of champagne to celebrate the new place. You know I still avoid the liquor aisle like the plague."

"Very funny, Mom." Elliott took the bags from her hands, glancing at the array of fresh fruit, bakery rolls and two bags of aromatic coffee. "This is great! Thanks." Elliott pulled Rebecca into the crook of his arm again and kissed the top of her head.

"My pleasure, Son." She rolled her eyes up to regard him happily, "I'm just so glad to have you guys back here. I can't tell you how excited I am!" Rebecca glanced around the house, her blue eyes resting on the unpacked boxes. "Sorry I had to work yesterday, and I couldn't be here to help with the big move. I talked to your grandparents this morning though. They said the day went well."

"Yeah, we had plenty of help," Lauryn agreed. "Your mom Rose and my mom helped me put stuff away inside the house, Jared put stuff away in the garage, and my dad and Elliott helped the movers with the furniture. We really don't have much stuff when you think about it."

"Well, I'm not so sure about that," Elliott spoke up, nodding his head sideways towards the unpacked boxes, "I know none of that stuff was around when I moved out to California, it seemed to mushroom once you arrived on the scene."

"That *stuff* is what makes our house a home." Lauryn laughed, thinking of the candles, lamps and various home decor items packed in the boxes. She turned to Rebecca with a grin, "Your son is talented at many things, but decorating a home is not one of them." Lauryn took hold of Rebecca's arm, "Come on, let me show you the place."

After the brief tour and once they had assured Rebecca that they didn't need her help unpacking anything, Lauryn left Elliott and Rebecca on the deck while she went in the house to get them something to drink. As she filled Mason jar glasses with ice water and lemon wedges, she stopped for a moment to watch Elliott and his mom through the paned glass doors leading out onto the deck.

To the casual observer, someone who didn't know the history between them, this scene would seem banal. Mother and son were sitting next to one another, soaking in the sunshine, with their feet up on the ottoman in front of them, and even though Rebecca was a tall woman, Elliott's legs stretched well beyond his mom's.

The neighbor's bird feeder seemed to be the topic of conversation as they watched a horde of yellow finch each struggle to keep their perch on the feeder which was swaying with the summer breeze and the weight of the birds coming and going. Lauryn found herself momentarily lingering at the counter as she watched her mother-in-law grasp Elliott's hand in hers and grip it tightly, her face lighting up with look of pure joy and pride as she laughed with her son.

Sometimes Lauryn couldn't quite believe they had actually come this far, having had no significant mother-son relationship throughout Elliott's teenage years. His grandparents had been the only parents that Elliott had ever known during those years. To see

Elliott now, learning to accept his mother back into his life – it was inspirational. And knowing all the hurt he'd experienced as a kid at his mother's rejection as the disease took over and she chose drugs and alcohol over him repeatedly, seeing him making peace with his mother –well, it made Lauryn love him even more.

Elliott will make a great father. The thought winnowed through her mind again, frustrating her with its familiarity. Of course, he will make a great father, she thought brusquely, and busied herself putting the drinks on a tray. But, to be a father, you must have a baby. And this morning you found out that wasn't meant to be this month. *Again.*

She hadn't told Elliott; he had guessed by the look on her face. And, of course, he tried to console her, but as she stood in the warmth of his arms, she was saddened to find her heart closing down, even to him.

Of course, it wasn't *his* fault they'd had three miscarriages and now couldn't seem to get pregnant at all. And the doctor she'd been seeing in California had assured her it wasn't *her* fault. But, if it wasn't her fault or Elliott's fault, then that left only God.

She didn't like where her mind was going, it felt scary and dark. But she went there anyway. It *must* be God's fault.

CHAPTER 3

2017, May

"I think it should be at the end of this block." Lauryn scanned her Google Maps app, sat up straighter in the seat of the Jeep and peered from behind her sunglasses, intent on finding the stucco house on the corner lot.

"This is a pretty neighborhood. It's good for resale to have a park across the street, right?" Elliott commented as he read the name Promise Park that was etched onto an ornate metal sign hanging from a black lamp post.

The lamp post marked the beginning of a winding sidewalk that looped lazily alongside a creek that gurgled around shiny rocks and low ledges until it cut at a diagonal across the park. In the distance, close to a picnic shelter, an old red-brick walking bridge graciously laced the two sides of the lush green park together. The town's main street with its red-brick sidewalks anchored Promise Park on the south side while rows of century-old houses bordered it on the other sides. The grand old houses, each with their own unique personality, all stood in quiet maturity and blended into the neighborhood as if they were all born in the same era and with careful maintenance, had all aged equally well.

"Yeah, no doubt that's a bonus." Lauryn appraised the park with its impressive canopy of oak, elm and cedar trees, teeming with kids on the playground equipment and people walking their dogs. It really was an exquisite neighborhood and had an aura of a small town, even though she knew there was a strip mall with a Starbucks and a Target store within a mile of here.

"Is this the one? You said 316 Promise Place, right?" Elliott pulled the Jeep to a slow stop with a confused frown on his face.

Lauryn turned in her seat to gaze at the house. A sloping yard of patchy grass was bisected by a pathway of broken concrete sidewalk that led through overgrown lilac bushes. The growth of the bushes and the scrub tree seedlings was so unrestrained that a person couldn't see the front door from the street where they were parked.

The porch that Lauryn had drooled over in the pictures was there behind the bushes, but it was badly in need of repair from the weight of the heavy vines that travelled the first and second story of the house. Obviously, the exterior photos she'd been sent had been taken at least three years ago - or, maybe more than that - from the looks of the peeling paint on the window casements and soffits.

A muted, putty-colored stucco covered the simple design of the two-story structure, which Lauryn would call a cross between Craftsman and Farmhouse-style. The steep roof was covered with shadowy, charcoal-gray shingles and the large-paned, casement windows looked in decent shape, but even from this distance she could see that the listing front porch floor had significant rot eating away at its bearings.

Lauryn sucked in a deep breath as she pulled at the door handle and stepped out onto the curb. She was accustomed to seeing past the cosmetic with exteriors, but she steeled herself to the disappointment of what might lie inside waiting for her. Typically, the interiors were what broke the bank.

"Well, it's true, the first impression isn't the best, but that doesn't always spell disaster, Elliott. I've seen worse." She waved him over towards her and reached for his hand as she led him around the side of the house towards the driveway. "Come here. I want to show you something."

There it was. The porte-cochere was a beautiful archway fashioned of stucco and stout, crimson-colored bricks that perfectly complemented the deep, burnt-red and cream window trim throughout the house. Attached to the south side of the house, the archway was designed as a protected area for carriages in a by-gone era and provided cover for an exquisite double-door and simple concrete stoop where Lauryn's imagination filled in the mind-picture of carriages depositing visitors on rainy evenings over a century ago.

"It's beautiful, isn't it?" She glanced up at the interior of the archway and noticed it must have been regularly maintained because it was perfectly preserved. Her gaze continued along the stone driveway towards the double-stall, carriage-house garage that sat off in the distance, towards the far end of the lot. Needs new shingles, but otherwise the garage seemed structurally sound she thought, mentally tallying the costs in her mind.

"Yeah, this is cool. I didn't see anything like this on any of the other houses around here." Elliott stepped onto the stoop and cupped his hands around his eyes to look in through the hazy windows of the doors. "Too bad we can't get a look inside while we're here."

"Yeah, I know." Lauryn joined him on the stoop, but the glass had been covered from the inside, so they couldn't make out anything behind the murky plastic. "Oh, well, I'll have to call the seller and find out who can show us inside. Let's go around back though and check things out."

After their tour of the backyard, they were pleasantly surprised to find a quirky stone patio off the north side of the house. A sliver view of a library/office was visible through the windowed French doors which had been covered with the same plastic on the inside.

They were standing out front discussing the potential costs to fix the concrete sidewalks, when Elliott elbowed Lauryn and nodded his head sideways in the direction of an old man who was walking gingerly across the yard next door as he leaned heavily on a cane.

"Hello? Can I help you two?" The man was balding, with the exception of the last gasp of hair that formed white puffs around the base of his skull and around his ears. He had on a pair of gray, heavy-rimmed sunglasses that if worn by a younger person, one might call them retro, but on this guy they looked like he had purchased them in the Men's department of a 1950s Dayton's department store, a testament to their classic style.

"We're just checking out the house, we understand from the owner that she's going to sell it." Lauryn smiled wide and reached her hand out to the man, who promptly returned a wizened, slightly trembling hand in her direction, "I'm Lauryn and this is my husband, Elliott. The seller sent me some pictures of the place, it's quite the home."

"Oh, yes, that it is! I'm Graves, the neighbor next door," He gestured back over his shoulder at the beautifully-restored Victorian home, "Actually, my name is Phillip Graves, but ever since I was a young man, I've always been known as Graves."

"Well, nice to meet you, Graves," Lauryn offered with a broad smile, "Do you know Bridgette Townlin then?"

"Oh, yes. I've known Bridgette since I moved from Winona five years ago when my sister became ill and I moved to help her. She's passed now, but I'm still here." He smiled a timid smile and pushed his glasses up further on the bridge of his nose, "Bridgette Townlin is quite the world traveler, I'll say. Never stays in one place long; in Hong Kong now, I think. She doesn't come back here much. Not since her parents passed."

"Yes, sorry to hear about the loss of your neighbors," Lauryn offered.

"Well, thank you. But they hadn't lived in this house for quite some time, from what I understand. Bridgette's parents built a new home on the edge of town many years ago and I really never did get to know them."

Graves turned slightly to regard the house with a squint and slightly tightened lips as he seemed to reminisce in his mind, "They never sold this house because it was part of the family, going back generations. A few years ago, they split it up into two apartments, you go through the front door for the upstairs apartment and through the side door for the apartment on ground level. They had renters in the house for years - some good, some bad - until a problem with the furnace a few winters ago and some water pipes froze and broke in the basement. Bridgette had things repaired after that and was planning on renting it out again, but then about two years ago she put it up for sale instead. I guess it's just too much for her, what with her being gone so much, ya' know."

"There's no For Sale sign out here. Do you know who has a key so we could see inside?" Elliott spoke up, never one to waste time with small chat when a decision had to be made.

"Well, yes, of course! What am I thinking? You must think I'm just the nosy, next-door neighbor." He fished deep into the front pocket of his too-large khaki shorts and retrieved a set of keys with a smile, "Actually, I'm Bridgette's go-to guy for showing the house. She canned that good-for-nothin' real estate agent a few months ago when his contract was up. She said all they want to do is sell tract homes in new developments, they didn't have a vision for this place. Here, let me show you inside."

So, they respectfully followed a short distance behind the stoop-shouldered old man with his cane, while Lauryn delighted in his plaid camp shirt that was tucked neatly into his shorts and his black socks and brown leather sandals combo.

Once inside, while breathing in its slightly dust-laden air and wandering room after lovely room, Lauryn fell more in love with the house. The deep, lush hues of the mahogany wood door trims and unique built-ins in the office, the oversized dumbwaiter that travelled from the basement all the way to the attic, the flow of the generously sized rooms, the stately paned windows with wide, original wood trim and the three fireplaces that all worked, according to Graves – each of these features solidified further in her mind that this house was perfect for her.

Yes, she loved the house. But, as is true in most love stories, the tale is much richer with a sprinkle of conflict and there were a few impediments with the home. Of course, it was to be expected that you wouldn't just saunter down the aisle towards your life of bliss without a few hurdles.

First, there was a wall that would need to be taken out between the kitchen and the dining room, requiring a new set of kitchen cabinets. Second, there was the ceiling issue caused by some water damage from a leaking pipe in what would become an upstairs master bathroom. Third, there was a lot of carpet to remove with the hope that the floors were good underneath. Fourth– well. There was quite a list.

None of that mattered, however. She was still in love with the house.

Over the next two weeks, with the combination of a few coffee dates with Graves where he shared some of the local folklore about the house and email correspondence with Bridgette where she shared some of the family photos taken inside the home, Lauryn was beginning to feel the house's history come alive. It was an easy decision. She must buy it and bring it back to its glory.

The house on Promise Place was originally built as a family residence for a young physician named August Berndt II, who left his wealthy family in Connecticut and moved with his new wife Minnie and their children to settle in River's Bend as the town's doctor, just before the turn of the century.

The Berndt's quickly became part of the social fabric in the small, close-knit community and even though the house was built with the expectation that they would have a large family - because Minnie loved children - they were blessed with only two children of their own, a son they named August III and a daughter named Lila.

It was rumored that the plans for the house were the same as the handsome home where August was raised in Southport, Connecticut, but it didn't have the feel of a colonial or primitive New England-style home, so Lauryn wasn't so sure about that part of the story. She was puzzled by the lovely, spacious library, however, which was adorned with custom-built mahogany bookcases and cabinetry and the most exquisite marble floor. These types of extravagances were not common in the more typical, no-nonsense Great Plains architecture of the time - even in homes that were considered opulent by frugal, Midwestern sensibilities.

At that point in history, doctors typically visited patients in their homes. It became evident, however, as Doctor Berndt settled in with his small family, that the library would become his office with a privacy screen installed in the corner for patient examinations and procedures and the small bedroom adjacent to it for the occasional overnight patient. This was considered a temporary solution, however, because the city had plans to build a community hospital in town after enough money could be raised.

As traumatic as it must have been at the turn of the century, the first birth by an unmarried woman at Dr. Berndt's office, was not noted in anyone's recollection. The woman likely stayed in one of the many unused rooms on the second floor, at least until she and her newborn were considered healthy enough to return home. Or more likely, they would travel to relatives living in another state, until the dust settled, and people stopped talking.

Some say it was Minnie Berndt, and her love of children, who encouraged the doctor to treat young, unmarried, pregnant mothers with such loving kindness. Some say it was his simply in his nature. Whether it was intentional, or accidental through word of mouth, within a few years, it became known around the area that Dr. Berndt would discreetly deliver a baby and then provide housing for the mother and baby for as long as it took to get them on their feet. Many times, these mothers and children stayed at the doctor's home for a year or better, the mothers helping with housework and cooking and some were even known to assist Dr. Berndt with his patients.

Dr. Berndt and Minnie's children - August and Lila - grew up accepting the patients and their babies were part of their lives and they shared their home, and their parents, not realizing until they were adolescents that this isn't how all doctors' families lived.

When August III began to consider the path he wanted his life to take, he too studied medicine. By then a hospital had been built in a

Minneapolis suburb many miles away, but not in their town. So, he chose to continue his practice out of his childhood home that had by then become his and his wife Patricia's and he drove to the hospital for only the most serious cases and for surgeries.

August III followed in his father's footsteps, interrupted for a brief few years by World War II, and continued the practice of helping young mothers through their pregnancy and delivering their babies. His practice was also conducted out of his library, which he called his office, even while raising his own young son, until the River's Bend finally built their own hospital in the early-1950s.

Dr. Berndt III became a founding member and the first doctor on staff at River's Bend community hospital which was named Riverside Hospital. With this move, the era of a small town doctor working out of his comfortable home office, with his small children perhaps sitting quietly in the corner, moved from everyday life for the small town's residents and into small town folklore, eventually forgotten by the next generation that walked these streets and lived in this home.

And, that's why she was motivated to restore this stunning home, with its layers of rich history. This house was like the others. She felt the energy of the people who had built it, those who had lived in it and even liked to think she could picture the ones who would move into it after she was done. It was like the other houses before. When she found the right house, somehow, she just *knew*.

"So, what do you think? Are you excited to get started?" Elliott held his cell phone in her face, taping her reaction as she joined him in the Jeep after their meeting with the attorney a few weeks later.

That sparkling mid-June morning, it was warm enough to enjoy the sun by taking the top off the Jeep and they had just signed the paperwork and handed over the check to purchase the house on Promise Place.

As he maneuvered the phone to get the best angle, Lauryn bemoaned secretly, he sure was taking his new job seriously, almost like her life was part of a reality television show. It seemed every time she turned around, he had new ideas on what to videotape like the phone calls with Bridgette in Hong Kong, and when she hired carpenters for the project and when she sketched out her renovation plans on her whiteboard. The mountains of video footage he had accumulated gave her a tension headache, but Elliott seemed to be in his own sort of cyber-geek heaven. Each night he spent hours editing footage into small snippets that he would upload to her social media and her website, which he had enthusiastically re-designed to make it "more engaging and user-friendly."

Lauryn had long known that Elliott was driven by a force not typical to most people. Obviously. This was a guy who started his own company while still a teenager. When Elliott focused on something he was passionate about, it was like he literally lived and breathed it, never tiring of it, he was almost electric with ideas.

"Yes, give me a moment to think about that question." She glanced out the window, away from him for a moment, while he held the phone a few feet from her face. She turned back to face him and the audience of viewers that would see this video later today.

"Uh, yaaasss, I'm excited to get started! So, we just closed on Promise Place and I know this is going to be the best one yet! Just you watch." Lauryn laughed a small laugh and rolled her eyes, trying to be authentic yet 'turned on' for the camera, "Okay, I know I say that about each one. But, really, this house is super special. I can't wait to get started. Tomorrow's going to be a big day, so stay tuned!"

She smiled and did a half wave before making the slicing "cut" sign across her neck.

"Enough, Elliott. We're good. And my hair is a mess so I'm not sure you're going to use that anyway." Lauryn glanced into the mirror on the visor and smoothed her fly-away hair down with her hand and then flipped up the visor with a sigh.

"You always say that," Elliott laughingly agreed, tossed his phone into the center cubby and put the Jeep in reverse to pull out of the parking spot next to the attorney's office. "And I always correct you and tell you that you're gorgeous." He reached for her hand, bringing it up to his lips to kiss it in mock gallantry, "And you are. Gorgeous, I mean. And smart. And successful and-"

"Okay, got it, Romeo. Thank you." Lauryn looked at him soberly, trying to bring him back to a more serious conversation, "So, now that we own this place, tomorrow we get started. Are you sure you want to follow me around for the next few months? I'll be asking you to do some manual labor too, you know. Especially with the demolition of the plaster and taking out that wall. I told Pete and Tyson to come next week once I got the basics done and prepped. No sense in having carpenters do the stuff I know we could do ourselves."

"Yes, I'm sure I want to do this with you. And, yes, I am capable of manual labor, Lauryn." He laughed at her doubtful look, well aware that his work typically involved computer keyboards and monitors rather than drills and hammers. "By the way, speaking of carpenters, I've been wondering, did you ever consider hiring Gabe for this job? He's still working around here, right?"

"Yeah, I think so. But I never even thought about hiring Gabe. That would have been a bit awkward, don't you think?" Lauryn watched her husband's expression as she considered the carpenter and previous business partner whom she had dated years ago. Her relationship with Gabe Holmquist had been serious enough to consider marriage back then. But that was before Elliott confessed his true feelings for her - which in turn forced her to recognize her true feelings for him - not just as a childhood friend, but as her lifelong soulmate. Once that realization hit her, it was clear that there was no one else that could fill that place for her.

The break-up with Gabe had been incredibly painful and the aftermath, where they extricated themselves out of their shared house projects, was extremely uncomfortable. Eventually, they parted as friends and Lauryn's parents had told her he was now married and had a new baby boy. It was all good and she was happy for him.

"Yeah, I guess you're right," Elliott agreed, still obviously a bit edgy about the whole concept of another man in Lauryn's life. "I can't say I'm disappointed. I mean I know you guys worked well together, but still, I'm glad I don't have to see him every day. All that – that life before 'us' – I don't know. I guess I just would never want to go back to that." Lauryn noticed something unsaid in his tone of voice, something was off.

"Well, that makes two of us." Lauryn assured him and she wondered why he would even say that. Could he be feeling insecure in their marriage because of moving back here, with reminders of their life before? Or, did his comment have something to do with her roller coaster of emotions over having a baby? The thought sobered her, and a feeling of conviction and dread bubbled from somewhere deep inside.

"Elliott, I know that I have been super stressed lately – you know, about a baby. Then, selling the business and us moving. And, now taking on this house. But I don't want you to think any of that changes you and me. Because we're tight. Right?"

He turned at her statement, which had somehow, unintentionally, ended with a question. The green-gold eyes that had captivated her for years held hers in a look so full of honesty that it left her breathless and suddenly she realized that things between them that had seemed so secure for the past few years, now felt just slightly *off*. Like a picture that was hanging just a little skewed on the wall above a couch. Most people might walk past without noticing, but if you were attentive to detail, it would really bother you and you couldn't help but straighten it, putting everything back in order again.

"Of course, we are." With his answer, Elliott gathered his wind–whipped hair away from his face and settled his baseball cap backwards on his head so that his eyes were clear for the drive back to their house.

CHAPTER 4

2017, June

"I'll just set these up here and over there while we demo," Elliott was sweeping the air with his head because his arms were full, "That way I'll have some close-ups and some further-backs and then I'll switch them up when we start taking out the cupboards-" Elliott hurried ahead of her through the opened door, lugging two cameras over his shoulders and tripods under each arm. He stopped midway across the dining room and turned to her with his eyebrows raised in a question, "Unless you had another idea and wanted them set up somewhere else?"

"No, that's great, hon. That will look really legit." Lauryn set down one load of tools and stood up again, putting her hand on her hip while she surveyed the expansive rooms while standing just inside the porte-cochere doors. So much to do, Lauryn assessed the workload, naturally sorting it out in her mind, but first things first. What's under this carpeting?

Taking her hammer out of the belt on her hip, Lauryn knelt low and carefully pulled away some of the wood trim board. Pulling on one corner of carpeting, she took hold and gave it a jerk. There it was! Hardwood flooring, in its perfect, slightly worn but always timeless beauty. She shook her head in disbelief and confusion, why would anyone cover *this*?

She turned around, sensing Elliott nearby and laughed in surprise at him, camera already in hand, videotaping her discovery.

"Why? You just ask yourself, why?!" She spoke into the camera and smiled through her puzzled look while she tacked the carpet down again for protection, knowing the abuse the floor would be sustaining as they renovated this main level of the house.

"All the better for the next owner though," She continued in an animated voice, "From the looks of it, I'd guess this carpeting was installed in the 60s or 70s and these floors have been protected ever since. I can't wait to pull this up and refinish these beauties!"

With Elliott's cameras set in position and with Lauryn providing an easy banter for the audience, they recorded the demolition of the shared wall in the kitchen/dining room and after that was accomplished, they moved on to the upstairs. There, they were re-configuring the second-floor apartment with its efficiency kitchen and awkward living room/dining room into a flow more in keeping with the original footprint of the house.

By removing some walls and planning to add some walls, they would be fashioning smaller bedrooms into bathrooms and walk-in closets, making this a five bedroom, four and a half-bathroom home. As the morning hours passed into a warm afternoon, Lauryn was becoming ever more grateful for Elliott's help; he was an excellent assistant, and she told him so. She especially appreciated his attention to the wiring as they hammered away the old lath and plaster walls and his tireless optimism in the clean-up afterward.

In addition to his role as "assistant carpenter," he was also contemplating the video product he was recording, hoping to have abundant footage to edit. Around nine o'clock that night, as they finished up their last task for the day, Lauryn found herself watching him as he geeked out over the shot angles in the new closet/bathroom space in one of the bedrooms.

Frequently during the day, she found herself distracted by how cute he looked in his light blue t-shirt with the sleeves cut out and those crazy camouflage-pattern shorts he bought at that little store in Berkeley. Most of his shopping was done on-line, but once she got him into the store and convinced him to try them on, he liked them so much he bought three pairs, all in different color combos. It was just so Elliott of him, hating the act of shopping, but liking cool stuff. And, it didn't hurt that he looked great in everything, but then again, she might be biased.

"So, you're planning on removing this wall too?" Elliott commented as they passed through the vestibule off the front door that had been created to access the upstairs apartment. "This stairway is so pretty, it should open directly into the living room, right?"

"Yeah, they added this wall and this door when they sectioned the stairway off from the main level. If we take out this wall and this door, it will be opened back up to the way it was originally built," Lauryn opened the door to the main level and glanced along the base of the wall, hoping they hadn't taken any time to install electricity in it. Luckily, they hadn't.

They were walking through the main level when she remembered something that had been nagging her in the back of her mind all day. On a whim, she turned to her left and crossed the wide hallway that ran through the center of the house towards the gorgeous wooden sliding doors behind which hid the office.

She could see the last vestiges of daylight outside as the sun set across the street, leaving the office drenched in an iridescent orange-pink color. Reaching around the wall, she flipped the light switch and glanced towards the wood casement ceiling and the brass and glass chandelier. Wrinkling her forehead, she stood pondering its placement, her hand on her hip.

"What's up?" Elliott joined her, hoisting a camera more securely onto his shoulder.

"Something about this room was bothering me. Now, I know what it is. It's this light and the coffered ceiling. It's not centered." With a motion of her hand and a perfunctory nod, Lauryn walked towards the bookshelves where she opened up one of the lower cabinets and using her pocket-sized flashlight, she glanced around inside. "Yep, that's it."

She stood up again and rapped her knuckles in a random pattern along the wall, listening for hollow spaces, while she surveyed the wood trim and the coffered ceiling again.

"Okay. What's *it*?" Elliott sighed, confusion in his gaze.

"At some point in time, someone put up this wall, creating that butler's pantry on the other side, off the kitchen. Come here, I'll show you."

They walked back through the hallway and around the now-open kitchen area towards the butler's pantry which was a separate small room, housed behind the west wall of the kitchen.

It was a convenient and rather pretty storage space, with its iridescent white and gray-veined marble floor and newer, white-painted cabinets with leaded glass fronts. She had always considered the cabinets in this pantry odd; one wall had newer white cabinets which stood in stark contrast to the mahogany shelves and cabinets on the opposite wall. Now she knew why. Those mahogany cabinets, and this marble floor, were part of the original office, just the width of a wall separating them.

If she wanted to keep the original footprint of the house on the main level, and if that coffered ceiling and the chandelier in the office were ever going to look spectacular again, this butler's pantry would have to be sacrificed and the original office footprint resurrected.

"Oh, boy. I'm not liking where my mind is going." Lauryn turned to face her tired husband, who let out an exaggerated sigh and rolled his eyes.

"Well then, stop that thought right there. Tomorrow is another day. Let's go home. Some of us gotta eat, you know."

"So, when do I get to meet him?" After visiting with Rebecca for a short time that morning, Elliott dropped the teasing question into the middle of their innocuous conversation about the renovations they were making at the women's shelter where she worked. The abrupt question startled her, and Rebecca tried to cover her nervous smile by studying the silk tassel that hung from one corner of the throw pillow she held in her lap.

"What- did your grandpa tell you he saw us the other night at Max's?" She felt a little cornered and uncertain about where the relationship was going, but she was still happy that the news of it was out. Rebecca chided herself silently, she should have known it wouldn't take long for her father to share the news with Elliott after he saw her with Kyle at the coffee shop two nights ago.

"Well, yeah, of course. He said that you were all cozy with this guy, holding hands, all dreamy-eyed - well, you can probably imagine how Grandpa described it, with his usual charming sarcasm." Rebecca's face felt warm under her son's continued inspection, "So, who is this Kyle guy? Does he have a last name?"

"You wouldn't know him, and I told your grandpa and grandma they won't know him either. I wish Dad would've just come over and asked to be introduced instead of making it all secretive and dramatic. Kyle's from Woodbury, he's an insurance agent there and he has a cabin on Lake Belle." Rebecca finished the quick summation and rose from her chair and escaped to the kitchen to make them some coffee.

"Grandpa told me that much. Come on, Mom, I expect a little more detail than that from *you!*" Elliott called over his shoulder to her.

"Ha ha, that's because there's not much more to tell!" Rebecca called back to him and reached for the coffee in a cupboard above her shoulder. Turning around to measure the it into the coffee pot, she found Elliott had joined her in the kitchen and now sat at the counter, watching her expectantly, obviously looking for more information, so she continued, "I met Kyle at a donor's luncheon, his company has been a supporter of the Lake Belle Women's Shelter for years and he was there representing them. That luncheon was a tremendous success, by the way, we raised enough funds for-" Rebecca stopped talking when she noticed his eye roll, "What? Okay, so we were seated next to each other at the table and we hit it off and he asked me out to coffee. Not much else to tell you."

"Well, the day Grandpa saw you obviously wasn't your first coffee date, from the sounds of it. How long have you been seeing him?"

"Well, since you are so interested, I guess it's been close to six months now. His wife died about five years ago from cancer and his three kids are all grown and living in the area. He's a good guy."

"I'm sure he is but since it sounds like you're really into him, I think we should meet him to check him out." Elliott's teasing tone had an undercurrent of caution to it, "You know, Lauryn was right. She said she knew something was up with you."

"Oh, is that right? Well, that women's intuition can be a double-edged sword, you know. You can't get away with much, better keep that in mind, son."

"Yeah, you got that right," Elliott paused at the comment, his internal thoughts drawing his gaze out the kitchen window over Rebecca's sink.

"How's the house project going?" Noticing the change in his demeanor, Rebecca cautiously tried to draw him out, as she busied herself with the coffee again, "Are you having fun helping her or are you starting to get restless?"

"You mean looking for the next IT thing?" Elliott turned his eyes back towards his mother, "No, not really. I mean there are some opportunities floating out there that could turn into the real deal, but for now, they're all just talk." He sat forward, "I'm having fun doing the video and media thing, it's a nice break. Lauryn is so good at this and now that she's got a team of carpenters there, everything seems to flow."

"I know, I've been watching. Like I've told her before, her mother-in-law is her biggest fan! The house is phenomenal, and the history is so interesting. It's fascinating to see how she brings all that together when she's working on these houses."

"Yeah, she's been talking a lot to a local guy and the great-grand daughter who we bought the place from. We've got some old pictures and stories, but Lauryn is working on a segment that will cover the history of the doctor's practice there and the young mothers they took in. It will be amazing, but she wishes she had more personal stories - like from women who stayed there with their children."

"Maybe you can get more information by posting a request on Instagram or during one of your videos? You never know who might be watching and have a connection to the house."

Rebecca moved from behind her kitchen counter and handed Elliott a cup of coffee. She noticed again that he looked tired. They had been working on that house night and day for the past two weeks.

"Yeah, that's a good idea. I'll mention it to Lauryn." Elliott agreed as he took the cup, blew slightly over the coffee before taking a swallow. It was the slight frown on his face and the troubled look in his eyes that prompted Rebecca to continue.

"How is Lauryn doing, Elliott?" Rebecca ventured quietly.

"She's doing okay. Why?"

"Just wondering, that's all." Rebecca paused and as she took a sip of coffee, she debated with herself. Did she have the right to hope he would open up about his personal life to her? After what she'd put him through his whole life, had she earned the right to be his mother again?

"Okay–" Elliott drew out the word with a sigh, "I know that tone of voice, what is it you'd like to know, Mom?"

"Only what you feel comfortable sharing." She paused again, and the awkward silence hung between them.

"Well, she's not pregnant, if that's what you're trying to ask." Elliott spoke as if he was quite sure that was what she was trying to ask.

"Yeah, I guess that's what I was wondering. Sorry to hear that. I know how much she wants a baby." Rebecca's heart broke again for them, knowing how deeply they had been hurt by the miscarriages in their past, "But, this house project must be a good distraction."

"Yeah, it is. But even though she puts a lot of energy into her work, it doesn't ever seem to be enough for her." As a layer of his guard fell away, Rebecca's instinct was to gather him in her arms and try to help him, but something held her back, so she just waited. Finally, he continued slowly, his shoulders bent forward as he looked into the coffee cup on the counter in front of him.

"Sometimes, I wish we hadn't gotten pregnant right away after we were married. You know we didn't plan that and still, we were excited by it. But, as time passed and the miscarriages happened, it seems like something shifted in Lauryn. It's like having a family became the most important thing about marriage to her."

"And, you think you don't matter as much to her as having a family?" Rebecca said softly.

"Well, the doctors told us that it's common for couples going through pregnancy issues to lose sight of each other because so much is focused on having a baby. I guess that's what I'm feeling."

Rebecca reached across the space between them and put her hand on his shoulder, hoping to offer some reassurance.

"Have you discussed this with Lauryn?"

"I've tried, but she gets all skittish with me and panics that I'm ditching the idea of kids altogether, which isn't true. I want a family too someday, but for right now, I like taking time to be together, and with God."

"Yeah, I can see that. There's no rush." Rebecca agreed.

"Yeah, I tell her it's no rush. Plus, these pregnancies have put her through a lot physically and mentally." Obviously, Elliott had been thinking a lot about this, and Rebecca was reminded that her young son had become a man and she had almost missed it.

"That's true, Elliott. I'm amazed at how hard she works, and in such a physically demanding job. She is a tough girl, no doubt." Rebecca paused as it suddenly dawned on her that Elliott may have other reservations about having a family. Reservations that had less to do with Lauryn's physical state and more to do with the way he had grown up. Without a father, or a mother.

"You had a difficult childhood, Elliott. When I think about what I did, the people I allowed around you, the places we lived, that time we lived in that van-" Rebecca abruptly halted the litany of hurtful memories before the black hole of the past could swallow them, "- Well, I guess what I'm trying to say is you're so resilient that sometimes I don't think you realize how much you've actually been through and the impact it's had on your life."

"Okay-" Elliott half-smiled in resignation, "Now you're going to enlighten me with some psychotherapy, right? No offense, Mom, but we've been through all this already. I don't hold anything against you, and I know that you've straightened out your life. That - other person - she wasn't you. *You* are my mom." Elliott swept a hand towards her and smiled an endearing grin at her. As usual, trying to lighten the conversation.

"El, I am so grateful that you see that was not the whole me - you have no idea how grateful I am that you can forgive me." Tears pricked from behind her eyes at the enormity of the simple declaration she had just made, "But sometimes these things from our past, they may not seem like they've survived to our present, but somehow they linger underneath and we don't even know it."

"I don't know what you mean. I'm not hanging on to any of it, I'm trying really hard not to anyway." He frowned a little, as if checking his heart right there while he sat in her kitchen.

"I know you aren't hanging onto it - with me - you aren't. But, when you think about starting a family-" Rebecca moved closer and

60

reached for his hand across the space between them, "El, I sometimes wonder if you don't trust that you'll be a good parent because I was so - absent - during your life for all those years. And, you've never known your father."

"He's not someone I even think about, Mom. I don't need to know him. Honestly, I've prayed about this a ton. I know my heavenly Father, that's enough for me." His voice was urgent and sure, as if trying to impart his wisdom and his faith onto her.

But, no matter how often she tried to deal with it, the burden Rebecca felt about Elliott's father Donovan not being part of his life was sometimes so acute, it would overwhelm her with despair. It was just another facet of his life that she had messed up for him, by her inability to make things work with his father.

That he could now see the missing relationship with Donovan as a hole that God filled for him? It left her speechless for a moment and brought fresh tears to her already watery eyes.

"Yes, that's true," She breathed out with a sigh, "I'm so glad you know God, El. And, it's okay that you feel that way about not connecting with Donovan, it's totally up to you. I just want you to be confident that you aren't limited by your past. I know - and Lauryn knows - that you will be a great dad." She reached over again and brought her son into a close hug.

"Thanks, Mom." He nodded as he continued, "Well, someday hopefully, I will be a dad and I hope you're right."

"–I found them in the attic, in that little alcove space between the dormers on the north side." Lauryn was sitting in the living room window seat at Promise Place as she spoke to Bridgette Townlin on her cell phone, a pile of black and white photos, some with curled edges, sitting next to her, "There are at least twenty pictures that are dated between 1910 and the 1940s. Some of them show the house in the early 1900s with your great-great grandparents August and Minnie. She sure was a classy lady – the hats she wore were sweet! Like, really, they were works of art!"

"Oh, my gosh, Lauryn! I think I remember seeing some of those pictures at some point. I remember her in those dark, high-waisted skirts and pointy-toed satin boots. I can't believe you found them!"

"Yeah, and I found a few more pictures of your great grandparents August and Patricia, too. Some of them with him in a military uniform. I have to say, you come from some really good genes, girl!"

"Oh, yes, I know, he was very handsome, wasn't he?" Bridgette laughed at the compliment, "He was in the Navy and served as a medic in the South Pacific for a while. I've seen some pictures of him in uniform, but mom said he didn't talk about the Navy much, so I'm sorry but I don't have any war stories from his service."

"That's okay. I'm starting to put together some things in my mind and you have already been such a great help. I have heard some stories of people who were patients here with broken arms or legs, and even a guy who stayed here for a couple weeks while he was treated for a stomach virus that he picked up overseas. But I'm really hoping to find some first-hand accounts from one of the babies that your great grandpas delivered - or a mother who stayed here. Trouble is, it's so long ago, I'm beginning to think it's not likely. I'm going to keep asking around though."

"That would be great, wouldn't it?" Bridgette paused and Lauryn heard her speak to someone else in the room with her, "Oh, I guess we're leaving, so I will have to hang up. By the way, Lauryn, I will be out of touch for a while on this trip. We will be helping some villages set up medical clinics to provide primary care. They say cell service is really bad and almost no internet in this part of Bhutan, so I will check in with you when I can or when I get back to civilization, whichever is first!"

"Okay, that sounds good. By the time you get back to Hong Kong, you might not even recognize the place!"

"I bet. It's so exciting that you are bringing it back to its original beauty. That house has a lot of good memories in it."

"That's good to know, I feel the good memories in this house. Take care and safe travels, Bridgette."

Lauryn hung up her cell phone and set it down on the smooth, wide wooden planks of the window seat. As she leaned back against the wall behind her, with a self-satisfied sigh, she glanced through the window at the lazy sprays of golden sunset rays as they played on the lush green grass in the front yard.

From this vantage point in the living room, now that the fake wall and door that created the vestibule for the upstairs apartment had been removed, she could see the grand, mahogany stairway that rose eight steps, paused at an extra wide landing and then turned and continued up another eight steps before disappearing.

Frowning slightly, faintly remembering a photo, she flipped through the pile until she found the one that she was looking for. It was dated 1940 and was an ideal photo to authenticate the design of the original stairway. As she held it in front of her, Lauryn scrutinized the image; the staircase hadn't changed at all in the decades since. It still emitted its timeless, old-world charm with its shiny wood banister and spindles and its antique lanterns set upon the intricately carved wooden newel posts.

Lauryn smiled at the photo, noticing for the first time that the original subject hadn't been the beautiful staircase or the ornate lanterns, but was instead a little blonde-haired boy, about two years old, whose face was peering out from between two spindles midway up the first flight of stairs. She looked at the date again. 1940.

This must have been Bridgette's grandfather, but because they had been so focused on the medical practices of her great-grandfathers and all the history of the early years of the house, they hadn't really spoken at all about the rest of her family. As Lauryn regarded the bright eyes and the mischievous smile on his face, she wondered what had become of him. What a cute little boy.

Lauryn dropped the photo back onto the pile and stood up to stretch her legs. She had made a point to call Bridgette at 10:00 am Monday morning, Hong Kong time, to catch her before she left for the airport, which meant it was 9:00 pm Sunday evening in River's Bend. She'd spent the afternoon and evening at the house catching up on a multitude of smaller projects while Elliott went to visit his mom.

As she stood at the base of the impressive open stairway, she looked upwards at the fruits of her labor today. Earlier, she had felt a sense of solitude - a familiar feeling for her when she repaired older homes - when she removed the upstairs apartment door and then demoed the small wall that supported it.

Now, at sunset, with the grand stairway completely open again, the gorgeous floor to ceiling stained glass window at the landing bathed both the upstairs hallway and the main floor living room in brilliant shades of red, blue and yellow. This was what that window was designed to do, just be breath-taking, Lauryn thought as she gazed up at it.

She turned towards the office, remembering that she wanted to see how much work it would take to repair the ceiling now that the carpenters had removed the wall between the office and the butler's pantry. The sheetrock guys were coming tomorrow to rock the kitchen and they said they would make the repairs to the office, if she was ready for them.

Flipping on the light, she studied the ceiling that was now completely exposed. Not too bad, she surmised, just a few cosmetic issues to repair on the moldings and the cross beams. Her eyes travelled along the marble floor and noticed that it too was relatively unharmed by the false wall; it just needed a good polish.

The bookshelves, however, were a different story. At the time when the butler's pantry was built, someone had installed a fascia board over the section where the original cabinets would have been. The board was now badly scuffed and faded. She would have to repair that for sure. Unless? Could she hope that the original cabinets were left intact behind that board?

Lauryn moved closer to examine with her flashlight and then began to lift the fascia board away from the cabinets with the claw of her hammer. It fell away easily, revealing a cupboard near the floor which was missing its door and a set of bookshelves that matched those on either side of it that travelled from about waist high to the ceiling.

This is perfect, she thought, as she knelt low and felt around inside the cupboard for any rot or holes. They look in decent shape and now all I have to do is get a custom door for this bottom cupboard, she thought. It might be hard to match the patina of this wood stain, but–

Lauryn frowned in confusion as her fingers briefly touched something and she heard the clink of metal falling to the floor of the cupboard. When she drew out the item, she found an old skeleton key that must have been resting up behind the frame of the cabinet door.

Why would someone hide this key inside this cabinet that had been covered for probably fifty years? Crouching lower to look more carefully inside, the beam of her flashlight revealed that inside this compartment was a second door.

When she tried to pull it open, however, it refused to budge. Obviously, it's been years since anyone opened it, so it was likely just stuck, she thought as she encouraged it to open by putting pressure on the two top corners.

Pressure on the top right corner finally did it; the door swung open as if she had uttered the secret passphrase. With its opening, however, her flashlight revealed a smaller drawer, hidden inside the inner cupboard. But when she tried it, the drawer seemed to be locked.

Her eyes found the skeleton key and she couldn't help but notice her heart was pumping a little faster. Sometimes, these old houses had the most enjoyable surprises, like cabinets disguised behind fake walls or hidden nooks behind cabinetry; often, these secret hiding places protected historical gems including antique jewelry and hat pins or ornately embellished calling cards, or sepia-toned photos and newspaper clippings, all the forgotten mementos of lives lived generations ago.

Lauryn turned the key in the ornate locking mechanism and when she pulled the drawer open, she found an old, long-since-dried-up ballpoint pen inscribed with a Skelly Oil logo and a set of vintage, leather-covered journals, each in pristine condition because of their air-tight environment, protected not only by a hidden drawer, in a hidden cabinet, but also behind a wall. Who would have ever guessed she'd find something like this?

She moved back from her haunches, tucked her long hair behind her ears and sat down heavily on the cool marble floor. As she crossed her legs in anticipation, she opened the first of the three journals, the one with the year 1966 inscribed in bold black lettering on the front of it.

Had she stopped and thought about it, she might have felt a little embarrassed, somewhat presumptive and basically like a major creeper, to just peruse through someone else's obviously secret ponderings. But, most of the time, she wasn't the type to stop and think about things. Sometimes, you just went for it and worried about the consequences later.

She touched the first yellowed page of the 1966 journal reverently. Whoever had written this had exceptional penmanship, each line was written precisely in long hand, with decorative swooshes on the first capital letter of each paragraph and strong, intense lettering for every word that followed.

From the first passage, Lauryn was captivated. Not by the handsome visual appearance of the handwriting and not by the intriguing historical significance of her find, but instead by the sheer presence of the person. His words were written in a way that they seemed alive, as if they were pouring from his mind and out of his mouth as he stood next to her in this room. His words vibrated with life as if he was telling her his story in 2017, not writing in a journal in 1966.

Cameron Berndt was his name. He had written it on the inside cover of the 1966 journal. Pastor Cameron Berndt.

Chapter 5

1966, June

As I start this new journal, I look forward to another day with you, Lord! Today I will remind myself to count my blessings and when I am tempted to see my circumstances through my own eyes and rely on my own understanding, I will instead look to you because your plans are perfect and your love is without end. I know this, Lord. Please help me remember-

The muffled sound of the Sunday morning newspaper dropping through the slot in the kitchen screen door onto the orange and green floral-patterned linoleum floor startled Cameron out of his prayer. Noticing then that the wooden door hadn't even been shut last night after the party guests finally left, he rubbed his early-morning, tired eyes, slid the pen back into the wire binder of his leather-covered journal and closed his Bible with a sigh.

Today's sermon, written neatly in outline form and tucked into John, chapter 3, weighed heavy on his mind given the argument he had with his wife Cassie last evening. How was he supposed to stand in front of those people - be "Pastor Cam" to his congregation - when his own life was in such a precarious state?

He was weary. This constant tug of war between them, it was making him weary.

As he crossed through the kitchen on his way to retrieve the newspaper, Cameron's eyes travelled over the empty beer bottles on the kitchen counter and the wrinkled cigarette butts in the overflowing ceramic ashtray sitting amongst them. Along with his cold, disapproving glance at the state of the kitchen, a cold, deep disappointment in his wife wormed its way into his heart.

Cassie's college friends' get-together, a night that Cameron had been dreading for weeks now, had sure been quite a party. Not content with an evening of dinner and drinks at a local supper club, the four women had returned to the Berndt's house late last night so Cassie could show off her recently updated living room with its wall-to-wall carpeting and its new Home Interiors wall decor.

And, while two of the friends lived close by, two others lived in north-side suburbs of the Twin Cities and it would be over an hour's drive home for them. Still, none of them were in a hurry to leave, so they settled in and continued to drink into the early morning hours.

When Cameron finally came downstairs, drew the blinds and asked them nicely to please quiet down so they wouldn't wake the kids, they all looked at him as if he was the fun-hating father and they were the fun-loving, rebellious teenagers.

His wife's response to his request? A derisive laugh and a sweep of her arm towards him, "I'm sure you can take care of it, dear. I told you already, this mommy's off-duty tonight." Which, of course, made the group erupt into fits of laughter.

Frustrated at the memory and the feelings in him that it evoked, he snatched the garbage can from under the sink and with one swipe of his arm and with a loud clatter, he gathered the whole lot of empty bottles and the ugly gold ceramic ashtray into it, not even caring if he woke the entire household with the racket. She needs to wake up and take a shower anyway, he thought, resentment seething in his mind; they were expecting her in church early today for the Sunday school planning committee.

After tying the bag shut to hide the evidence from his young children, he leaned against the kitchen sink and tried his best to control his anger. He knew why Cassie did these things, why she carried on this way. Her rebellion was obvious. And she was right, of course.

After all, Cassie hadn't married a pastor six years ago; she had no idea what was in store for them and that this was what would become of her life. That May afternoon six years ago, the day they were married, he was still a medical student, in his first-year residency, just steps away from being a doctor. And, *nowhere* near a pastor.

He was the one that changed the trajectory of their lives –and began the battle of wills between them that day two years into their marriage - not her. Sometimes he found himself so entrenched in the battle with her that he would forget God had anything to do with it at all.

A movement in his backyard drew his attention and he peered out the window above the sink as he watched the paperboy slide the back tire of his bike over the newly planted grass by his driveway, leaving a nasty looking streak of torn turf and slippery mud from the morning dew. Isn't that just wonderful? He reprimanded the kid in his mind, and with a hard frown, he turned towards the stairway to wake his family for church.

Nothing renewed Cameron's spirit quite like summer Sunday mornings when the birds in the park across the street sang with noisy abandon and the sun shimmered over the top of his dew-covered front lawn. He often found solace while observing the quiet nature of God through these simple gifts of life. Today, he literally sucked in the fresh air as he loaded his two small children in the car, willing his spirit to be calmed by the solitude.

Once the children were settled, Cameron glanced into the rear view mirror of their '61 Bel Air and winked at his five-year-old, freckled-faced son Aaron who looked rather tiny and timid in his crisp blue shorts and white shirt and tie as he sat in the massive back seat. Even though this two-door model was smaller than the four-door version, the back seat had abundant space for Charlotte when she would eventually join her brother back there.

For now, their three-year-old daughter, with her honey-colored curls tied into pigtails, sat next to Cameron on the front seat. She was opening and closing the top of her small, white-wicker purse, double checking that her quarter for the Sunday School offering was still safely tucked inside. The purse had been a gift for her birthday last week.

"It's only for special occasions like church, Charlotte." Cassie had told her, but that didn't stop her from carrying it around everywhere she went these past few days, filling it with crayons, pencils, keys and other household trinkets that the family would surely need and be forced to search for at some point in the future.

Cameron smiled as he noticed one of his daughter's chubby knees had a nasty scrape and a grass stain on it from when she toppled off the step just now on her way to the car, as she informed him, "I don't need to be carried, Daddy! I'm a big girl now, I'm three!"

As they waited for Cassie to join them in the car, he rolled down his window, wiped some morning dew from the side of the car with his handkerchief and gently rubbed the grass stain away from the soft skin as she laughed at him, telling him it tickled.

A few minutes later, when they finally pulled into the church parking lot, Pastor Cameron Berndt had prayed his way to a smile. And as he stole a glance at her, thankfully, his wife Cassie also looked the part.

She had teased and sprayed her hair "just so" and was dressed in a rose-colored, polyester-blend suit with a neatly trimmed jacket and matching pencil skirt. Cameron didn't really know they called it a pencil skirt. Cassie had informed him of the name when he complimented her on it. He just knew it fit snugly to her curves and made it difficult for her to get into and out of the front seat of the car. But he had to admit, she looked great in it.

And even though Cassie had one that matched this suit, she refused to wear a hat and Cameron agreed that hats were unnecessary church attire now that it was the 1960s. Truthfully, he thought hats aged her and they hid her pretty, shoulder-length, brunette curls. He loved her hair, especially when she pulled it back from her face with a white ribbon like she had done this morning.

Of course, that was his ultimate dilemma. Because even though they battled each other daily in their thoughts and their words, Cameron loved his wife. He loved everything about his wife, even her willfulness. God never promised this would be easy.

Cameron's arrival back in his hometown River's Bend two years ago had not been exactly how he or his parents had planned it. Yes, he did bring his wife and children with him and yes, he did take up residence in the house where he'd been raised, but he didn't arrive in town as a doctor ready to pick up the medical practice his locally-beloved physician father had left vacant when he and Cameron's mother retired and moved to San Diego two years ago.

Instead, Cameron had arrived in town as a recently ordained pastor to the non-denominational Freedom Church. In this newly planted church, people raised their hands and sang to Jesus with or without the accompaniment of an organ. They welcomed anyone in this church, no matter the color of their skin, what their last name was or the size of their bank account.

And in a small Minnesota town, this close to the ring of the Twin Cities suburbs, you never knew who might show up. That made his congregation an interesting mix of prim Scandinavian and African American ladies who favored colorful hats complete with little nets on the brims sitting alongside some rather rough-around-the-edges factory workers and stoic farmers. Mix in some younger people that were struggling to bridge the gap between the white shirt and tie of the 1950s with the more popular long hair and striped polyester, hippie pants of the 1960s, and there you had his congregation.

Cameron liked to think the only common denominator in his congregation was Jesus and frequently that was the glue that he relied on to keep doing his job. Because he was a young pastor, often he felt ill-equipped, often he felt inadequate. But, when he chose to invite Jesus to help him, he never felt left alone.

Ever since the day during his residency when he first witnessed a person die in front of him on an ER table, he had known Jesus Christ had changed his life forever. That morning the patient, a seventeen-year-old girl named Mae Churchill, had been severely injured in a car wreck. As the nurses rushed her into the ER, even as he prepared the necessary equipment and was assessing her wounds alongside the doctor on call, Cameron's eyes were drawn to her face.

She was smiling at him, unabashedly, almost flirtatiously. He looked away, in some way embarrassed for her. She was in shock and not in her right senses, probably not expecting her doctor to be a young med student only a few years older than she. But as he did so, he remembered feeling guilty for looking away because surely, she needed comfort. He reminded himself that it was his job to not only provide medical attention but also to provide whatever comfort he could to the patient.

As he scrambled to stem the blood flowing from multiple wounds to her body, Cameron looked back into her eyes, but by then she was gazing intently beyond his shoulder as if someone else was standing behind him. He turned his eyes and quickly glanced over his shoulder but saw only the chaos of the ER nurses pulling equipment to the table and urgently working, speaking in short, clipped commands.

When he looked back, the girl's clear blue eyes were focused again on his, staring straight through him. When she spoke, it was a weak, breathy voice, barely a whisper, "He's beautiful, isn't he? Just look at Jesus. He's so beautiful."

And with those simple words, she left this earth.

Cameron froze, his hands still on her body, fruitlessly pushing the gauze into her wounds to stem the flow of blood. It was at that moment - when she spoke those words - that he felt the chaos surrounding him strangely ebb away and he felt like he was left all alone with her in a quiet, white room. In that same moment, Cameron felt the shift happen inside him. Something just moved.

He knew he had witnessed something tragic, yet within that momentary blip of time, he had witnessed - *he knew* - that something awe-inspiring had happened to Mae Churchill.

Everything in his world quaked and was thrown on high alert. He knew instantly that he wanted his last moments on this earth – the ones that bridged from this place to the place eternal - to be like hers. He wanted to see Jesus.

Cameron began to comprehend the extent of his own sin through a daily pursuit of God's divine plan as outlined in the Bible. As his recognition of God's unfettered grace began to sink into his cells, Cameron was seeing more clearly that it was God's plan to be in relationship with Him on earth and in heaven. To see the sacrifice

God's son made on the cross to make this relationship possible, and then ignore it? Impossible, in his mind.

At first, he convinced himself that this recognition of God's true presence in his life would develop him as a more complete – more human and more humane – doctor. He was determined to somehow force the tragedy of Mae's death and his resulting transformation to fit into his world as a husband, father and doctor.

As God worked in him, however, it felt like layer upon layer of apathy was being lifted like a shroud off his heart. With each layer, he was filled with more joy until he began to realize that *he no longer fit* the constructs of the life that he'd built up to this point.

When Cameron thought about living his life as a doctor, he felt a sense of loss, not one of anticipation. He just couldn't shake the feeling that he was meant to do something else. It was like he woke up in the wrong body every day, doing all the wrong things, thinking about all the wrong things. It just didn't feel right. At least not for him.

Cassie had tried to be supportive with his decision to leave medicine and attend seminary and there were moments early on when Cameron felt that she was allowing God to work in her too. But those moments had become less frequent over the past two years or so.

Cassie loved him and she loved her children, but it saddened Cameron to know that her relationship with God was one driven by duty, not inspired by joy. Mostly for appearances, her walk with God was something that she did on Sundays and because she was a pastor's wife.

The truth was, she hadn't seen Him yet. She didn't know how beautiful He was. Cameron prayed that someday something would happen to rock her the way he had been rocked. It was a simple request; he was sure God was listening and surely, he was capable.

Chapter 6

1966, July

I look to you, my heavenly Father, for strength and inspiration to live my life for you completely; every moment of every day I will turn to you. I need to remind myself that you are my rock in the storm, my strong foundation on which I build my family and my source of joy in my role as a pastor-

"Excuse me, Pastor Cam. Vivienne is here to see you." Glenda, the church secretary, a petite African American woman in her early sixties with a halo of gray hair, knocked her knuckles softly on his partially opened door and stepped aside to allow the woman into his office. Cameron closed his journal and his Bible and stood as Vivienne stepped inside, acknowledging Glenda with a hesitant smile as she passed, her eyes downcast.

"Yes, come in and please sit down, Vivienne. Thank you, Glenda." Cameron walked around his desk, nodded at Glenda in quiet dismissal and softly shut the door behind her. As he turned towards Vivienne and sat back down in his office chair, he noted her uncombed speckled gray hair and the dark circles under her silvery-blue eyes. These cues when combined with the slight puffiness of her reddened face told him she'd been crying and that her visit had nothing to do with her role as the church social director.

"Thank you for making time to see me, Pastor." Vivienne's voice cracked when she spoke, and she reached into her large, blue-vinyl purse for a tissue to wipe at her silvery eyes that were swimming in unshed tears.

"Of course, Vivienne, anytime. What can I help you with?" Cameron sat forward in his chair and folded his hands in front of him on his desk, unconsciously preparing himself for almost anything. She hadn't given him a specific reason for her visit today, just that it was urgent that she see him.

In the few short years he'd been pastor of this church, he had counseled his parishioners on a wide variety of matters running the gamut from spats between neighbors to dealing with rebellious teenagers to serious health scares and the loss of loved ones. Cameron accepted this as part of the job, even though most of the time he felt inadequate to offer meaningful advice. He was young after all; he had not experienced many of the problems and concerns that were brought before him. He had learned early on, however, that the best response was to listen, open his Bible and turn to prayer.

"It's our son Bradley, Pastor Cam, the one that's an enlisted Marine in Vietnam. He's been injured, they say it's serious. He was in a field hospital and now they've moved him somewhere, but I don't know where." She twisted the tissue between her shaky fingers, bit her bottom lip nervously and continued in a faltering voice, "Do you know how hard that is for a mother? I know my son is hurt ... but I don't know where he is."

"Oh." Cameron sighed heavily, his whole body reacting to her shocking words. He knew her son Bradley, one of the young men in the church. Drawing in his breath to calm his voice, Cameron said, "I'm sorry to hear that, Vivienne. What else did they tell you about his injuries?"

He couldn't help it, Cameron's immediate instinct was to assess the situation medically to help her understand the gravity of her son's prognosis, as any trained med student would. But on another level, he realized that his soul had already begun to pray, and that realization calmed him in a way that understanding the medical prognosis never could.

"Nothing. They've told us nothing! All I know is that he was injured by an explosive and that he is still - they said he is still alive." She finished weakly before she doubled over, hugged her knees tightly and sobbed with her face buried in her lap. So shocked by the normally even-keeled, middle-aged woman's sudden raw emotion, Cameron sat motionless for a moment before he gathered himself together and shifted around his desk to sit in the chair next to hers. Reaching a hand to her, he patted her shoulder lightly as he tried to comfort her. But all the while he felt hopelessly inadequate - this is where God had to show up because this is where he felt so lost.

"I'm so sorry, Vivienne. I'm just so sorry." Cameron paused for a beat as she continued to cry and he tried to disconnect himself from the conversation they were having, desperately wanting to talk to God. What would God want her to know at this moment? If He were to speak with an audible voice right now in this office, what would He say?

"I never supported him enlisting," Vivienne continued suddenly, speaking into her hands with her head still lowered, her shoulders shaking in anguish. "His father was almost killed twice in France and Bradley grew up knowing that. Why would he choose the service? He's only nineteen years old. I just –" She shook her head again more urgently, "I just can't make sense of it." Her rush of words finally receded into tired silence.

As they sat in the quiet office, kind words of support rippled through Cameron's mind because, of course, any number of platitudes would be expected at moments like these. But, what would that accomplish? How would trite words ease the pain of a mother grieving over something such as this?

"Vivienne," Cameron spoke gently, "I know you are scared. But I also know that you trust God. So, knowing just those two things, could we pray for Bradley right now?"

She raised her face to search his eyes for strength and in her bewildered, watery gaze and the deep creases between her brows, Cameron saw clearly that her whole world was teetering on the edge. He felt the tenuous thread that held her here with him, the thin line she walked between sanity and losing her grip completely – that razor thin line between belief, faith and hope on one side and the vast wasteland of hopelessness that laid on the other side.

"Yes," She whispered finally, and her lips settled into a firm, determined expression. "Please, Pastor. Let's pray." With her words, Vivienne gripped his hand with the strength of a hardened lumberjack, bowed her head and allowed God to show up once again.

A short time later, Cameron watched as the distraught mother squared her shoulders with a deep breath and left his office to return to work at the variety store that she and her husband owned on Main Street. She would make a brave attempt to go on living, but he knew her everyday existence would be inextricably altered by this. Her every thought would now be darkened with the knowledge that her son lay injured somewhere in a hospital halfway around the world and she could do nothing to help him, except pray.

Cameron was secure in the power of prayer, how it changed people, how it brimmed with mystery, how it gave strength to people in dire circumstances. Still, as he watched Vivienne leave through the front doors of the church, he couldn't help but wonder what his response would be if faced with such a traumatic event as the potential loss of a child. If he wasn't mistaken, he felt a tinge of something – he wouldn't call it outright doubt in God's ability to do miracles – but still something inside him felt unsettled, just not quite *certain*.

He turned back to his Bible, still open to the verses in Second Corinthians that he had read with Vivienne just moments before, after his prayer. He read 2 Corinthians 12:9-10 again and drew his journal across his desk towards him. Rubbing his eyes roughly, as if by clearing his eyes he could somehow see better, he tried his best to focus on the goodness of God.

Summer afternoons in River's Bend seemed to meander along with their own sense of time. It was as if the hours were measured by the summer vacation activity of children instead of the arc of the simmering sun.

At lunch time, the day was full of promise as cool breezes rustled through the oak trees along the city boulevards and children rushed home from vacation Bible school or summer recreation activities to dress for afternoons at the community swimming pool. By three o'clock, they would seek refuge from the hot sun under the awning of the poolside candy stand and by five o'clock they would be tearing through the back doors of their homes as their mothers called them in to wash up for dinner.

It was just that kind of day, pleasant and carefree, Cameron thought as he sat in his car waiting to turn into the church parking lot. As he flipped on his turn signal, he watched as two kids dressed in dripping swimsuits pedaled past on their bikes, obviously having just come from the public pool three blocks away. The sight of the boys laughing, not a care in the world, reminded him of the many summer afternoons he'd spent doing the same thing on these same River's Bend streets. It was just over ten years ago, but somehow it seemed like a generation ago.

Having grown up in this town, he felt a certain comfort coming back here with Cassie and the kids to make his home here. He felt like he understood the place and the people who lived here. He could relate to their struggles, he enjoyed sharing in their triumphs.

As he pulled into his parking spot near the back door of the church, he caught his reflection in the rearview mirror and found himself frowning behind his sunglasses and he realized that the look on his face said it all.

Today was another reminder that underneath the picturesque, small-town, middle-American veneer lay the real deal. And it wasn't so pretty.

Just after lunch, Cameron met Al Newsome, the pastor at their sister church in Brookside, a town located about forty minutes away. Al had been an invaluable resource and supportive mentor to Cameron ever since he accepted the job as pastor of Freedom Church. And while the two men differed in style – Al was much more gregarious than Cameron could ever hope to be – they both had wives and families and had developed a friendship over the past few years.

Today, Cameron met with Al about the upcoming church convention in Minneapolis at which the two pastors were hosting a Q&A session about their church youth programs. Seated in a booth towards the back of the diner, they worked through their presentation materials and were confident they had more ideas than they even had time to present at the conference.

Truthfully, as he admitted to Al, Cameron was a bit intimidated to speak in front of a group of seasoned pastors – he had a hard time seeing himself as an "authoritative source" – and his wavering confidence was further undermined by Al's frequent little comments like "you dress like a college undergrad" and "a tie might help."

This was a lesson that Cameron was learning over and over as the early days of being a pastor now turned into years – it was challenging being a young pastor in a small community. Often it seemed Cameron had to work extra hard to gain the respect of those in his church and the other area pastors, most of whom were ten and twenty years his senior. With his blonde hair trimmed neatly short, instead of the increasingly popular styles of long hair around the ears, and his clean-shaven face, Cameron felt every bit presentable as a pastor. It annoyed him that people were so superficial to judge him by what he wore or by the way he looked.

But surely Al was different, he knew Cameron personally, he knew better. That's why his continued comments on so many levels, seemed shallow and unkind. Then again, Cameron had reasoned to himself while they drank a second cup of coffee, perhaps Al was right. Maybe he should consider dressing a bit more formal when he went out on church business. Was it his own willfulness that made him so resistant to it? It was something to consider.

As happened frequently when they were together, once they dispensed of their business at hand, Al asked Cameron how things were going generally. Today, Al also shared some stories about things happening in his church and in his personal life.

In the beginning of their friendship, Cameron had felt honored and humbled by Al sharing his confidences with him. He had always shared them anonymously enough, concealing names with pseudonyms like "long-standing member" or "treasured soul." But as the months went by, Cameron began to see that Al tended to be heavy-handed and sometimes unabashedly judgmental when dealing with his parishioners. Even more troubling to Cameron were the instances where Al would shift his perspective to fit a desired outcome.

Sometimes, the truth seemed relative to Al. Today's conversation was undoubtedly the starkest example of that.

As the waitress took away their empty pie plates, Al leaned across the table and spoke in low tones so as not to be overheard by the two women sitting in the booth behind them, "I want to share something with you so that you might pray for me to have wisdom when dealing with a very delicate situation."

"You see," Al continued in measured tones, "We have a long-time member - a treasured soul who has served on the church board for many years - he's a critical pillar of our financial support and has been married to his fine wife for over thirty years. But recently it's been rumored that he is having an affair with another member of the church, a young mother - a divorcee with two children - in an unfortunate situation, to be sure." Al paused for dramatic effect, pushing himself back into the cushioned bench of the booth, never dropping his gaze from Cameron.

"Apparently," He continued, "His wife is acting like she has no idea, but in such a small town, this is highly unlikely." He stopped talking then, as if waiting for Cameron's response. When the moment drew out, Cameron felt obligated to acknowledge him.

"Whoa. That *is* delicate. What do you think God is prompting you to do in this situation?" It was a sensitive and hurtful affair to all involved. And sinful, Cameron added in his mind, but certainly Al already knew that.

"Nothing. For now, I will do nothing." With his comment, Al leveled his steady gaze downward at his hands which sat folded on the table in front of him. Then, casually, he picked up his spoon and stirred more cream into his coffee cup.

Stunned by his response, Cameron struggled to understand his reasoning. Certainly, this was a tough one; Cameron had a hard time imagining a worse situation to face in a church, especially with someone in church leadership. And, of course he understood everyone sinned and everyone was allowed the gift of redemption through admission and repentance, but no matter how Cameron looked at this situation, it appeared that Al was condoning it by choosing to do nothing.

"I'm surprised by that, Al." Cameron uttered aloud in confusion, "I don't understand why you wouldn't lovingly confront the man and counsel him and his wife so that they can repair their marriage. And, also the young mother. This is serious."

"Well now, that would be foolish of me, Cam. This man has given much to the church over the years, both of his time and his resources. He is a beacon to all the members of our church. The way

I see it, this is a matter between him, his wife and God. If these parties all decide to avert their eyes, and are learning to live with this, then who am I to step in?"

Cameron sat dumbfounded on the red vinyl seat in the booth, his mouth going dry and his heart hitching in his chest as if someone had walloped him. He couldn't help but think maybe Al was just too close to the situation to see clearly. Maybe he just needed a little clarity.

"Al, I don't see how you can possibly feel this way. If you know this to be true, certainly something must be addressed with the parties involved. This is sin. It's not a situation to gloss over."

Al lifted his coffee cup and took a long, slow swallow before carefully setting it back on the ceramic saucer. As he leveled his gaze across the table at Cameron, a wry frown settled on his mouth and his voice was dripping with syrupy condescension when he spoke.

"Cam, let me give you some advice. Sometimes a pastor has to know his limits and when to keep his mouth shut. We need to do our best to keep people in the church, not give them reasons to leave."

His response landed like a heavy thud on Cameron's spirit and left him speechless. Without waiting for a reply, Al changed the subject and Cameron, for the first time ever, wished he hadn't ordered the cherry pie. The sugar in it was making him sick.

As he sat in his car now a few hours later, the sun cooking through the windshield, Cameron felt like a veil had been lifted from his eyes. Now, he saw things just a little clearer than before. Trouble is, he didn't like what he was seeing.

He had begun to trust Al's advice as a pastor but obviously Al was mistaken in his approach to this situation. Sure, Cameron thought as he got out of his car and began walking towards the church, pastors are frequently called into unpleasant situations because people are imperfect, but that's why we as pastors and believers rely on the perfect one to lead us, right?

But still, Cameron couldn't help but feel isolated and alone, and the question that kept rolling around in his head was, *If this was ministry, was it the right profession for him?*

CHAPTER 7

2017, June

"So, you think these journals have been hidden in there since the 1960s and no one else has read them?" Elliott was as interested as Lauryn at her find but he was undecided on what should be done about them. As he opened the door to the trendy new coffee shop two blocks from the house on Promise Place, he stepped back to let Lauryn pass by and the scent of her perfume was suddenly overwhelmed by the scent of roasted coffee beans.

"Yeah, I think so," She responded. "I mean, why would someone lock them in there and then build a wall in front of the cabinet if they wanted someone to read them?" Lauryn moved towards the line of customers standing at the counter, all of them dwelling in various states of impatience and boredom.

"Maybe they were just forgotten there." Elliott stood behind her and thought again how stunning his wife was that she could make a simple ponytail pulled out the back of a baseball cap, some faded jeans and a flannel shirt look *so great.*

"I suppose that could have happened," Lauryn pivoted to face him and caught him staring at her but was oblivious to his admiring gaze, "The drawer *was* hidden." She continued with her brow knit in deep thought.

Elliott smiled at her, finding it ironic that she always said he was the one that was obsessive about things. Her intense interest in this house and these journals was a case study in obsession.

"Are you going to tell Bridgette you found them?" He asked as he studied the coffee selections on the sign behind the counter, thinking maybe this morning he would order something different than his usual dark roast with a shot of cream.

"I already sent her an email, but I don't think I will hear back from her soon." Noticing his interest in the coffee board, Lauryn asked with surprise, "Are you thinking of switching up your order or something?"

As he stood contemplating all the choices, Lauryn ordered her usual coffee from the cheerful young woman in the green apron behind the counter and Elliott followed, having decided to stick with his usual after all.

After they ordered, they paid for their coffee and continued the walk along the counter while they watched three coffee shop employees rush around, making expressos and other coffee creations.

"Do you think it's totally nosy of me to read these? I mean the guy could still be alive somewhere, that feels kinda creepy of me." Lauryn spoke over her shoulder as she walked with her coffee towards the odd little booth near the front window, the one with a single bench seat where they sat next to each other instead of across from one another. Their usual table.

"I don't know. Who do you think he is?" Elliott spoke as he slid next to her and then blew off the steam rising from his cup.

"He must be Bridgette's grandfather because he mentions two children, a boy named Aaron and a girl named Charlotte, which would be Bridgette's mom."

"And Bridgette never mentioned these people living around here anymore?"

"Well, she mentioned an uncle in passing once, that could be Aaron, but she said he moved out to the west coast when he joined the Navy and that they've never been close. I suppose I could try to find him though. Do you think I should?" Lauryn watched him, obviously wanting his opinion.

"I don't know. I thought your story angle with this house was the doctors that worked from there at the turn of the century. What did you say this guy from the journals did for a living?"

"He says he almost followed in the footsteps of his father and grandfather to become a doctor, but he became a pastor instead." Lauryn paused while she took a swallow of coffee and then continued as if she was having a debate with herself, inside her mind, "I suppose it's a tangent that could get confusing ... I don't know, though, he's kind of interesting, there's just something about the way he writes ... something about it just moves you."

"Huh. Well, we could see how it fits in once you've talked to Bridgette." Elliott offered, his attention focused not on the journal or the house or their video logs but instead on how his wife's eyes sparkled from under the bill of the baseball cap.

"Yeah, you're right. For now, I've got my hands full just pulling together the story on the other two Dr. Berndt's. This third guy, coming out of left field, maybe he should just stay anonymous." Lauryn stated, her mouth set in a firm line.

"So–" Elliott reached over and lifted her cap slightly to look directly into her eyes and teased, "You think you're going to keep reading, even though that's kinda creepy?"

"I'll try not to–" Lauryn stammered in the most adorable way, Elliott thought with a smile.

"Uh huh, sure, whatever you say–" Still smiling and obviously not convinced, he took another swallow of coffee.

As was common with her projects, renovating the house seemed to be taking over her life; it had been many days since Lauryn found the journals and her discussion of them with Elliott. In the meantime, she hadn't had much time to contemplate Pastor Cameron Berndt or the problems he had in his life some 50-odd years ago.

She had mountains of problems of her own.

Elliott wasn't videotaping today because he had scheduled a meeting for this morning and it was just fine with her that he wasn't around, Lauryn thought with frustration. She didn't like the idea of tip toeing around him all day; her work around here was stressful enough without having to deal with all that extra drama.

He had mentioned the meeting before to her – something about an IT security firm start-up – but how was she to know that this one was worth extra attention? After all, he'd taken many calls about different opportunities since he sold EL Go a few months ago.

The sale of his company, though microscopic by Silicon Valley standards, still put him on the radar of those firms searching for business investors. Someone was always trying to sell him something, trying their best to make a buck on their new big idea. So, when he mentioned this security start-up to her one day a couple of weeks ago, she didn't give it much thought.

This morning at home, while he was making his morning protein shake and telling her the outline of their proposal, she had zoned off for a moment, distracted by the fact that she had missed her period two days ago which, given her history of inconsistent periods, may or may not mean something important. And, okay, maybe she had zoned off for more than *a* moment, it might have been a few moments, but Elliott could tell immediately that she wasn't listening, and he called her on it.

He might have been on-edge about his meeting. Or, more likely her comment might have bugged him, the one where she said the small bedroom next to their master bedroom would make a great nursery. But whatever it was, something set him off. And this time they had an official argument, which was something she could honestly say didn't happen often.

In fact, she couldn't really remember Elliott ever raising his voice in anger to her before this morning; their arguments were mostly what he liked to call "spats." Most of the time, he'd come around to her way of thinking; he'd smile at her with his charming smile, make some lame, adorable joke about them being "a duet, not a solo" or something like that, and then they'd move on.

She couldn't really remember a time in all the years she'd known him where, if he disagreed with her, he held rigidly firm and stood up to her. And, she couldn't remember him ever shouting at her in anger.

Until this morning. It had all started out like a murmur, just a little spat, but it ended with a shouting match, like a battle.

"Lauryn, enough already about a baby! I'm trying to talk to you about something else here. Can you at least pretend to listen to me?" Elliott slammed his shaker bottle on the counter loudly as if to get her attention.

"I am listening!" She countered defensively, "Sheesh, I thought you were done. Besides, you know that I can't offer you any advice on your business deal since I don't know anything about IT security."

"I wasn't asking you for advice on it, I was just telling you about it." Elliott looked at her, his frustration evident on his face, "And, it's *our* business deal, not *my* business deal. It's different now that we're married, you know. We're a team now."

"Yeah, I think I know we're married and that we're a team, Elliott. That's why I mention the nursery-" She had planned to share with him her excitement about possibly being pregnant, because she was sure he'd forgotten the significance of the time of the month. But something held her back. Elliott's way of dealing with the previous pregnancies and miscarriages had always been to retreat, and it seemed like he was worried about her all the time. She just didn't want to start all that until she was sure what this was.

"Well, since you brought that up–" Elliott interrupted her without letting her finish the thought in her mind or speak it out loud, "I've been thinking a lot about that lately. I think we should just wait on having a baby. I don't want to go through all that again so soon after the last one. We have plenty of time to start a family, there's no rush."

He delivered this proclamation with a measured tone in his voice, but his gaze was resolute, as if he couldn't believe he'd spoken the words out loud but was still relieved his thoughts were finally known. Obviously, he had been thinking about this for a while.

To hear him say this, though, took Lauryn by surprise and immediately she was overcome with anxiety mixed with an unsettling sense of abandonment and loss.

"What's that supposed to mean?" She didn't really want to continue this conversation and she felt squeamish with fear, but she had to know.

"It means exactly what I said," Lauryn could tell Elliott felt cornered, but he still spoke calmly, as if he could convince her this made sense because he was so sure of it, "There's no rush, Lauryn. I want time to be with you, get our life figured out – enjoy our time together – before we bring a kid into the picture."

With the first baby, they found out they were pregnant just after their first anniversary and because they weren't specifically planning it, the sudden surprise was part of the magic of it all. Telling Elliott that they were having a baby was one of the most precious memories she had with him.

At eight weeks, they told their parents, they told their friends, they talked about names and dreamed about what their baby would look like. Then, after a horrible night of cramps and bleeding, they no longer had a baby.

They thought like most people do, that this would not happen to them a second time, so a few months later, they became pregnant again. At about ten weeks, they told their parents but no friends. They didn't talk about names, but they couldn't help dreaming about what the baby would look like. Then, during a doctor's visit, she was informed that there was no heartbeat, the baby inside her wasn't alive any longer. The doctors helped her with the cramping and the bleeding.

After the second miscarriage, Lauryn insisted they keep trying, over Elliott's misgivings. A few months later, they were pregnant with their third baby. They didn't tell anyone about it. No names were discussed, no dreams were dreamt. It happened so fast, one day she was pregnant, the test told her so. And, the next? The baby was just ... gone.

Now, as she stared at him and his statement reverberated in her mind, it all made sense. Elliott had always been supportive during the miscarriages, amazingly so. But now with perspective, she could see some things - his support was for her physical health and her mental state. And, while he was sorry to lose the babies once they were conceived, it was clear that he was still missing an important element. He mourned the children, but he didn't mourn the loss of the dream. With each miscarriage, Lauryn mourned the *lost dream* of having a family. It was clear to her that Elliott did not.

"I knew it - I *have* been right all along. You haven't been fully committed to having a family, have you?" Lauryn uttered the words, the hurt she felt laced through each syllable.

"Well, I was, at first," Elliott glanced away from her accusatory gaze, but continued, "It all happened so fast, I wasn't really prepared for it. I don't think we were prepared for it." He looked up at her then, as if expecting her to agree with him. But all she could think of was how deceived she felt. And, angry. She had trusted him. She had believed they were in this 100 percent together.

"So, all along - through all that we went through - you were saying how much you wanted those babies, but you really didn't, did you?"

"What?" Elliott's eyes darkened and he frowned, almost in disgust, "How can you say that? Of course, I wanted those babies."

"Well, it doesn't sound like it to me! You seem ready to stop trying all together now. As if they didn't count for anything. It's like you thought they were mistakes!" Lauryn wasn't thinking anymore, her words were falling out of her mouth, they were coming from someplace deep, someplace painful.

"Stop, Lauryn!" If it was possible, Elliott's face darkened even further and his voice bellowed in the small space of their kitchen, "I can't believe you'd even think that. It's not fair and you know it!"

"All I know is that I thought my husband and I agreed on having kids, but now I hear that he doesn't want to be a father!"

"That's not what I said! I said I think we should wait! There's a difference." In frustration, Elliott grabbed his empty bottle and tossed it into the kitchen sink, forgetting completely that his finished shake was still in the blender and then turned back to her as he grabbed his car keys, "Besides, it's supposed to be a mutual decision, you know – one made between a husband and a wife. Or, are you so caught up with the thought of being a mother that you forget you're a wife?"

Stunned at his dig, Lauryn winced, and her mouth dropped open in shock.

"That's a pretty selfish perspective." She gushed in shock, bereft of a better reply.

Deflated now by all the emotion but still obviously angry, Elliott turned away and spoke over his shoulder as if he couldn't get out of the room fast enough.

"Well, okay, I guess I'm selfish. All I know is that we work hard, we don't have a lot of extra time. So, my bad – I want my wife to myself for a few years. I don't think that's selfish. I think it's love. But you think whatever you want, I gotta go."

Elliott hadn't called or texted her all day – not even after his meeting – so she knew he was really mad, but so was she. As she worked on various jobs in the house throughout the day, she ran their argument over and over in her mind.

She couldn't honestly say she was *sure* he didn't want a family, that really hadn't been fair. But she was pretty sure that he regretted the past pregnancies. The incredible euphoria of knowing you had a baby inside, a life you'd made together growing inside you, and then- it's gone. All the dreams you had for that little person, enough dreams to fill a lifetime - just gone.

Yes, Lauryn knew he regretted the pregnancies, not the babies themselves, saying that to him had been wrong, but she knew he regretted each pregnancy ordeal. With a little time to cool off today, she had come to some conclusions.

Elliott was a person who had lived his entire life guarding himself, protecting his heart against the pain of a childhood without loving parents. To find that they were being denied the gift of their own baby, again and again? It was obvious that Elliott was trying to avoid the pain.

Lauryn thought about the pregnancy test she'd picked up at the drugstore on her way to the house this morning. In the past, she would have tested immediately, the anticipation driving her crazy. This time, all day, she avoided the thought of that test sitting innocently enough inside its box, inside her purse. It was too upsetting to know. Because if she knew, she'd start to dream, and if she started to dream, she was sure to be let down again.

As always, when Lauryn was upset, she turned to whatever kept her the busiest - like renovating an old house with a million small jobs that needed to be done. It was her release and allowed her to cram her frantic thoughts into a box at the back of her mind. She would just ignore that pregnancy test, and all its implications, for a while longer.

The ceiling had been repaired, they were wrapping up the sheetrock throughout the house and had begun preparing the kitchen for the custom-built, new cabinets with their hardware and edging inspired by the original cabinets.

From the first time she walked into the kitchen that day back in May, Lauryn knew that after they opened the space to the dining room, the kitchen's design would be inspired by the white and gray marble flooring used in the office. Of course, marble was extremely expensive, and it had totally blown her kitchen budget to do marble countertops and to cover one entire wall from counter-height to ceiling in it, but the result was everything she'd dreamed about, plus some.

In these houses, Lauryn solved problems, she made her design visions a reality, she was in control. In her personal life however, much like Cameron Berndt, she was anything but in control.

CHAPTER 8

2017, July

A lawn mower droned monotonously two doors down, and the kid next door had been shooting hoops for about an hour according to the clock on Elliott's computer screen. Bounce, bounce, swish, shuffled steps against the concrete driveway, then a few sporadic dribbles to set up his shot, then bounce, bounce, swish again. Repeat.

The faded, white window casement was propped open in the upstairs spare bedroom that now doubled as his office and a light breeze floated the blinds back and forth in a soothing rhythm against the screen. As he squinted against the setting sun through the half-shuttered blind in front of him, Elliott hit the enter key on his keyboard, leaned back in his office chair and let out a long sigh as his mind checked off this last task of his day.

He had just posted the first video teaser for the history angle of the house which included old photos and stories they had been getting from locals. Overall, he was pleased with how it turned out. Technically, the teaser flowed well, and he should have been glad it was done since they had been talking about getting this done for weeks now. But instead he felt this weird, directionless feeling.

Lost in thought, Elliott sat, his elbow resting on the arm of his chair and his chin in his hand, his gaze was drawn to the tree branches moving in the breeze outside his office window.

At this level, he felt like he was sitting in a treehouse, positioned in the center of the bird world that was living within the oak and maple trees around the house. While he watched, three vivid yellow male finches chirped and flapped their wings at each other, never content to share a branch with each other. It was a convenient distraction and somehow it grounded him mentally, this bird life.

It was beyond strange, he thought. To be back here untethered to a job – it felt so out of body, he almost felt guilty. And to think it had been here all along, just one decision away. Just sell your business. That's all it took to really be present in *this* life.

But, of course, there was more to it than that. Without the joy he found in his faith and his marriage to Lauryn, he might have been content to stay on the bullet train of his business, going from one deal to the next, never selling it. And never really thinking about where his life was headed.

Basically, he realized that he had grown up, but he really couldn't point to a specific day or time when that happened. All these life events had unfolded so organically, it was as if they were meant to happen. It was only now, as he stopped and contemplated things, that he felt disoriented and honestly, a little fearful.

There were all these questions that sidled around in the back of his mind and their argument this morning was like a verbal eruption of the voices debating inside his head. Questions about where were they headed and, were they ready to add a child to this ride they called their life? Life was just so complicated.

The meeting this morning with the IT security firm investment deal left him pretty much how he thought it would: disappointed, dull and uninterested. And, while he tried to be professional and asked enough questions to be respectful, nothing about it excited him.

On the other hand, Lauryn's business was doing great, she was making money on the renovations and with YouTube monetization of her channel. It was a business that was 100% Lauryn and, having created his own business, he could appreciate the energy she got out of it, and the fun she was having with it.

They'd rarely argued about work, or the amount of time they were devoting to work. They both had come from backgrounds where hard work was expected, it was modelled and respected.

So, for Elliott, it was not surprising that the topic of having a family, and all the pain they'd gone through with the miscarriages, was always the source of their conflict. What was surprising to Elliott this morning was his own response. He was not used to feeling so angry with Lauryn.

He sat back in his chair and closed his eyes as he recalled what she'd said to him. To actually accuse him of not wanting his own children? Reflexively, his hands gripped the handles of the chair tightly and as he cringed, tears pricked onto his lashes.

He'd felt the sorrow of loss every bit as much as she had with those miscarriages. He held her each time as she cried, and he'd cried along with her as they'd prayed together that God would watch after their babies in heaven. Three times. So much pain.

After each miscarriage, for months, Lauryn would suffer a kind of sadness that nothing and no one could break through. Gradually she'd come back to life, just in time to get pregnant and then, horrifically, it would happen again, and they would be on the same torturous trek once more.

Of course, he had wanted each of those babies. His reticence about getting pregnant again wasn't that he was selfish or that he was insecure about being a father because he'd never known his own father, like his mom had theorized. In the end, it had nothing to do with his own childhood.

No, the real reason was that he just didn't want to experience the pain that came along with having a family. He knew why he resisted it – he just wasn't strong enough for it. He felt like he was going to crack if he had to go through it again. He just didn't know what he would do if he had to stand by while Lauryn went through it again.

He thought she understood his position, he'd told her before in his own way, but it always fell on deaf ears. And, now even talking about postponing a family was tantamount to not wanting children ever? Wow, he shook his head in disbelief, she'd said some really sick things.

But then, so had he. Replaying his own comments, he recognized that all his buttons were being pushed at the same time and he'd lost it on her. What a fail.

Elliott's phone buzzed on the desk in front of him, startling him. He picked up the phone, saw the profile picture announcing the text was from Lauryn.

My Wife Lauryn: Hi there. Have you eaten?

Me: No, have you?

My Wife Lauryn: No. Can I take you out for dinner?

Me: Like ..... on a date?

My Wife Lauryn: Yes, if you don't have any other plans for this evening.....oh, and by the way, forgive me?

Me: Always.

And then he texted without hesitation:

Me: Forgive me?

My Wife Lauryn: Never.

Within a moment, another text popped up along with a smiley face emoji:

My Wife Lauryn: And always.

With a resigned smile to the empty room and the finches still fighting for a perch outside his window, Elliott swiped the message shut. They would work through this argument too because what other option did they have? He loved her. He would always love her.

CHAPTER 9

1966, October

You know the storm that we are in right now, Lord - it's as if we are dismantling the very foundations of our marriage, brick by spite-filled brick. When I think back over the past few months, I find that we are arguing a lot more and making up a lot less. The weight on me is becoming almost unbearable. I want to be the husband and father that you can trust, Lord, but I feel untrustworthy. I am sorry for my anger, I am sorry for my bitterness, I am sorry for my resentment and my pride. I know that you are listening, Lord.

"Daddy, please hurry! You said I could jump in them if I raked a big enough pile, but Charlotte keeps messing it up!" Aaron's fist pounded loudly on the side door next to his office chair, and the rattle of the glass panes startled Cameron from the journaling he was doing at his desk.

Instinctively, Cameron reached towards the silver transistor radio that sat on the bookshelf and turned down the hypnotic melody of "Norwegian Wood" the song by the Beatles that was playing.

He wondered, a shaft of guilt piercing through him, if he'd been remiss in watching his kids. Cassie was forever reminding him,

"You never know with these two, you really can't take your eyes off them for a moment." And, since she was out again today, shopping with friends, he was the responsible party.

Glancing in the direction of Aaron's pointing finger, Cameron noted with relief that there wasn't any medical emergency. Instead, his daughter was burrowed chin-deep into a pile of amber-gold oak leaves, and as he watched, she threw some leaves into the air and turned her face into the flurry, laughing as they fluttered down over her eyes. Even feeling heavy like he did now, Cameron couldn't help but smile at the scene of his children outside his window.

Both were dressed in fall coats and flannel hats tied tightly under their chins to ward off the chill of the fall Saturday afternoon. As he watched, and before he knew what had happened, his children started tussling with each other in the rather paltry piles of leaves that Aaron had been raking for the past hour.

"Hey now, come on, don't fight!" Cameron, pulling his fleece sweatshirt over his head, called through the door to Aaron who was now standing over his sister as he unceremoniously removed her from the leaf pile, much to her chagrin. She wasn't having it and she pushed her brother away with both hands sending him stumbling until he landed on his bottom with a thud a few feet away from her.

"But, Daddy, you said to make the piles big and she won't let me. She wrecks everything!" Frustrated, Aaron pushed himself up, gripped the rake again and began to drag it through the grass in random swipes, gathering up the scattered leaves into the small pile next to the larger one where Charlotte was sitting.

"Now. Is that any way to talk about your sister? She certainly doesn't want to wreck everything." Cameron reached for Charlotte's hand, trying to instill a sense of calm on the eruption. As he lifted her into his arms, he leveled a mock-serious look into her heavenly, sky-blue eyes, "Now, Charlotte. You don't really want to wreck Aaron's leaf piles, do you?"

"Yes." She nodded with a mischievous grin playing around her mouth and she wrapped her small arms tightly around Cameron's neck and her legs tightly around his waist, "I like leaves!"

"I know you like leaves, so does Aaron." Cameron kissed the top of her head and set her down again, "Let's help him rake so you can play in them together."

They spent the rest of the afternoon raking the yard. The job, which should have taken a little over an hour, took three times as long, given the fact that two of the workers did more playing in the leaves than raking them.

Between her book club, bowling league and ceramics class, Cassie had made a new set of friends outside of their church circle which only added to the already-active church schedule. In fact, many times when there was a scheduling conflict, Cameron was forced to attend church events without her. Today, she was with some of her bowling league friends and had called just before dinner to tell him they were going to grab something to eat and have some drinks, so "just go ahead and get the kids some dinner, don't wait up for me, babe."

He felt the burn starting again in his stomach.

As always, when he started to condemn her in his mind, he instinctively retreated, a harsh, bright light of self-recrimination reminding him that he was no angel.

Truth was, between the two of them, Cassie had always been the more moderate person, not likely to swerve from the straight and narrow very far. She was the "good girl" who had fallen for the wrong kind of guy. She always said that while she was first attracted to the carefree, party-loving side of him, she fell in love with the nurturing, kind man underneath. Cameron always wondered about that because when he met her, that nurturing side was buried so far down, it was unlikely it was visible at all.

Cameron's life had always been privileged. His parents had money and both his mother and father had come from wealthy families going back generations. There was always more than enough money around and he took it for granted, using it to his advantage whenever he needed to. Money covered sins, it got you out of tight spots, it camouflaged you until at some point you couldn't even see who you were without the comfort of money.

He was raised with the expectation that he would continue this life of relative affluence by earning a good living, there really was no alternative. He would, of course, become a doctor; he had always been groomed for that path. This was obvious when, on his thirteenth birthday, his father gave him a book on human anatomy for his gift and said if he had any questions about how things worked, now he could just look it up for himself.

But, knowing this was his trajectory, and never really contemplating or questioning it, there were moments where he did things, acted certain ways, just to push it, to see how far he could go before sabotaging the whole thing.

For years he drank too much, smoked too much marijuana, he dated too many girls and his quick temper, fueled by alcohol and an inner rage, got him into way too many fist fights.

He lived this chaos all while attending medical school. And, even though he was passing his med school classes, he didn't study enough to excel in them. Honestly, even meeting and then marrying Cassie was yet another chapter of the reckless, irresponsible haze of his world at that time. In retrospect, at least that was one chapter that he could say he was proud of now that he was on the other side.

To say his life was messed up was an understatement. But somehow - underneath all the bad-boy "acting out" that he seemed incapable of controlling - he felt a more authentic person, a person who had a faith in God, inside him wanting to come out and breathe the fresh air.

That day when Mae Churchill died on the table in front of him and he felt something move inside him - when Jesus moved him - he took notice. He took notice indeed.

This took him on a gut-wrenching journey where he evaluated all aspects of his life, eventually bringing him completely to his knees with remorse for his lifestyle and the many sins he had committed. It was with a sense of exhausted freedom that he finally accepted the salvation that Jesus had bought for him with the cross.

Maybe *that* person had been inside all the time; maybe it was just the right timing. Or, maybe he just needed a push to free the chains he had bound that person with.

Now, years later, he had grown secure in the authentically Christian life he was living, the life he'd lived since he first experienced Jesus that day.

Trouble was, with each of these skirmishes with Cassie, his grip on the new Cameron, the security of his identity in this new life, was starting to feel a lot less solid and the haze of that old life crept ever closer.

1966, October

The phone was ringing. Cameron glanced up from his sermon notes and out towards the kitchen wondering if Cassie was still out there preparing dinner and would pick it up. He looked back down again, stuck on how he could tie these two thoughts together. Pride and Surrender. Surrender and Pride. He turned his Bible to Proverbs 11:2.

The phone was still ringing. With a sigh, Cameron pushed his notes away, stood up from his desk and peeked out his office door towards the kitchen. He could smell the pot roast and vegetables that Cassie had put in the oven earlier and the kitchen radio was playing, but there were no other signs of them anywhere in the hushed house.

Where had they all gone, he wondered as he reached for the hand receiver on the telephone which sat on the side table in the center hallway. Maybe next year they would be able to afford the additional monthly charge to add a telephone extension in his office, that would be so much more convenient, he thought.

"Hello, Berndt's residence." As he answered the phone, Cameron glanced out the windows of the living room and saw Cassie pushing Charlotte on the tree swing while Aaron played just beyond them in his sandbox. With her hair tied securely under a bright pink headscarf, he could see the pretty contours of Cassie's face as she laughed at something Charlotte said. She was a beautiful woman, his wife.

"Yes, may I speak with Cassie Berndt?" A woman's pleasant voice was on the line.

"Well, she's outside right now. This is her husband Cameron. Can I give her a message? Or would you like to hold on while I go get her?"

"No, that's quite alright. Just tell her that Julia Piper called from the law office. I forgot to mention to her that she will need to bring her social security card along with her on her first day. We went over so many things that I realized that I forgot to mention that." The woman paused, obviously expecting a response from him. What was she talking about?

"Uh, okay."

"Thank you, Mr. Berndt." She continued conversationally, obviously not noticing that he was in a bit of confused haze right now. "We are so excited to have Cassie join our staff and look forward to meeting you and the children. I told your wife that we have many work-social events where employee's families are encouraged to meet each other. You will find that we are like one big family." Julia Piper paused at the shrill sound of a ringing telephone in the background. "Well, I am getting another call, Mr. Berndt, so I must hang up. Tell Cassie she can call me if she has any questions before we see her next week. You have a good day now!"

"Uh, yes. You too, thank you." Cameron's voice drifted off quietly as he dropped the receiver onto the telephone with a slow thud. He turned around to look out the window at his pretty wife playing with their children, his mind full of unanswered questions. Maybe he missed something. Did she just apply for, interview for and accept a job without saying a word to him? How could she do that? Why would she do that?

As he watched her help Charlotte down from the swing and tighten the string of Charlotte's hat under her chin, Cameron's skin began to crawl in frustration. At first it felt like an uncomfortable itch, then it lit with a pervasive heat that travelled throughout his torso, an unpleasant reminder of a time in his life when this angry feeling was all too common for him.

He tried to control the anger by taking a deep breath and he tried to pray. Desperately, he looked back towards his office where he knew he had an open Bible and a sermon that he was working on. He should take a moment to reign in his thoughts and emotions, he knew he should, but, somehow, he couldn't force his legs to carry him there and instead he let his mind run rampantly forward to the angry place.

The months of arguments, the distancing that had been going on, this other life that she insisted she needed to feel "complete," it all suddenly felt vindictive and deceptive. Like *he* was the problem in her life. Like *he* was holding her back from something.

The nerve of her! To hide something like this. As if he didn't have a right to an opinion on whether she took a job or not. As if uprooting their lives in this way would have no effect on him.

Cameron strode out the back door and was standing next to her before he even realized it, his anger now seething through every muscle. As he reached them, Charlotte, not recognizing his mood, looked up with glee and started to pull on his hand urgently, lisping a little when she spoke in her stilted language, "Daddy! Can you push me on swing? Mommy pushed me on swing!"

He brushed Charlotte's hand aside roughly, startling her so much she lost her balance and her unsteady, three-year-old legs wobbled to the ground, prompting a stunned cry. As Cassie exclaimed in surprise and knelt to attend to their crying daughter, Cameron barely noticed Charlotte's distress, he was too focused on Cassie to really care.

"Cam! What's going on-" Cassie exclaimed, taking Charlotte into a loose hug and looked up at him with confusion, her eyes frowning.

"You tell me, Cass. You tell me what's going on." His voice was ice cold, hard and unbending. It was a voice he didn't even recognize anymore. But he didn't care.

"I don't know what you're talking about." Cassie said the words, but her eyes told a different story. Somehow, she knew that he knew her secret.

"Oh, I think you do know what I'm talking about. Julia Piper from the law office called. You're supposed to bring your social security card when you show up for your *first day on the job*." Cameron finished the sentence with as scathing a tone as he could utter. Immediately, the lights went on in Cassie's eyes and then they went out again, as if she knew what his reaction would be, and he was playing it out just like she expected. She stood up slowly, pulling Charlotte back against her legs, her fingertips resting on the little girl's shoulders.

"Cam, please. Let's not fight about it. Especially here, in front of the kids."

"I don't want to fight about anything. I want you to tell me what the hell is going on." As the angry words escaped his mouth, Cameron bit his lip. Too far. Too far. Get control of yourself, he scolded himself in his mind.

"Well, I would tell you, but I don't feel like you can hear me right now, you're too angry." Cassie picked up Charlotte, tucked her legs up around her waist and walked away from him towards the house, leaving Cameron in the yard with his son watching silently from the sandbox six feet away.

If her retreat was supposed to give him time to cool down, it had the exact opposite effect. His initial white-hot anger was quickly becoming searing, indignant resentment. How dare she act like she was the injured party? After all, she was the one who was deceitful, not breathing a word to him about looking for a job.

What, wasn't he providing well enough? Couldn't she stand to live the life of a poor pastor's wife? Maybe she was embarrassed by their life when she compared it to the lives of her new friends?

Just past his shoulder, Aaron rubbed a dirty fist at his watery eyes, catching Cameron's attention. Was the boy crying? Great. First, he made Charlotte cry and now he made Aaron cry?

Cameron squinted into the bright sun, shrugged a little and lifted his hands towards his son.

"Hey, bud. It's okay. Mommy and Daddy are just talking. Come here."

But Aaron sat rooted in the sandbox, shook his head slowly and then turned his focus back towards the amber-colored Tonka toy truck in front of him. He bent low, rested his round cheek on the truck's cab and as he muttered an engine sound under his breath, he burrowed the truck through the late autumn-damp sand, leaving deep ruts in its wake.

Cameron stood still, dismally watching his son. He knew this was one of *those* moments. He could feel in his bones how important it would be to connect with Aaron about what he had just witnessed. But, the dead, eerily disconnected feeling of gloom that had been inching its way to the forefront of his consciousness now seeped completely through Cameron, numbing him to everything and everyone in his orbit. Including his child. He just couldn't make himself care.

Frustrated, he turned on his heel and headed towards the house, readying himself for the next battle in the war.

"I couldn't tell you, Cameron. I can't tell you anything anymore because you don't want to listen to me. It's like I've ceased to exist altogether. It doesn't matter to you what I want." Cassie said in an even, steady voice after calmly pulling his office doors closed behind her an hour later, the smell of a recently smoked cigarette trailing her into the office.

While Cassie eventually had called Aaron inside and his family all sat down to dinner, Cameron had gone straight to his office, avoiding dinner altogether because he had no appetite to sit across the table and pretend that he wasn't utterly furious and deeply hurt at her deception.

Now, as the children sat outside in the living room propped in front of the television, he wondered, just what was she thinking? Was she thinking of them at all?

"Of course, it matters to me what you want, Cassie. Don't make me the bad guy in this. You looked for a job and accepted a job - all without even consulting with your husband. Who does that?"

"Well, it wasn't exactly like that. They found me. My friend Mary's brother is one of the partners at the firm. When I met Mr. Hearst at her house after bowling one night, we started talking about my work in dad's law office. One thing led to another, and they offered me a job."

"But you have a job. You're a mother. We agreed when we had Aaron that you wanted to be at home with him."

"Well, I didn't have much choice, did I? I had to quit college because you were in med school. Nothing really went according to *my* plan, did it?" Cassie said, her voice dripping with scorn.

"Oh, so that's it." Cameron spoke up, pouncing on a reason that might make sense for all this, "Now you tell me that you regret that decision, and this is your way of paying me back somehow?"

"No-" Her voice rose, and she reached into her pocket for her lighter and another cigarette, "It's not about you, Cameron. It's not always about you. We've already done *you*. You decided to leave medical school and become a pastor. And, I supported you. Now, I want to do *me* for a change." She finished with a plaintive tone, begging him to understand as she lit her cigarette and drew in a ragged breath, but he couldn't understand the logic. What else could she want anyway?

"But, Cassie, what about the kids?"

"What about them?" Cassie breathed out a plume of smoke with her question and her gaze became more emboldened as she leaned against the door, giving the distinct impression that she felt this argument was going nowhere, "I have already arranged with Mrs. Redfield down the street to watch Charlotte during the day and Aaron in the afternoons once he gets off the kindergarten bus. And, if she's not able to watch them, I will figure it out. Don't worry, I won't bother you to watch them."

"That's not fair. I think I've been watching them plenty over the past year while you've been living *this other life*."

"Oh, please, Cameron." She rolled her eyes dramatically, "You're just upset that I didn't tell you. And, okay. I should have, I get that. But it doesn't change the fact that I'm going to do this."

"Well, obviously, you could care less what I think about it-"

"You're right. I could care less." She interrupted firmly, "But I would hope that you would be supportive of me. Besides, you know we could use the extra money."

"We are doing fine." Cameron's bruised pride immediately flared with a vengeance, "You live in one of the nicest homes on the block, you're not hurting for clothes, you do pretty much whatever you want to do. What do you mean we could use the money?"

"I mean that when I married you, I thought things would be different." Cassie's voice rose again, "I thought I wouldn't have to worry about paying the grocery bill. I thought maybe we could take a vacation once in a while. I thought we would be able to afford to have a lake cabin or maybe camp for our kids in the summer. Lots of things."

"We talked about all this when we made this decision years ago. You know we did. We both decided that we were better off being happy knowing Jesus and walking out our faith rather than living the old way. We agreed on that, Cassie."

Cameron tried to recall their discussions a few years ago about becoming a pastor, he knew they had discussed it in detail, but he was having a hard time remembering the details of it now. His memory had been erased. It had been replaced with the here and now.

"Yeah, well, maybe I agreed then. I don't know. Now, I'm not so sure I agree." Cassie looked at the floor with her admission and took another nervous drag on her cigarette.

They stood in silence for a long, tense moment as her comment filled the room.

"What's that supposed to mean?" Cameron finally spoke breathlessly, and a sensation returned that he hadn't felt for many years now. He didn't just want a drink. He *needed* a drink.

"I don't know-" She looked up at him, tears in her eyes as she blinked through the smoke trailing from her cigarette, "I just don't feel like I fit this life sometimes. I mean I don't fit your new life sometimes. I'm just not that person."

"What kind of person is that?" He asked with a hollow voice and the sensation became stronger, his mouth started to go dry and his hand started to shake where it rested on his knee under his desk.

"Oh, Cam. Please. It's no big deal, it's just a job. Let's drop it." She pleaded but the cat was out of the bag, as they say. No stopping it now.

"No. I want you to say it. What kind of person is that, Cassie? What kind of person fits *my new life?*"

"Okay, then, if you insist-" Cassie breathed in deeply, her thin shoulders under her striped knit top rose and lowered slowly as she spoke quietly, "Cameron, you want a perfect wife. You insist on a perfect wife. Trouble is, you didn't marry a perfect wife." At her words, as he tried to interrupt her, she held up one of her hands slightly and put the other on her hip as she continued, "I just don't fit, Cam. And, I don't think I *will* fit. Ever."

Cameron felt like she'd landed a solid punch to his gut. In fact, he felt a painful slicing sensation through his stomach as her words sunk in. His mind raced in a thousand different directions all at once as he lost the ability to gather his thoughts into a coherent response. What was she saying? What was she not saying? What did she mean?

But just as he was about to interrogate her further with an avalanche of questions, his voice refused to comply. In a stupor, he put his elbows on his knees and dropped his heavy head into his hands.

Of all the thoughts in his head right now, the one that stood out was of a time when he was still a small child and he sat right there in the corner of this office, next to the heat register. As he sat there and obediently played with one of his toy trucks, he listened as his father discussed an upcoming surgery with a patient.

He was far too young to understand any of their conversation, but he remembered watching his father talk to the lady. Cameron remembered the way his glasses sat on his face, the kind, deep timbre of his voice, his steady, intelligent gaze. This was one of many times in his life where he felt a deep admiration for his father. He was a man who could control things. People trusted him to control things. People put their lives in his hands. He wouldn't let anyone down.

His father hadn't been a failure.

When Cameron raised his eyes a few moments later, desperate to connect again with his wife the way they used to, he was greeted with an empty room and the remote, inaudible tone of a television in the next room.

Turning in his chair slowly, dreadfully, he bent low and opened a door in the cabinet behind him. Closing his eyes in submission, he reached for the bottle and the single glass standing next to it.

There was only one glass, because this bottle wasn't meant to be shared. Only one person ever drank from it.

CHAPTER 10

1966, December

I ask that you remind me of your presence, Lord. Each day I find that I need more of you. And even though there is so much to learn about being a good father and husband, I find that you are patiently teaching me. Every time I look in my children's eyes, I see your blessings. Help me to see your blessings when I look into the eyes of my wife, Lord.

It was a winter-brisk, snow-laden Christmas Day that Sunday in 1966 and Freedom Church had been over-capacity with congregants and their visiting families and friends which required additional folding chairs in the aisles and along the front of the church.

Delivering the Christmas sermon was one of the services Cameron enjoyed the most. Even this year with the shadow of Cassie's new job hanging over his marriage, he found a simple kind of peace watching the children sing their carols, all dressed up in their Christmas clothes, the little boys in their plaid vests and ties and the little girls with their shiny hair and red velvet dresses.

Cameron's parents had been among the visitors in attendance this year, having arrived from San Diego two days ago to stay with Cassie and him at the house. They stayed in the guest room down the hall from the bedroom they had used as their master bedroom for the thirty-plus years before his father retired.

The whirlwind of last-minute shopping, food preparation and church activities of the past two days provided a welcome cover for the continued tensions between Cameron and his wife. But still, his ever-watchful parents had exchanged a few knowing glances. Cameron knew they suspected all was not well in their son's marriage and he dreaded the inevitable moment when the subject would be addressed head-on.

As always, Cassie had outdone herself dressing the house for her family and their Christmas guests. For his part, just after Thanksgiving, Cameron would stop at the Christmas tree lot next to the local hardware store and pick the most handsome tree he could afford. Cassie always said the living room with its high ceilings required a grand tree with an impressive stature.

Once it was securely mounted into the stand, Cassie would adorn (and overload) the tree with brightly colored, metallic ornaments in traditional reds and greens and heavily punctuated with some bright blues and flashy pinks and teals. The kids, anxious to help this year, proudly contributed some handmade snowmen and Santa Claus ornaments fashioned from pipe cleaners and painted clothespins.

After their Christmas tree work of art was completed, Cameron often found the kids sitting silently on the carpet fascinated as the twinkling lights danced off the puffy silver tinsel and mirrored bead garlands. Of course, the brightly wrapped gifts under the tree were also the objects of their attention, but if they had peeked at their gifts, they were mindful not to get caught.

Early Christmas morning, before they left for church, the children had finally been allowed to open their gifts, the numbers of which had quadrupled with the arrival of their grandparents. Amongst the deep red poinsettias that Cassie had set around the tree, the children opened box after colorful box of toys, books and games, each gift bringing another round of "thank you" hugs and kisses.

The chaotically poignant scene felt like a scene from a movie, and even though Cassie sat next to him on the couch with her hand resting on his knee, Cameron noticed a sad feeling of detachment as he watched it all unfold. He didn't ask himself exactly why he felt so sad when he had so much to be thankful for. Somehow, he recognized that asking too many questions might result in some answers he didn't really want to know.

Now, a few hours later, they had just finished Christmas dinner, and the kids were in the living room playing the Twister game his parents had given them. It was the newest thing, his mother gushed earlier when the kids opened it, she said they'd watched Johnny Carson play the game on his television program earlier that year. The twisting and turning it required were a little beyond Charlotte's ability and physical size, but she tried valiantly to keep up with her older brother.

As he sat in the overstuffed chair next to the couch with the Sunday paper unfolded across his lap and a small benevolent smile on his mouth, Cameron's father took a sip of his after-dinner coffee, a look of introspection in his silvery gray eyes.

Cameron's father was a complex man. Dr. August Berndt III embodied a generation that learned by going through the fire of war what it took to survive. His quiet, unassuming demeanor often disguised the brilliant, sharp clarity of his mind. He was loath to speak without a purpose, often preferring to stay silent until something or someone moved him to speak.

"That was quite a sermon this morning, Son. You made your mother and I proud today." August spoke quietly as he set his cup onto the saucer he held on his knee.

"I appreciate you saying that, Dad. I always pray that the words I find help people grow in the things of God."

"Well, that must be what happened because there were moments during your sermon today where I completely forgot you were my son."

"Ha. Well, that's the way it should be, Dad. Thank you for telling me that."

They sat in silence for a few moments and Cameron wished anew that his father could understand the sentiment of what he was sharing, how his faith truly inspired his words. But, long ago, Cameron had realized that his father's faith held a private place in his heart and that it looked different than his own faith. It had taken years to feel comfortable with this realization, for both of them. They were still working on it.

"Do you miss medicine, Cameron?" The question came out of nowhere, surprising Cameron with the abrupt shift in topic.

His departure from medicine years ago had always been a touchy subject, fraught with discord. To his father, his decision had never made any sense and had been viewed as a wild, impulsive move destined to drive him and his young family to the poor house.

All this turmoil only served to make Cameron more adamant in his defense that he'd made the right choice. But, as the years passed and things settled in, Cameron was able to honestly reflect that sometimes he did miss aspects of his life before.

"Sometimes I do, yes." Cameron admitted, "When I think about medicine, it feels more certain than ministry. It was something I could train for."

"Yes, I think I understand what you're saying." His father nodded before continuing quietly, "I always knew you would have made an excellent doctor."

"Thanks, Dad. Life sure would have been different, wouldn't it?"

His father paused and sipped slowly from his coffee cup before continuing again, "But, still, you didn't. You made a choice for you and your family. At the time, you were sure it was the right choice. Have things changed?"

It began to dawn on Cameron that perhaps his father's deliberate line of questioning might be his way of ascertaining the reason behind the tension between Cassie and him the past few days. And, while his choice of profession was weighing on their marriage, it was only one of many reasons for the tension they lived with every day.

"Well, there have been many adjustments, that's for sure." Cameron tried to find words to summarize honestly some of the struggles he was facing, "As for me, I find the expectations of ministry are daunting sometimes. You know, leading a group of people in something as personal and critical as their faith with their Savior. Honestly, sometimes I don't feel up to the challenge. I suppose that's something you can't relate to. You always seemed to be up for the challenges you faced as a doctor."

Cameron smiled hesitantly at his father, wondering if he would hear the vulnerability in what he was saying. His father met his gaze and took in a deep breath, as if giving himself a moment to collect his thoughts before speaking.

"Cameron, I have spent my entire life tending to the physical needs of people, not their spiritual needs. But when you told me that you needed to go in a different direction and tend to the souls of people rather than their bodies, I tried my best to understand."

His father paused and took another sip of coffee and Cameron waited, intuitively knowing that he had something else he wanted to say. With his father, the subject of his career choice never seemed to be completely resolved and for reasons that were tangled in duty and respect, Cameron always heard him out.

"I'm not pretending to understand any better now," His father eventually spoke quietly with sigh, "But if you're feeling at a loss with tending to people's souls, isn't that the beauty of the arrangement with God? He's there to step in and fill those gaps?"

Maybe it was that deep respect he had for his father or maybe it was that everything he said seemed seasoned and wise to Cameron, but something about his father's simple analysis of faith resonated through him with a clarity that immediately seemed to relieve his mind and brought a smile to his face.

"Yes, it is. That's exactly what he does, Dad."

Distracted by the children playing Twister in front of them, Cameron rose to pull Charlotte, whose body was much too small to play the game, out from under her brother.

Cameron returned to his easy chair, pushed a pillow up behind his back and got comfortable. They sat there together for a few minutes in peaceful silence as his father watched his grandchildren playing on the carpet in front of them while Bing Crosby's Christmas Greetings LP serenaded them on the stereo. With flames crackling and spitting in the fireplace and the children playing contentedly for once, Cameron was just starting to nod off into a nap when his father suddenly spoke again.

"I didn't know that Cassie smoked."

Startled awake, Cameron glanced towards the kitchen where his mother and his wife sat at the table looking at some old photographs that Cassie had found in the attic last month. As he watched her draw on a cigarette, Cameron turned back to his father, feeling a bit sheepish, as if they were disobedient teenagers.

"It's just something she's picked up again over the past year or so." Even though Cameron disliked her smoking, he still felt defensive for her. Certainly, his parents couldn't tell her what to do.

"Yes," His father continued, a paternal tone in his voice, "But it is a nasty habit with significant health consequences according to the Surgeon General."

"Yes, Father. I'm aware of that." Cameron sighed with a roll of his eyes as he watched his wife laughing with his mother at the pictures spread out on the table in front of them. "I don't think it's a habit for her. I think it's something else."

Okay, here comes the conversation, Cameron thought. This is where I have to tell him what's going on.

"What *something else* would that be?" His father's tone was measured yet inquisitive as he emphasized the words carefully.

"It's many things, Dad. We're going through many things right now, that's all. It's a lot of change." How could he tell him exactly what was happening? The arguments, the excruciating tug of war between Cassie and him? That he'd started drinking again.

Cameron had never so much as heard his parents raise their voices to each other. How could he explain to his father that sometimes he felt an anger that he couldn't control? And, he was a *pastor* and a *father*. *He was supposed to know Jesus...*

"Well, it seems your life with Cassie is reflective of our times, Cameron. Things are changing, families are changing." His father watched Cassie from across the room, a look of kindness in his eyes, "It must be challenging to manage it all – her job at the law office, providing care for the children and the demands of being a pastor's wife."

"Yes, all that." Cameron muttered, shutting down the thought in his mind when he really wanted to ask, What about your son, Dad? Why didn't anyone ever think about how any of this affected him?

His father turned his attention back to Cameron, obviously hearing the irritation in his voice.

"Well, how do you feel about all *that*?" His father asked, opening the door for Cameron to finally share with him more details. Debating in his mind how much and what to share, finally, the desire to get it all off his chest won and his words gushed out.

"I haven't been completely honest with you and mother over the past year. It's been pretty rough." Cameron sat forward in his chair while he watched the women carefully, speaking quietly enough so they wouldn't hear him, "Cassie took this job without even discussing it with me. And, once we worked through *that* and I forced myself to get over it and be happy for her, it's like that was just the doorway to *so much more*." He hesitated, never having said the words out loud before, but knowing that he had to let it go, the urge to share the burden with someone else was so overwhelming.

"Dad, it's like she's always pushing the envelope with her choices, the way she spends her time, the people she chooses to be with. Her personality is even changing. It's like she's going through some type of identity crisis right in front of me and I am powerless to do anything about it. I just have to sit by and watch as this torrential flood alters the landscape of my life."

His father reacted to the dramatic deluge of information in much the same way that he had always reacted to dramatic news. He blinked slowly and his shoulders lifted as he drew in a deep, introspective breath while he rubbed his chin thoughtfully before he responded.

"But even so, you're dealing with it well, Son. You have compromised in some areas and marriage is about compromise."

"Yeah, I guess so. But I just don't know where this is all going. One of the attorneys she works with is encouraging her to finish her History degree and then go to law school, which could mean she'd have to move to another state for all we know. Talk about compromising."

"Oh. That is a lot," He agreed, "But, of course, none of that might happen. After all, you have two children and Cassandra is a good mother. I think she will make choices that are in the best interests of the children."

"We *both* make choices with the children in mind. That's why we are here in the first place. Choosing to be a pastor was *supposed* to be the mutual choice." Cameron stopped awkwardly at the hollow sound of his statement, knowing full well that Cassie regretted their decision. So, here they were. And, where were they going? Who knew? And, what could his father do about any of it?

Nothing, Cameron thought desperately, his heart rate rising. His father could do nothing about it.

This was fruitless – this sharing of information - he was done talking. Cameron stood up suddenly, and needing to get some air, he let himself out the front door onto the porch and breathed deep of the December icy air, not even aware that he hadn't stopped to grab his coat.

CHAPTER 11

2017, July

It was just past midnight according to her cell phone, and a light breeze lifted the sheer curtains she'd hung on the window next to their bed and carried the faintest hint of rain spatter, reminding her that the forecast had been for scattered showers tonight. But, somehow, she found herself too exhausted to even climb out of bed to close the window.

With a quiet sigh, Lauryn shut the journal and ran her tired hands over the cover, unconsciously praying for Pastor Cameron and his family and all the unrest they were going through. Vaguely, the recognition that this had all happened decades ago dawned on her again. And, although some of the issues he wrote about, like the distress around the issue of his wife having a full time job while also raising a family seemed to be from a by-gone era a generation ago, many of the other issues he mentioned were completely relevant now. This juxtaposition was one of the things that made his journal so captivating.

With each reading, Lauryn wanted to know more, and, like an engrossing novel, she found it almost impossible to put the journal down. Tonight though, she felt a strange sense of weightiness reading his journal because it was becoming exceedingly clear to her that this man's life was something precious and private. Rarely did he spend time documenting inconsequential trivial details of his life. In fact, each page was like a window into his soul, leaving her feeling like a time-travelling voyeur.

But even though she felt conflicted to read it, she knew she couldn't stop. Of course, at some point she'd have to admit to Bridgette that she'd read it. And when she did, she'd have to convince her she had no choice because her grandfather Cameron is – or had been, because she still didn't know if he was alive or dead – a thoroughly captivating man.

As she squinted away from the table lamp's bright beam, her eyes felt like they were dragging over sandpaper with each blink and she rubbed at her thighs trying to relieve the dull pain. Much of today she had worked on a ladder fixing the trim on the garage while the carpenters re-roofed it. It had been a long, hot day and her muscles were in full-on revolt tonight as fatigue travelled throughout her entire body, finding its final resting spot in her legs.

Exhausted, Lauryn glanced over at Elliott, sleeping soundly next to her, his arms cradled around the pillow on which he laid. He was on his side, his face turned towards her with his dark, glossy hair loose on the pillow and falling in light waves over his eyes. She watched him for a moment, her eyes travelling over the familiar planes of his face, thinking he looked like an angel, his face was so peaceful. Was it possible, she wondered, to love a person more than she loved him?

She remembered a sermon she'd heard once about the different types of love and about how it was God's delight to give humans the ability to love, how important love was to him. Even though, honestly, she felt a little distant from God right now, this feeling of love somehow always connected her back to him. If God could bring a love like Elliott into her life, he had to be faithful to her in other aspects of her life too, right?

Lauryn reached out to smooth Elliott's hair away from his eyes and bent close as she kissed his forehead softly, slowly breathing along with him, while trying to calm her tired body and anxious mind.

This body-numbing fatigue and her short temper were very familiar to her. He should know the signs too. Maybe Elliott was subconsciously trying to ignore them so he wouldn't be forced to recognize that their lives had been set on a familiar path once again - and he wasn't in full knowledge or full support this time.

The test had been positive. She was pregnant. What should have been an exciting announcement the night she saw the two distinct lines, was instead a secret, riddled with anxiety.

She hadn't told Elliott yet, it had been over a week since she took the test, but still, she hadn't told him. And she wasn't sure when she would.

"- That would be great! I look forward to meeting you and please bring any pictures you can find. We'll take special care of them and return them once they've been scanned."

From where she knelt, painting carefully around the rugged edges of the bricks near the dining room fireplace, Lauryn glanced over at Elliott with an excited grin and a thumbs up sign. Finally!

"Yeah," She continued into her cell phone, finishing up her call, "We are trying to find as many connections to the Berndt house as possible so if you think of anyone else, please let us know. See you Friday!"

Lauryn straightened her legs, swiped her cell phone with a flourish and held her hand up for a high five. Elliott walked towards her, smacked her palm and then threaded his fingers through her hand, while he turned it around to kiss the back of it.

"Congratulations, babe! Persistence always pays!" He turned back to where his paintbrush sat balancing on the edge of his ladder and returned to his job painting along the ceiling molding.

"Yes, it does, doesn't it? Patient Baby number five is named Milton and his mom was one of the women who stayed here to work with Doctor Berndt, the second. Can you believe it? Depending on the pictures he has, I think we can finish writing the history story for this house!"

The five "babies" they had found had all been born at Promise Place between the years 1920 and 1945. Two of them were already dead, the contact with Lauryn had been made through their children. But these children had happily shared their stories and had pictures to document their loved ones' lives with their once-single mothers, all who went on to marry and have other children.

This last baby, Milton, had been born in 1941 to Nadine, a young mother aged seventeen. His father - her "boyfriend" at the time - was twelve years older and married, unbeknownst to her. The scandal of the affair forced the young woman to travel across the state from her small, western-Minnesota hometown to live with relatives in eastern Minnesota, where she met Doctor August Berndt III and his wife Patricia during a prenatal visit.

Once the doctor and his wife heard her story, and they noticed the disdain the young woman's aunt displayed towards her niece during the visit, the Berndt's offered the young mother free room and board in exchange for her work assisting them in their medical practice. It wasn't the first time this arrangement took place and it wouldn't be the last, but it was the only one where Lauryn had first-hand account of it, and she was thrilled to get more details from Milton at their upcoming meeting.

"I think there were some other contacts that messaged through Instagram though," Elliott spoke up as he glanced down from his perch on the ladder, "I saw one from a guy named Clive who said he knew a Dr. Berndt and two or three others from ladies in the Minneapolis area. Did you look through those messages?"

"Yeah, I did. They were all patients who had other issues, no unwed mothers with babies. After talking to all these people about this, it's really obvious how difficult it was for these women, and how secretive it all was, isn't it?"

"No doubt. I suppose as a doctor, though, it came down to caring for their patient. It was just their job."

"Right. I wonder what people in town thought about it though. I suppose it was a challenge for these doctors to deal with the stigma in a small town."

"I guess they came to terms with it. They were probably too busy to care."

"Or, they didn't care what people thought because they really just loved people."

"Yeah, or that."

Because they had been invited to her parents' home in Lake Belle for steaks on the grill that night, they packed up early and took the twenty-minute drive mostly in amicable silence while Lauryn debated with herself how and when to tell Elliott about the pregnancy. Her most recent thoughts had centered around visiting a doctor before telling him. If everything looked good after her OB-GYN visit next week, then she would have that as extra reinforcement and she could convince him that this time it would be different.

As the first clues of pregnancy became evident, like her loss of appetite and frequent visits to the bathroom fighting nausea, Lauryn was concerned that he would just guess anyway.

Now it was becoming almost laughable to her that Elliott hadn't pieced together even the obvious ones like her mindless distraction two days ago when she'd ordered the wrong paint color for the bathroom upstairs and yesterday when she'd locked her keys in the work truck and today when she repeated herself three times during the videotape session they had while she sanded and refinished the front door. But no. Elliott hadn't noticed anything was awry. He seemed oblivious.

As they waited at the stop sign at the end of Main Street in Lake Belle, Lauryn glanced at him across the front seat of the Jeep. Elliott was on his Bluetooth talking to his grandpa Jared. As she listened to their shared sense of dry humor and easy banter, her mind travelled back over the many moments where he had turned to his grandparents for their calm, loving presence to help him through rough times in his life.

As the years passed and her love for Elliott matured, she noticed that his circle of people was deep, not wide. And the most beautiful thing about his relationships with people was that he allowed relationships, and people, to *be*. He didn't feel obligated to move things along on a schedule, force people into something they weren't.

Lauryn regarded him as he finished the call with his grandpa and turned the car onto the steep street that bordered the lake in Lake Belle and led towards her parents' home. Resolutely, she decided, instead of waiting until next week, she would tell him tonight. It was the right thing to do. She would convince him not to worry about her and together they would look forward to the birth of this baby. It was wrong to keep this secret from him, no matter how he reacted, and she felt better already, now that she had a plan for it.

Passing a few lakeside homes with their manicured lawns and trimmed trees, Elliott turned into the steep driveway that led down the embankment towards her parents' home, a century-old, two-story gabled house with shuttered windows and a deep, wrap-around porch. The noise of their doors closing in the peaceful yard disturbed a red squirrel who a moment before had sat perfectly still, like a statue, on the bottom step of the deck. They both laughed at the furry blur he made as he scampered up one of the yawning oak trees and chattered at them from his safe-space twenty feet above them.

Taking in the pretty sight of her mom's colorful quilt of flower beds around the deck and the lawn that invited bare toes to dig into it's deep-pile, green carpet, Lauryn breathed in the fresh, outdoorsy lake air.

She was so glad to be back in Minnesota, she had missed so much about this place - the people, the sights, the smells, the energy of it.

As usual, her mind returned to the baby inside her.

On a whim, she grabbed at Elliott's hand and drew him across the lawn towards the steps that led down towards the water, the plan taking shape in her mind. Why wait to tell him later tonight? Why not just tell him now? And what better place to tell him the good news about this baby than the place that held such sweet memories for them from their childhood?

The decades-old, flat-rock steps leading to the lakeshore at her parents' lake house were steep and lined with wildflowers and tangled shrubbery on either side. After a few turns through the fragrant greenery, a person would end up at the bottom, where they were greeted by a warm, sugar-sand beach and a broad dock with a swimming platform at its end and the shimmering purple-blue water of the lake beyond.

It was down at this dock where, as kids, she first met Elliott. And, it was down at this dock where, ten years later, he first told her he loved her - in *that* way - and wanted to share his life with her. It was the perfect place to tell him about this baby.

"What's up," His laughing voice interrupted her daydreaming, "You want to go swimming or something?" His eyes were crinkled in confusion as he gently resisted her pull.

"No–" Her mind was racing now that the moment was upon them and she was about to say it out loud. She hoped he would be as excited as she was about this news and she stammered in haste, "I just miss the water so much, let's go down to the dock for a while before going inside."

"But, I smell the grill going," Elliott demurred and glanced over his shoulder at the smoking grill on the deck, clearly he was imagining thick-cut steaks sizzling away under the hood, "Your dad probably started the steaks already since we were running late. Let's go down to the water after we eat, ok?"

Lauryn pushed down her immediate disappointment as she glanced towards the house, but she had to agree, this was the kind of news that couldn't be rushed – especially since Elliott was likely to be less than thrilled at the timing of it. She had to be prepared to win him over with her arguments that all would be different this time. It might take a few lines of argument. But the bottom line was the bottom line. It was too late for "let's-wait-and-see-what-happens."

"Okay, fine. Let's go eat." She agreed reluctantly.

They walked together across the lawn, onto the deck and past the grill which, after Elliott's quick glance inside, revealed that it was pre-heating, no steaks were cooking yet.

Lauryn rapped lightly on the screen door before pulling the door open and glanced around the kitchen, surprised that her mother wasn't inside making the spicy southwestern chicken pasta salad with green chilies in it. Although it was Lauryn's favorite, tonight the thought of it made her stomach queasy.

Following the sound of her parents' voices, Lauryn and Elliott walked through the spacious kitchen and around the oversized center island which was a haphazard mix of marinating steaks, garlic bread on trays and a watermelon, half cut. After dropping off the bottle of wine they brought, Elliott passed a tray of colorful, fresh vegetables and ranch dip and plucked up a cut of celery, munching it as he followed Lauryn down the wide hallway towards her dad's office with its open door.

Her mom Gabrielle, with her curly, dark hair piled high on her head with a barrette, was dressed casually in a loose-fitting flowy top, white denim shorts and flip flops. She was facing away from the doorway, standing behind her dad and resting her hands on his shoulders, while Todd sat in the office chair in front of her. Both were unaware that Lauryn and Elliott had arrived and were fully engrossed in the video call in progress on her dad's large computer monitor.

Lauryn glanced around her mom's shoulder to see her sister-in-law Madison's smiling, tanned face on the screen, her long blonde hair pulled back in a ponytail and her wide smile glossed with a pretty shade of vivid pink lipstick. She was holding something, a piece of paper with a flash of black and white, which was whisked out of her hand suddenly as Lauryn's brother Daniel joined her in the space of the screen, as he hugged her in the crook of his arm and laughed with an infectious excitement.

"–they say it's a boy! But I can't see how they tell that, Madison says she can see it, but I sure can't." He stopped his gushing for a brief second and kissed his wife's cheek before turning his bright blue eyes towards the screen again, continuing breathlessly, "I don't care though, I don't care if it's a boy or a girl, I'm just so pumped, can you believe it–"

By now, Lauryn and Elliott had walked far enough into the office that they were visible behind the shoulder of her mother as evidenced by the smaller screen in the bottom of the display. Daniel's eyes travelled above his parents and shadowed slightly in confusion as a look passed immediately through his eyes and across his face. He stopped talking abruptly, and Lauryn felt something twist inside her stomach, not the baby, it was something else.

"Hey, sis." Daniel laughed uncomfortably, trying desperately to adjust his emotions, "Hi, El. Sorry, I didn't know you two were even there." Daniel's eyes shifted towards his father as Todd and Gabrielle both turned away from the monitor to face them as they stood inside the doorway of the office.

"Well, hey, Snickers! Hi, Elliott. We didn't hear you guys come in." It was a nickname that Todd had given Lauryn as a child, one which she had never outgrown. Todd rolled his chair away and unfolded his long legs from under his desk, immediately strolling across the few feet between them to take Lauryn into a big hug. As she watched the look pass between her parents, Lauryn recognized it as the same one that had been on Daniel's face. The look of pity.

Daniel and Madison had obviously called from their home in Kansas City with some exciting news, and they had an ultrasound for added dramatic effect. A baby. A healthy baby boy.

"Daniel and Madison called to tell us their happy news. They're having a baby in November, isn't that great?" Her dad pulled away slightly to look into Lauryn's eyes, his arms still around her protectively, "We are so excited for them! Wow, God is so good." Todd turned back to the screen, including both of his children and his daughter and son-in-law in his praise.

"Yeah," Lauryn spoke first and swallowed hard against the hurt, but of course, she really was happy for them. This was a moment they would never forget, "Hey, you guys - that's great, congratulations! Oh, my gosh, you're going to be a daddy-"

Lauryn smiled at her brother, but she couldn't help it - her smile was shaky at first. It almost felt fake. *What was wrong with her?*

She turned out of her dad's hug and against Elliott's waiting arms behind her. She just needed something for support, her legs felt like they would give way any moment. She felt as Elliott tightened his arms on either side of her waist, and she took comfort in the gentle rumble of his voice against her back as he spoke.

"We're so happy for you guys. A boy, huh? Poor Madison. Two against one for the big screen TV on game days-"

"You're dang right!" Daniel laughed in relief at the light-hearted response, "Well, I hope he likes football as much I do but - whatever, it's cool. He's going to be my little gopher - run get your dad more chips and salsa, go find the remote, would ya, buddy - ahh, the life ..." Daniel laughed at the thought while he gazed lovingly at his wife. Then, he turned back towards the screen and found his sister again.

"Lauryn, I'm glad you guys are at mom and dad's tonight so you could hear about this from us first-hand. It means a lot that you're happy for us, given all you've gone through. We love you guys so much."

Elliott and Daniel had always been extremely close friends and Lauryn and her brother had a bond that was super tight. He had been on the other end of many telephone conversations supporting them through the miscarriages they'd suffered. He knew how hard this was for them.

"Of course," Lauryn said, and she desperately wanted him to know how much it meant that he was so considerate, that even in his joy he found empathy for their pain, "We're happy for you! We love you too." Lauryn found comfort that as she spoke, her voice strengthened and the stormy sea that was swirling around in her stomach calmed enough for her to focus on her brother and his wife and think, *I really am happy for them.*

The conversation with Daniel and Madison continued for a few more minutes and the dinner with her parents continued for a few more hours. The steaks were sweet and the easy conversation was cool, but the entire night Elliott felt like he was on the verge of losing his mind.

He was sure Lauryn wasn't telling him something. He could tell by the way she was acting, all jumpy and odd. She couldn't sit still for more than a few minutes, she hardly ate anything at dinner and while she sat there next to him the entire night, more than once she wandered off in their conversation, only coming back when someone asked her a direct question.

It could have been the news of Daniel and Madison's baby that was distracting her, Elliott pondered to himself. It was a gut punch to hear it, no doubt they were happy for them, but still, it was hard to be brought back to those times over the past few years when he and Lauryn made the calls to family with exciting news that a baby was coming - only to follow up with devastating calls about miscarriages a few months later.

Come to think of it, she'd been acting weird for a few weeks now. He'd attributed it to everything that was going on with the house project and this guy's journal that she was so wrapped up in. Could it be something else? Could it be- ?

The stark realization jolted through him, electrifying his nerves to the point he felt the hair raise on his arms. Elliott stood up from the deck chair suddenly, interrupting Todd's conversation about the fish he caught last weekend and the massive fish fry they had with their next-door neighbor. Todd glanced up at him in startled confusion.

"You okay, Elliott?" Todd spoke, but his voice sounded had a disturbing, echoey timbre to it, like he was speaking to him from the safety of a boat and Elliott was under water struggling to breathe.

"Yeah- I - I just remembered something - uh, no big deal. I think I'll go get Lauryn. We should probably head home." He glanced towards the kitchen where Lauryn sat at the counter with her mom who was on her laptop showing Lauryn some new Belle Homes real estate listings. Gabrielle's real estate office, located in a renovated house just off Main Street in Lake Belle, had some of the best listings in the region.

Elliott pushed open the sliding door and strode across the room towards the women as Todd followed behind.

"Hey, Lauryn, you ready to go soon?" He interrupted their conversation with an abrupt, loud voice; he felt kind of bad about it, but not really. Lauryn turned to face him with a weak smile. And just like that, he *knew* it. She was pregnant.

The thought washed over him like a cold waterfall, stifling his breath, making him want to be sick. Joy, sweet anticipation and dread all mixed together. She's pregnant. *Sick.*

"Sure. I am kind of tired, it's been a long week." Lauryn's eyes were nervous, as if she knew her secret was no longer so secret from him. She squinted at him slightly and then smiled hesitantly before turning back to face her mother.

"Mom, I'll have to let you know on your job offer. I do miss selling real estate, but right now this house project is more than enough for me. We haven't decided exactly what comes next." She hefted herself from her chair, walked behind her seated mother and hugged her shoulders tightly. "I do miss you as my boss though, Mom. You're pretty great. I miss our coffee breaks."

"Ha, well, remember, the goal is for *you* to be the boss. Your dad keeps talking about his ten year plan to retirement and he seems to want me there along with him-" Gabrielle patted the arms Lauryn draped around her shoulders and she kept chatting to the room as she smiled across the kitchen into Todd's eyes, but Elliott couldn't focus on a word she said.

He wasn't surprised to hear them discussing a position with her mom's real estate office because Lauryn had been a successful agent a few years ago before she joined him in California after their wedding. In the years since then, Gabrielle had lobbied Lauryn to come back to Belle Homes more than once. A change like that would change their lives for sure and they'd have to spend some time thinking about that; but right now, Elliott was more interested in finding out if his suspicions were correct.

He couldn't help it. His eyes were drawn like a laser towards Lauryn's flat stomach in her denim shorts and the figure-fitting light blue t-shirt, the one he bought her a while ago, it was covered with printed white daisies and a simple message in white script across the front that read "Loved."

She looked adorable to him, as always. She didn't look any different to him, but still.

Still, he was sure of it. He was sure they were pregnant. Again.

CHAPTER 12
2017, July

"I guess I'm just not ready for this- I'm sorry, I'm just not ready for you."

Tired and hot – *was that air conditioner even on?* – Rebecca fanned her face with the print version of last week's Target advertisement and turned the volume to four on her television remote, hoping to drown out the dialogue that was on a loop in her head.

It had been three long days since Rebecca had told Kyle that she thought it best they move on with their lives, separately, as friends. But now, in retrospect, she realized that she had known it for a while, but some things are just really hard to say.

This movie is about as lame as they get, she grumbled to herself, and flipped the channel. Every program she landed on seemed to be a sappy romance or a stupid detective movie. She stopped flipping channels when she found House Hunters. It was a rerun, but it was something. She turned the volume up to five.

It wasn't helping, the voices were still there.

She'd chosen to tell him as he was leaving Tuesday evening, after they'd cooked dinner together and watched a movie on Netflix. She didn't want to hurt him and she'd practiced in her mind ahead of time what she'd say, but in the moment, with his gaze piercing through her resolve, the words came out in a flurry, blunt and harsh in their honesty. Once she had spit them out, she clamped her mouth tightly shut, actually pressing her lips with her fingers, so that not even another sound could escape her lips.

As she breathlessly watched his reaction, which was a mix of surprise, confusion, hurt and a look of something else that she couldn't quite define, her thoughts ran wild inside her head.

How could she tell him? How could she tell him in a way that he could understand? It was impossible to say the words that were screaming from somewhere deep inside her at that moment. Recriminations that had nothing, absolutely nothing, to do with him.

Rebecca flicked the On/Off button on her remote in frustration, finally giving up on finding a distraction for her mind tonight. As House Hunters disappeared, the room fell into darkness, leaving a silvery-yellow glow of moonlight quivering over the couch where she sat in the only source of light. Rebecca focused her gaze on her fingers that lay in her lap and remembered his words from a month ago as he softly rubbed the back of her ring finger and said, "Have you ever considered getting married, Rebecca?"

Was that the beginning of the end for this relationship, she wondered. What was it about that question that sent her into such a spiral? She wasn't sure, but ever since he'd asked her that, she had been unable to function in this new life she'd been building. Instead, she found herself mired in the memories that she tried to keep in the folder in her mind marked B.S. (Before Sobriety).

Her B.S. memories were of a life on a completely different planet – entirely removed from this reality. They included memories of the years she spent stumbling around, living her life as if in some kind of semi-coma, itching, aching for the next high so she could forget the dredges of the one she was in at any given moment.

Reaching sobriety after all that had been a torturous climb. It took everything, every living thing, out of her to reach this place. So much, in fact, that in the end, she relied solely, completely and irretrievably, on Jesus Christ to finish the climb with her.

Often, she pictured herself leaning against Him, treading on a rocky, steep mountain path- just a little further, just a few feet further... The air was shallow, her energy was gone, she was emaciated from the journey, but the higher she got, the scenery was beyond spectacular, and all the while, He was there. Her rock, her support. Her shoulder to lean on, her heart to beat for her, her strength to finish.

Now, she was here. *Sober*. Clear-eyed. And, present.

Feeling *everything*. Even when it hurt.

And, God help her, she knew the signs of danger of losing it all. She was clear-eyed in this too. The whispers of temptation, like sneaky glances, sly winks from her past coming back to winnow their insidious lies into her life again. She called them out – sometimes verbally aloud to the mirror in her bathroom - and they slithered away again, under the rock, deep inside her soul. And, she would rejoice at her control over them. Through Him, she had control over them.

But, then, things like this happened.

Dreams.

Dreams, like falling in love with a good man, like the sweet feeling of falling in love with Kyle. A man who wanted to put a ring on her bare ring finger.

She realized sadly that although dreams weren't exactly like the sly temptations, the constant triggers, that tried to knock her off-balance and off her sober track, they were *every bit as terrifying.* More so even, because she couldn't help but *want* them. She couldn't help but think she *deserved* them, these dreams.

But even as she was swept along the past few months in the bliss of this simple life and the love she'd found, there was something that hung around the edges of this dream of her and Kyle together. It was like an ominous dark cloak that might lift for brief moments, but then always returned, reminding her that she'd been pretty pathetic at every relationship she'd ever attempted in her life.

What were the chances that sober Rebecca would be any better than wasted Rebecca at making a relationship work?

She was highly aware that she was re-building some important relationships in her life with Elliott and her parents and constructing some important new relationships with a few friends, her co-workers and her clients at the women's shelter.

But, all of this was building into some sort of relationship-overload for her, which was probably a common feeling for a person coming out of decades-old addiction. In that life, relationships with people were hollowed out by-products that flamed bright as you used them and then were discarded like used needles when you didn't need them anymore.

This was a different life. In this life, relationships were the flowers that needed extra attention and careful tending, especially when you didn't have a green thumb.

Yes, this was best. She was right about this, she assured herself as she took a swallow of lukewarm coffee, curled her legs underneath herself on the couch and turned the television on once again.

This situation with Kyle just needed the correct perspective. Even though she would miss their fun times at his lake place where they'd laugh as they sat on the end of the dock and watched fireflies and they'd talk about his kids and grandkids and her son Elliott and–

Even as she contemplated not seeing him again, she reeled in her thoughts with a scowl, *she knew it was best for him that she let him move on.* This was best for him.

It was a painful learning experience – but she was beginning to comprehend that some dreams were meant for the safe, sleepy comfort of the quiet, dark night, enjoyed within the protection of the subconscious mind, they just weren't meant to see the harsh, bright light of day.

The rhythmic rise and fall of Elliott's shoulders and the relaxed, weighty feeling of his head against her stomach told her that he had finally fallen asleep, even though she couldn't see his eyes. Lauryn shifted slightly, thinking maybe she was putting too much weight on the arms Elliott had threaded around her waist as she half-sat in their bed and he laid across her, holding her. She didn't want to wake him, he might think she wanted him to move, when in fact, after the conversation they'd just had, she wished they could stay intertwined like this all night.

A few hours ago, the side door of her parents' house hadn't even clicked shut before he urged her to confirm it.

Tell me, Lauryn, you're pregnant again, aren't you?

After a heated discussion where they'd covered all the basics of ... The doctor said we should wait before trying again, you told me that you were going back on the pill, I thought we'd agreed ... in the end, Elliott came around like he always did. Even though he couldn't understand it, he knew how much she wanted a baby.

Still, she did feel kind of manipulative about the way this one played out. She'd relied on the fact that for so many months they *couldn't* get pregnant, maybe it was a sign that they *wouldn't* get pregnant. Why take a pill?

She frowned as she threaded his dark hair through her fingers and let it drop in a fan across the printed design on her pajama top as she mulled it over in her head. Could she really help it that her cycles were so out of whack and unpredictable? Light spotting seemed like a period to her and she'd felt the regular cramping and other signs, so how was she to know?

Well, now, it was too late. They were having a baby and what really bothered her about their discussion tonight was that he wasn't going in 100% sure this time would be different, and they'd be successful.

His doubt was needling her, it was becoming her doubt, and she didn't like that one bit. Lauryn knew that the key was to keep focused on other things in their lives like work, their families and friends. And, like Elliott told her all the time, God would take care of them, right?

Each day would blend into the next one, and one day they would wake up and this pregnancy would be in the clear. They would be safely on their way to making a family of their own. She just wouldn't allow herself to think too much, she wouldn't allow herself to dream too much, about the little person inside.

Now she knew she was just too jacked to sleep so she reached for Cameron Berndt's journal which sat within arm's length on her bedside table, while Elliott continued to hug her, his head resting on her stomach, as if he was listening to the little person inside her.

CHAPTER 13

1967, February

Lord, this verse will sustain me today: Every good gift and every perfect gift is from above, coming down from the Father of lights with whom there is no variation or shadow due to change. James 1:17.

I pray that the eyes of my heart are open to see your unending grace and love, Heavenly Father. Amen

With a small silver spoon, she swirled the cream into the steaming cup of coffee, once around, twice around, over and over again as she drew on her morning cigarette. Cameron stepped slowly into the kitchen that Saturday morning and sat on the yellow, vinyl-covered chair across the table from her, feeling like the weight of the world rested on his shoulders. He watched as she brushed a stray brunette curl behind her ear and pursed her lips a little tighter around the Virginia Slim. Upon closer inspection, he noticed that her eyes looked dull and listless this morning, the circles under them deepened in intensity by the residue of the light gray eyeshadow she had worn last evening.

As the silence weighed heavy between them, Cameron glanced down at the fried eggs and toast on the plate in front of him. The eggs were cooked just as he liked them, the same as she'd prepared them for over seven years now. Even after a night like they had last night, Cassie still felt obligated to make him breakfast. *People and the parts we play*, he thought as he picked up his fork.

"So." He muttered as he dug lifelessly into one of his fried eggs. He wasn't hungry and he didn't really want to talk, but he knew one of them would have to break the ice the morning after that kind of night. Otherwise, how would they overcome such a thing?

"So." She glanced at him while her sky-blue, bloodshot eyes perked up in edgy anticipation. She took another brittle drag from her cigarette and her fingers were shaking a bit unsteadily as she placed it in the ashtray on the table, but her voice was caustic and firm. "So, Cameron. What's it going to be this time? Anger or disappointment? Let me assure you, I'm prepared for either one."

Last night was their "date" night. It had been planned a few weeks in advance, they had a neighbor girl come over to watch the children and they made reservations at the supper club in town. Cameron ordered a steak which had been prepared perfectly and Cassie ordered her favorite, butterfly shrimp. Things had been going rather nicely, and even though Cassie insisted on having a second glass of wine with her dinner and Cameron could tell she was getting slightly tipsy, they were enjoying each other's company.

There were moments during dinner, like when she grasped his hand and told him earnestly how she missed these times together, that Cameron thought, we should do this more often. Maybe this is what she needs, just some time alone together to unwind, without the kids around. Maybe this is what we both need.

They were almost out the door, within moments of safety, happily existing in that bubble of marital contentedness that Cameron missed so much. But just as the waitress returned with his change upon paying their bill, Cassie's face suddenly lit up with recognition as a small group of people entered the bar attached to the restaurant – three men and two women, all laughing together at a shared joke. She told Cameron that they were people she recognized, people she worked with at the law office, out with their spouses. Two couples and one odd man out. The single guy, a tall, dark-haired man somewhere in his thirties immediately advanced to their table when he saw Cassie. After she introduced them, Cameron found out his name was Devon Hearst, a partner and her boss at Hearst and Hearst, Attorneys at Law.

Nothing about this seemed out of the ordinary, in fact, him seeking them out the way he did just seemed congenial and friendly. It was the way he spoke her name, however – all familiar and personal – that's what set off the alarms inside of Cameron.

"Hello, *Cassandra*."

Yes, that's what bothered him. Immediately, Cameron recognized something about the way he said her name and the smile on his face when he said it – something about all that *really* bothered him.

"Well, to tell you the truth, I'm not angry or disappointed." Cameron did his best to wipe away the residue of irrational jealousy and anger he still felt this morning, "I don't know what I feel. Maybe...just confused, I suppose."

"Oh, please. I had too much to drink, that's all. Did I embarrass you?"

"Yeah, I was embarrassed. But not just for myself. For you too."

"Why? They all had too much to drink, and in hindsight, we probably shouldn't have gone back to Devon's place with them. But, I'm sure none of them will remember things too clearly from last night. Don't worry. They don't travel in the church crowd. Your pristine reputation shall remain untarnished." She made a sound that Cameron thought might be a laugh, but it dripped with sarcasm so thick that he wasn't even sure what to call it.

"Cassie, you say that as if I'm the only one who should be concerned about their reputation." Cameron paused, as usual, he resisted pushing her too far. "And you know that it's not a reputation I'm concerned about. I want – I want *both* of us – to lead a life pleasing to God."

"Mhmm, sure, whatever you say." She took a long drink of coffee and rolled her eyes, making clear her feelings on the matter.

"That's not fair. Have we really gone so far off course that I'm not supposed to care if another man shamelessly makes passes at my wife right in front of my face?" The memories of last evening were sharp in Cameron's mind, if not in hers or anyone else's.

After sharing a round of drinks at the supper club, where Cameron abstained, the group of them arrived at Devon Hearst's home in a newly built, upscale neighborhood of brick and stucco homes on the south side of town. Cameron did his best to be courteous to Cassie's boss even while the man mostly ignored him when he spoke, he was much too distracted by Cassie to pay attention to what Cameron had to say.

As they talked about Cameron's position as a pastor at Freedom Church and Cassie's new job at their law office, the first round of drinks turned to a second round, and the conversation started to quickly deteriorate. Devon Hearst's sly innuendos about a pastor having such an attractive wife - *"what a shame"* - coupled with a series off-color stories about clients and work around the office, just set Cameron's teeth on edge. Not long into the conversation, Cameron had to escape the room in search of the bathroom, just to keep from lecturing the guy on his utter lack of professionalism and his deficiency of compassion overall.

When he returned a few minutes later, Cameron found the guy's arm draped around Cassie's shoulder and his head bent low towards her, whispering something into her ear. It was the first of a few awkward moments where it seemed Devon Hearst had no shame and Cameron's anger began to build. He seemed like the type of guy who always got what he wanted, he was confident that this life was centered around him; it was his party and everyone else was an invited guest. All of it made the hour and a half they spent at his home pure torture for Cameron.

"That was nothing, Cameron. Devon is harmless, he didn't mean anything by that." Cassie looked at him over her coffee cup with a tired, slightly teasing smile. "Ok, granted, it has been a few years since we've been in that type of situation. But remember your promise - you weren't going to let that type of thing bother you anymore. We both know where your temper has gotten you in the past."

"Exactly. It has been a few years. And that's why I'm confused, Cassie. That *was* our past, we gave up that life." He searched her eyes and he felt his anger and frustration replaced with a sincere confusion and uncertainty. They had given up that life, hadn't they?

For some reason he had to hear her say it, so he remained silent while she watched him over her steaming coffee cup. Finally, she rolled her eyes in exaggerated submission.

"Ok, Cameron. I get it. I'm married to a pastor. I will try to behave like a lady." She reached across the table and rubbed his forearm lightly, her touch burning through the cotton of his dress shirt.

He couldn't shake the feeling that Cassie had acted hurtfully and disrespectfully towards him last night. But whatever wedges last night's infractions had built between them, at her touch, Cameron forgave her. He knew God asked us to forgive seventy times seven times. That's a lot of times. He was nowhere near that number with Cassie.

And, Cameron knew that he loved his wife. In the end, he knew he would forgive her of anything. It wouldn't matter how many times he would be asked to forgive her.

Freedom Church's sanctuary was simple. No ornately carved wooden pews or ceramic statues adorned its inner sanctum. No intricate stained-glass windows or soaring ceilings were in this

163

church. Instead, this church had functional wooden pews lined up on either side of the white walled sanctuary which was covered by a ceiling of finely polished pine and strong oak beams. A muted, blue carpet runner started at the back doors and ended up front at a low stage with a small podium positioned in front of four large windows. The stark simplicity of the surroundings invariably drew the attention of anyone entering the sanctuary to the eight-foot tall, wood-framed cut-glass cross, donated by a local craftsman, that hung from the ceiling rafters above the stage.

Later that Saturday afternoon, the sanctuary was empty except for Cameron who sat in the middle of the left-side front row, his head in his hands. It was here, in this church at the foot of the cross, that Cameron found peace. He found Jesus everywhere, yes, but it was here, when it was quiet and with light filtering in through the front windows, shimmering with prismatic color through the glass cross, it was here that Cameron found strength. Because that's what he needed right now. Strength to deal with all matters, big and small. The kind of strength that could only come from his Savior.

He'd arrived early for today's church board meeting. He wanted to review a few notes and look over the agenda again before the board members started to arrive because when he first reviewed the agenda Glenda brought to him Thursday afternoon, he'd had a faint sense of foreboding.

It seemed that there were some "issues" disturbing the normally calm waters of their church, including some trepidation with the fundraising efforts for their kitchen renovation. The fund was seriously short even after multiple community potluck dinners and a garage sale.

There was also a general disagreement about the level of supervision required for the children's nursery during Sunday services. A few mothers felt that two teenage girls were simply not enough supervision, especially after one of the girls was found sleeping in the nursery rocking chair on a recent Sunday morning. It didn't matter that the baby she was carefully cradling was also peacefully napping.

And finally, there were a few members advocating for a formal dress code. It seemed that some of the older people didn't approve of the more casual attire that younger members were starting to wear to church in recent years.

This subject of course was a little sensitive to Cameron, given his own proclivity towards casual dress, but as he stood at the podium on Sunday mornings and looked out over the members of his church, he honestly could not understand the basis for the concern. He was simply glad to see so many young people engaged in church at all.

Consequently, over the past couple years, he'd tried to brush aside the comments as he suspected that the issue had more to do with the looming generation gap spoken of so often rather than anything to do with clothing.

" … So, Hank will check with the contractor to see what else we can take out of the kitchen renovation budget," Cameron summarized later that afternoon after covering a financial review and updates from their missionaries abroad, "And we have decided that we will restructure the nursery workers program to include one adult and one teenager from this point forward. Thanks for rearranging the volunteers, Glenda." Cameron nodded towards the church secretary who removed her eyeglasses and smiled in return as she shut her notebook.

"Oh, and one more issue – the dress code. I hear the points a few of you have raised and I am trying to be sensitive to the source of the concerns. I understand that change is never easy, and I'll admit, change is not *always* a good thing. I don't want to add the word 'but' here, but I'm going to-" Cameron smiled as he turned towards board member Sam Cooper, a fifty-seven-year-old postal delivery man and board chairman Reginald Perkins, a sixty-two-year-old business owner, both of whom were most concerned about the issue.

"I see that our young people are actively searching for Jesus Christ right now." Cameron continued in an encouraging voice, "These people are our members too, they are our brothers and sisters in Christ. They may dress differently, and they may have different concerns- different social viewpoints than others in our church – but we are all one body here. I think that their souls are more important than what they are wearing."

"Pastor, I think you're missing the point," Long-time board chairman Reginald shuffled uncomfortably in his chair and was quick with his rebuttal, "It's not *just* what they're wearing, it's the way they are acting. It's disrespectful to a place of worship to be so

... casual. Some of these kids are rowdy – we've heard rumors about the way they carry on in school –and the manner in which some of these young women dress – like they are flaunting themselves, even in church. How does that reflect on our members in the eyes of the public?"

"Well, that is a tricky one, you are right. We cannot control what people in public will say about any of us, can we?" Thinking of his own sketchy past and the resulting public embarrassment for his parents, Cameron paused and noticed Reginald sat up straighter and nodded his head, obviously assuming that Cameron was agreeing with him, when in fact, the opposite was true. This would require a much more delicate argument than he had prepared himself for, Cameron thought as he continued cautiously.

"Reginald, have you ever considered that your father may have said the same thing about you and your friends – that you were disrespectful of tradition and perhaps a bit sassy – when you were a teenager? I know my father said it about me and I'm sure I will say it about my children. Each generation brings something new because we continue to evolve. Now, it's true that God doesn't change, but I can't see how enacting a formal dress code will help us fulfill our mission here – bringing all people, young and old, to know God."

"Well, that's probably because you're part of this new generation, Pastor." Reginald sputtered and then, as if he felt he stood on the solid ground of consensus with the rest of the board members, he continued, "And I, for one, am disappointed that we have to draw you a picture of something that should be pretty obvious."

Often easily riled, Reginald puffed up with red-faced anger. He glanced across the table at his frequent cohort Sam Cooper who, looking extremely uncomfortable, took off his dark-rimmed glasses and slowly rubbed away a spot with his handkerchief. Not getting any moral support verbally from Sam, Reginald surveyed the table of silent on-lookers.

Shocked at the public and personal rebuke Reginald threw at him, Cameron took his own glance around at the others, trying to gauge their input on the topic. What was he missing here? It seemed there was more to this than he imagined, and a feeling of dread began to seep over him.

"Pastor," Reginald continued in a haughty tone of voice, "Let me be brutally honest with you, if I may. There are members of this church who have voiced concerns regarding you - and Mrs. Berndt - in this regard. There are many who believe you have a casual, laid-back manner because you're- well, you've been open with your testimony - your past life drinking alcohol and doing drugs and all manners of carrying on." With a rough guffaw, he paused for dramatic effect, as if declaring your pastor is a recovering low life during a church board meeting wasn't quite dramatic enough.

Then, he continued, trying to spiritualize his insult, "Well, our God is mighty forgiving and we accept that you have been saved. But, you see, with a man, that type of activity is considered more acceptable. But - ehmm - Believe me, I take no pleasure in telling you this." The words he was searching for seemed difficult for him to utter as evidenced by his hard swallow.

Reginald glanced again at Sam Cooper for moral support before he forged ahead, "But, that being said, there have been many comments regarding Mrs. Berndt's choices in attire and her-attitudes. We are surmising that your past life colors your view of these things. Like those skirts she wears, way above the knee like that- well, some say you should reign in your wife a little. After all, she's wearing the very skirts we think should be banned. She is simply not a proper example of how a Christian woman should dress and act."

As he finished his speech, the room fell deathly quiet and Cameron felt a collective breath held as the words floated in the stifling air of the Bible Study room. Each board member sat frozen in place, all in various stages of stupor at the words Reginald spoke. The only sound to break the silence was the sudden rush of warm air puffing out of the black heating vents on the north wall.

Could they all possibly feel this way, Cameron wondered. Why hadn't anyone ever told him they felt this way? He looked at Ken Sieberts and Dave Mansing, two guys who he considered his friends because of their many shared interests and history together in this town. Certainly, they would have told him if they felt this way about Cassie. Right?

Cameron looked at Glenda, who while working with him every day had shared hundreds of stories of her children and grandchildren and her interests in gardening - did she feel this way?

Glenda was a kind woman, capable and thoughtful. The dark skin of her face was decorated with deep laugh lines around her full mouth and her deep, brown eyes, the color of dark chocolate, were usually cheerful and gentle. Now, Glenda's gaze was steely hard and unwavering as she met his eyes before she spoke.

"I just want to say, Pastor," Her firm voice, the first to be heard in the room after Reginald's tirade, was clear and purposeful, "I don't share that sentiment. I have never seen Mrs. Berndt be anything but a respectful and generous person."

Even in his stunned state, Cameron appreciated the guts it took for her to break from the ranks, in her position as secretary, not a voting board member and the only woman in a room full of men. Gradually, Glenda's bravery prompted a few others around the table to start nodding their heads in varying degrees of mediocre agreement with her statement. But, by now the damage was done.

Cameron felt completely off-balance, as if he'd been sucker-punched in a street fight by Reginald, a gray-haired grandfather with an overly large spare tire around his middle.

Of course, he knew the struggles they were having in their marriage - Cassie's willfulness and independent streak affecting many areas of their lives - all of this may have seeped outside the walls of their home and become evident to others that she interacted with. It surprised him though that, if they all knew about the issues in his home, why hadn't anyone said anything to him?

And, as far as her "attitudes" and dress, it was part of who she was. Cassie had never been a traditional person and most of the time, that's what he loved about her. For her to be the target of this type of malicious talk made him angry, and as he sat there waiting for someone to say something, he felt his thoughts were reaching a rolling boil in his mind.

Belatedly, he noticed his skin burning under his shirt and his hands were clenching and unclenching his knees under the table. His mouth itched to unleash a torrent of scorn on Reginald and the others who agreed with him, *how dare they judge his wife that way?*

He was also tempted to bare to the whole group that Reginald had his own issues relating to a gambling addiction for which his wife Maribelle had come for prayer. *How dare he set himself up as an example of a proper Christian?*

He wanted to yell at them, if this is what they thought about his wife Cassie then he was done with all of them *and* this church. *How dare they think they were better than her?*

But, as he sat on the hard metal chair in the Bible Study room, instead of doing any of that, the chaos in Cameron's mind was abruptly going numb and silent while one question was presenting itself loud and clear - what was God wanting him to say, and do, right now? Finally, having no idea what would come out of his mouth, he spoke.

"I'm going to be honest with you all right now. I don't know what to say. I'm at a loss how to react to this." Cameron sighed heavily, his mind overwhelmed with the duty to defend his wife and the responsibility to lead this church, "I guess whenever I find myself in a situation where I don't know what to do, I pray. So that's what I'm going to do now. Thank you for your time."

Cameron pushed his chair away from the table and without even a sideways glance at any of the people he once thought were his biggest supporters – the people he relied on and prayed with – he left the room.

CHAPTER 14

1967, April

The clouds were drifting along above me today and I was mesmerized by your glory, overcome to the point of tears. In the rolling meander of those silvery clouds, I saw the patience in your plans for me and I saw your undeniable pursuit of my heart.

Just as those clouds are pursuing the wind on a never-ending journey towards the end of that path, You pursue me. You will never stop pursuing me, your love has no end, just as those clouds will never find their destination. I saw your grandeur, Heavenly Father, and at the same time, I felt your nearness. You are my forever loving Father and in your son's name I pray, Amen.

With life, sometimes you just live each day like the offenses of yesterday never really happened. Cameron's mother had always called it his "gift," this ability to "forgive and forget."

You are so blessed, son, that you are able to just shirk things off. It is a gift, I tell you. She always used to say that it was a blessing from God and told him once that it was unfortunate this unique gift was bestowed on an only child, because it seemed such a waste that the ability to forgive and forget was bestowed on a child without a sibling.

Although he had a mercurial, ferocious temper, it was true, he didn't hold onto hurt feelings for long. Although he'd never be vulnerable enough with anyone to admit it aloud, Cameron knew the rightful source of this "gift" wasn't God at all.

Instead, the source resided somewhere deep in his subconscious because Cameron was deeply, irretrievably aware of his own flaws - he recognized that he was never fully righteous, never clean, without sin. At a deeper level he recognized this warped view of himself flew in the face of the whole notion of Christ's forgiveness in general - he had always lived with this nebulous feeling of self-disgust and even now, after years of prayer, it hadn't been completely assuaged.

Given this propensity to focus on his own flaws, Cameron found it difficult to judge someone else for their shortcomings, and if he did feel judgment, it was nearly impossible for him to hold it against the person for long. After all, Cameron reasoned, he had an explosive and sometimes irrational temper. How then could he be upset when he saw his children display their tempers occasionally?

Cameron was self-centered with an inordinate amount of self-preservation spirit mixed in. How then could he judge Cassie when she displayed some of those same attributes?

As he sat with his journal open in front of him, he thought back two months ago when he was forced to address the issues in his church and Cassie's dress choices and "attitude." It was with this spirit of acceptance and non-judgment that he'd tried to reconcile things. It hadn't been easy. Or comfortable. But it had been right and that's what mattered.

"He really said that? He actually said that my skirts were too short?" Not quite recognizing the severity of the issue, Cassie had laughed at his portrayal of the board meeting while she poured spaghetti into the strainer and backed quickly away from the escaping steam.

"Yes, he did." When she said it like that, it did sound rather ridiculous and Cameron struggled to put his feelings into perspective. He'd spent about fifteen minutes driving around town and praying before coming home to tell her, but he still was surprised at how insignificant the offense seemed now that he wasn't sitting in the hot seat amongst the board members.

"Did you tell him that you happen to like my skirts? If I remember correctly, you told me that I looked- what was the word you used? Oh yes, *enchanting* was the word, I believe." She smiled mischievously as she crossed the kitchen and rested her arms around his waist, smiling up at him and blinking her eyes coquettishly, the heavy dark mascara she wore making her eyes even more alluring.

"Well, there is that one particular light blue outfit ... and yes, enchanting was the word I used." Cameron smiled weakly back at her and felt the heat rise in his cheeks as she watched him carefully. Gradually, she started to sense the gravity when he didn't continue the joke.

She edged away from him, a question deepening in her blue eyes as she pulled away completely and leaned against the kitchen counter, crossing her arms over her chest.

"Are you serious about this?" Incredulous, her voice had risen an octave, "I mean, are *they* serious about this?"

"I'm going to be honest with you. Yes, they are serious." Cameron softened his tone at the hurt expression on her face. He knew exactly how she felt. "*Some* of them are serious, Cassie, but just so you know, the entire board doesn't agree. In my opinion, you have become the poster child for a general unease about youth culture in general. And, you're not alone. They want to say the same thing about me and have said it in their own passive-aggressive ways. But it doesn't matter, I know they think it-"

"Well," Cassie interrupted him, "Let me just say, I have a mind to tell them where they can put their opinions about my wardrobe." She turned to the sink and ran cold water from the tap over the spaghetti before dumping it into a Red Wing crockery bowl that sat waiting on the counter.

Cameron was moved by the injured expression he saw in her eyes before she turned away. Instinctively, he crossed the breadth of the kitchen and hugged her from behind, resting his chin on her head, as he breathed in the lemony scent of the Breck brand shampoo she used.

"I know, Cass, I know. Don't let it get to you. It will work itself out. I will take care of it, I promise." He frowned deeply, thinking through how to react to it all, as he watched the seconds tick on the red and yellow plastic kitchen clock above the sink.

Her shoulders shuddered and with a heavy heart, he knew she was crying. She resisted at first, but finally she allowed him to turn her into his arms where she then buried her face in his chest, refusing to look at him.

"Cass, don't. Please. Don't cry." Cameron whispered, his heart dropping in a free fall.

But she wouldn't look at him and the tears continued, her shoulders shaking in his arms. He hated to see her cry. It always reminded him that he had no control over her emotions. Really, he had no control over her at all.

"I've told you, Cam." Her halting voice, when she spoke a few moments later, was muffled by his chest as she shook her head against the front of shirt, "I've been telling you all along. I don't measure up. You're just the last one to see it, that's all."

Cassie pulled back suddenly and looked him squarely in the eyes, her dark, now-smudged lashes heavy with tears and her nose reddened slightly as she sniffed back a sob. She had the look of someone who was lost - someone so precious to him - lost and hurting so badly. The protective spirit he felt in the boardroom roared back inside him, but he did his best to keep it under control. He needed to be the adult in this thing. He needed to stay focused on the long game.

"Cass, I see how you measure up." Cameron smiled weakly and smoothed some stray brunette curls from her cheek as he wiped a tear from her cheekbone with his thumb. "God sees how you measure up. That's what's important."

Over the next two months, the shortest dresses were relegated to the back of their closet and Cassie made a point of attending the Ladies Bible Study every Sunday evening, even though it meant the kids had to be with a babysitter because Cameron led the Men's Bible Study on Sundays.

Reginald Perkins never apologized for his comments about Cassie, although Sam Cooper pulled Cameron aside after church one Sunday and stammered his way through an apology, of sorts.

For his part, Cameron never brought the topic up to anyone, including his friends Ken and Dave, until after he preached his sermon the Sunday after the board meeting, the one he pointedly named "Jesus Died For Them. Now, Can We Just Love Them?"

In it, Cameron laid out the age-old lesson, love thy neighbor. In times such as these with all the political and cultural turmoil and the widening differences between races and generations, he stated from the podium trying his best not to stare directly at Reginald, we don't have to agree with our neighbor, but we are required to love them. Just as Jesus loved them.

At the next board meeting, held a month later, Cameron made a point of listing Dress Code as the first item of business. It was perhaps a risky move, because he wasn't sure what his response would be if it didn't work out the way he hoped, but he requested that the board vote on whether or not to enact a Dress Code. The board voted 5-1, the Opposed won. There would not be a formal dress code in Freedom Church.

Cameron abstained because he had a conflict of interest. After all, he had skin in the game.

Things in the congregation had settled in again. A recent board vote brought in two new members, for the first time in their short church history an African American was elected, a man named Sibley Thomas who owned a shoe store on main street and whose wife was the choir director at Freedom Church. The other new board member was a young dairy farmer, who with the help of his wife raised four children, milked thirty-five cows and delivered milk for a local creamery.

Cameron felt a certain rhythm to his life, which was typically the case as the long winter months turned to spring and Minnesotans emerged from their respective homes and workplaces and started to enjoy the outdoors again.

Even as the chaos continued to unfold and deepen in Vietnam that April and a recent peace march in front of the United Nations building led by Martin Luther King called for a cease fire, Cameron's life was finding a comfortable rhythm, even in his home.

Cassie was succeeding in her job, had gotten a raise already and was exploring ways to continue her degree at a local private college with a combination of flexible work scheduling and night classes. The last proposal she shared with Cameron would put her on track to start law school, hopefully in Minnesota, just over a year from now. Although Cassie was the beneficiary of some college grants, they would still need to take out student loans before this was all said and done.

The thought of this new student loan debt didn't please Cameron, but he tried his best to be supportive, even as he imagined what their life would be like with Cassie working and going to school full time, all while being a mom to two young children and the wife to a busy pastor.

That April afternoon, Cameron pulled into his yard slowly, hugging the left side of his driveway to avoid Aaron's red bike which was laying on its side directly in the middle of the path, its back tire still spinning from an abrupt stop and dump. Frowning, Cameron glanced around for the children, knowing they must be nearby. At the sound of a shrill squeal, coming in loud and clear through his open car window, Cameron turned his head just in time to see Aaron chasing Charlotte from around the back of the house. One of his fists gripped his sister's pink sweater and the other was tangled with a fistful of her hair as he tried to pull her to a stop.

When she finally realized that to keep running meant more pain than it was worth, Charlotte stopped abruptly but not before she threw Aaron's prized GI Joe action figure into the shrubs alongside the house. As he dived into the shrubs in search of the doll, Aaron could be heard calling his sister "such a brat" and "so annoying."

"Charlotte!" Cameron called out as he opened his car door, "What are you doing?"

"Daddy! You're home!" Already forgetting her taunt of her older brother, Charlotte ran with abandon, arms outstretched, towards Cameron. Once she reached him, he gathered her up as she hugged her legs tightly around his waist, while he made sure to first to secure her dangling black Mary Jane shoe onto her foot so she wouldn't lose it.

"Hello, baby girl!" Cameron bent to kiss her soft, pink cheek which was cool from the brisk afternoon air, "But, what was that I just saw you do? You know you're not supposed to play with Aaron's GI Joe. That's his toy. You can play with it only if he says so."

"Or, if you say so or if Mommy says so." Charlotte countered, her blue eyes lighting up with hope.

"Yes," Cameron agreed, thinking how adorable his little girl was when she negotiated in her innocent way, "But we didn't say so, did we?"

"But I want a GI Sho. Why can't I have a GI Sho?" Ignoring Cameron's question, Charlotte lisped her reply with a pout and pushed some unruly curls out of her eyes.

"You got Dolly Ann, remember? Grandma gave you Dolly Ann because you said you wanted her for Christmas. You didn't want a GI Joe for Christmas."

Without a reply, Charlotte dropped her head onto Cameron's shoulder and pondered life's choices as her father ambled along the back walkway towards the house, stopping first to ruffle Aaron's hair and give him a conspiratorial wink.

"Honey, I'm home!" Cameron called as he deposited Charlotte down on the kitchen linoleum, helping her to remove her shoes which had a spattering of spring mud on the soles.

Cassie wasn't in the kitchen, although a pot of beef stew was bubbling on the back burner of their new olive-green electric stove top. Checking out the contents, Cameron turned down the burner since it seemed to be ample hot given the steam rising from the black kettle.

He continued through the house, down the wide center hallway while calling Cassie's name but did not hear a reply. With a glance up the open staircase, he stopped with his foot on the bottom step when he realized he heard a sound coming from the front porch.

Opening the front door with a smile, he found her in the screened-in porch, a cup of coffee and a pack of cigarettes laying open on the metal side table next to the black, wrought-iron settee where she sat. Her eyes were red-rimmed, as if she'd been crying and Cameron's gaze was drawn to the piece of paper that sat open in her lap.

"What happened, Cass? Is something wrong?" Cameron glanced around for Charlotte to make sure she was occupied elsewhere since it didn't look like the letter was good news. When he saw their daughter lying on her stomach, her head propped in her hands in the living room, occupied with a picture book, Cameron pulled the door closed behind him for more privacy.

"What happened?" He walked towards Cassie, reaching out for the letter but she snapped it away from him before he could touch it and crumpled it up roughly, pushing the letter under the green and orange floral seat cushion of her chair.

"Nothing! Nothing happened." The brittle, edgy tone of her voice belied the truth though as Cassie turned her head sharply and stared out the screened window at her right side, glaring at nothing in particular. Obviously, she was upset about something and the letter had something to do with it, Cameron thought.

"Well, something happened, that's for sure." He countered softly, "What is it? Is it something about your classes? Something about tuition?" For the life of him, Cameron couldn't figure out what else it could be. Things seemed so settled at church, he hadn't heard anyone making waves of any kind there. He had paid the monthly bills on schedule a few weeks ago, so it was unlikely it had anything to do with finances.

"Yeah, it's about my classes all right." Cassie interrupted his thoughts, as she spoke robotically and glared at the shrubs on the right side of the house, as if she was not even inhabiting her own body at the moment, "Actually, it's about the classes that I *won't* be able to take now."

Her face was a blank page, she showed absolutely no emotion at all as she spoke, continuing to stare out the window in stone cold silence. Then, she turned her eyes towards the pack of cigarettes sitting on the wrought iron table near her knee. Cameron watched in dumbfounded confusion as she slowly grasped the half-full cigarette pack and lifting her eyes towards his with a hard stare, he watched while she crumpled the pack into a small uneven ball inside her tightly clenched fist, bits of tobacco littering the wooden floor of the porch.

Cameron frowned, trying to comprehend what she was trying to tell him and becoming more frustrated by the moment. Somehow, he was the target of her anger. Something about a letter and something about him - what had he done now?

"That letter was the doctor's report confirming it. I hope you're happy, Cameron. I'm pregnant."

CHAPTER 15

2017, August

Elliott wiped his glistening face with the hand towel, and leaned down again, his face within inches of a spray of yellow and purple wildflowers rising through the gravel by the side of the roadway. Absent-mindedly, he brushed away a curious black butterfly from his face as he desperately tried to rub his thighs free of the tightness. The sloping hills around Lake Belle weren't a strenuous ride, but after pushing his speed for the past few miles, he realized that even easy hills weren't always quite so easy.

It was his third hard bike ride this week and still he felt like it wasn't enough. He hadn't quite shed the slightly queasy, sick gut feeling that had persisted since Lauryn confirmed the pregnancy a few weeks ago already. He realized that it was nervous energy more than anything else and that there was probably a more productive way to burn it, but instead he took full advantage of the light breeze and scattered clouds and rode until he couldn't possibly ride any further.

It sucked though, he acknowledged to himself as he lifted his bike and snapped shut the hook that held it to the back of the Jeep. He didn't feel any better now that his ride was done. He still felt this constant, unnerving fear in the pit of his stomach. And now he could add two burning legs to the list of ailments.

He'd chosen a different ride today, one a good distance from their home, this one closer to his grandparents' farm, hoping the change of scenery would allow his mind some escape, that maybe he would focus instead on some things he was reading in the Bible. The fascinating podcast he listened to today on his ride was a deep dive into the old-testament prophecies pointing to the arrival of Jesus Christ as Savior and the incredible, upside-down thinking of God's plan to send his own son to be born in a barn, raised the son of human peasants. And, still the son of God.

This study, and really any study of the Bible, put perspective on life. It put perspective on his life experience and reminded Elliott of life's purpose in the first place.

He leaned against the side panel of the Jeep, took a long swallow of water from his water bottle and gave his body a moment to reboot, while he watched two more black butterflies flutter around a flower near his knee as if assessing that he was no threat and the promise of nectar was too enticing.

The unrelenting thought rushed at him, never allowing him respite. He would be a father soon.

Backspace that.

Now. He was a father already and how this pregnancy would go was beyond his control. *Right now, there was a baby* and he or she was growing inside Lauryn and–

He was happy about it. To anyone else, that recognition would of course be obvious, the feeling expected and normal. But to him, given their history with pregnancy, sadly, happiness hadn't been the first emotion he'd felt when she told him.

But now he wondered, maybe he had been misjudging this ache in his stomach, thinking it was fear, calling it concern.

Maybe instead, the ache in his gut had morphed into something else, something like - butterflies? Like anticipation. A delicious exhilaration that refused to be extinguished by past heartbreak. Maybe because the nectar of what was coming was too enticing.

He was *beyond happy*. And he let the realization soak through him, calming his spirit.

Somehow, even given all the past pain, Elliott knew that God wanted them to be happy about this baby. He straightened up, shook out his right leg to loosen the muscles before he climbed behind the steering wheel of the Jeep for his drive to his grandparents' house.

Inside the Jeep, he jacked up the air conditioner and flipped the vents to blow onto his face. Maybe God just wanted them to be happy and content in this season of life, every day. Like, just find another level of trust in Him - maybe they didn't need to understand anything else.

Elliott decided then that he would have to lighten up on Lauryn a little. This baby business was starting to drag them down, pull them apart. He recognized it on some level, but he knew he resisted bringing it up with her because they never really resolved it. Once they made it past the safe mark in this pregnancy, everything would work itself out and they could go back to the way it was before.

"I love this, Lauryn! You have done an absolutely fantastic job - my gosh, this kitchen-" Gabrielle walked along the marble countertop, her fingers floating reverently along the smooth, rolled edge. She turned back towards her daughter, who stood leaning against the newly-enlarged opening to the dining room, "Honey, seriously, this is amazing. Your videos don't do it justice."

"Thanks, Mom, that means a lot, especially coming from you. You've sold a lot of nice homes in your day. This will be just one more in your portfolio."

"Yes, that I have. But this is really special. I can't wait to see more! Like, for instance, what's up this stairwell I wonder-"

Lauryn smiled at her mother's enthusiasm as she followed her up the curved, simple wooden stairs, originally designed for use by servants, that led from the kitchen towards the second floor. Lauryn had purposely left the stairwell barren, with its white beadboard walls and plain wooden railing anchored to the wall with ornate iron mounts. The steps were not covered or replaced, instead they were cleaned and polished to a warm luster because, in every worn edge and slight depression, she found a connection to the history of the house that she was sure the next owner would appreciate.

After their tour of the still unfinished upstairs - Lauryn figured it would be another month before they completed the plumbing and electrical - they returned to the main floor, ending up in the office, commenting on the beauty of the bookshelves and the French doors that led out to the small side patio.

Everything inside her wanted to tell her mother about the journals she'd found hidden in that shelf, over there, near the corner. She had always been close to her mother, and she knew she could trust her to keep this a secret, but still, something held her back. Cameron Berndt's life was so real, his pain so personal. It would feel like a betrayal of a friend to share it with a stranger. Even though her mom Gabrielle wasn't a stranger to Lauryn, she was still a stranger to him.

"Something is different about this house, Lauryn." Her mother, perceptive as always, had her arms crossed in front of her, first looking outside and then around the room again, her gaze zeroing in on Lauryn with a quiet appraisal as she tucked some dark curls behind her ear, "You feel different about this house than the others, don't you?"

Lauryn bit her lip at the comment. Her mother was sensing something was different, that was obvious. Maybe Lauryn hadn't been very good at hiding the pregnancy; perhaps there was some imperceptible pregnancy vibe emitted through increased hormonal activity or something. They had purposefully not said anything to anyone yet, even though her recent visit to the OB-GYN surprised them by confirming that she was actually close to sixteen weeks pregnant and they were supposedly "safe."

"You're right," Lauryn agreed, "This house is special to me, the story of the doctors who practiced and lived here at Promise Place-you don't find that kind of story every day." As she spoke, Lauryn walked to the fireplace and removed some stray protective plastic sheeting that covered the wooden mantel. Now that the sheetrock work and cabinet repair was done, this room was finished, she thought with self-satisfaction.

"Well, yes, that's been an interesting storyline," Gabrielle agreed, "I love those old photos you found showing the baby cribs and hospital beds upstairs with the nurses and the doctors; it's like the house is coming alive again in your videos. But, being here with you-" Her mother's voice drifted off gently and her eyes softened into a smile, "Honey, be honest - maybe you don't want to sell this house when you're done? Maybe you and Elliott want to keep it and start a family here someday?"

"No! I hadn't even thought about that, Mom. That's not why I wanted to show it to you." Lauryn's voice came out sharper than she'd intended; she wasn't ready to deal with the conversation of children yet, even if it was couched in the phrase "someday" as her mother delicately put it, to avoid hurting her.

"Oh," Her mother's eyes frowned in confusion and then moved on, obviously not wanting to dwell on the touchy subject of Lauryn's someday-family, "Okay. Well, I was just going to tell you that I think you'd be making an excellent investment if you did that. The comps totally support the price you were thinking of asking. To be honest, I think you could start even higher if you want. I've heard that they are building a new sports medicine clinic in town. That's sure to bring in good earners-" Her mother had turned and was starting to leave the room as she mentally clicked through the dollars per square foot in her head.

"Mom, I'm pregnant again." Lauryn was frozen, standing alone in the middle of the office, as the words escaped her lips, as if her cautionary thoughts from a moment ago hadn't even happened. To say the words out loud though felt so vulnerable, almost forbidden, like she was condemning the pregnancy by announcing it. But, for some reason, she just couldn't help telling someone else. If she and Elliott were the only ones to know, it was like it wasn't real.

"What?" Gabrielle turned on her heel so quickly her sunglasses toppled off the perch in her curly, dark hair and went sliding along the slick floor of the wide hallway, ending up at the base of the front stairwell. "Did you say– did you say you're pregnant?"

"Yes." Lauryn smiled tentatively, her eyes suddenly dripping tears off her bottom lashes as she walked over to retrieve the glasses. It felt so good to say it. And, even though the "safe" date loomed large in her mind, she was still glad it was out.

Now, maybe she could allow herself to think of this as a *baby* inside her, a little person with a Grandma Gabrielle, not a pregnancy – a *condition* – that she had to *manage* until they passed a date on a calendar. Reading the journal entries about Pastor Berndt and his wife expecting a baby only highlighted the normalcy of pregnancy for so many people; it was so normal that sometimes it occurred at inopportune, unexpected times in life. It was such a common fact of life for so many people. Why was it so hard for her?

"Really? Oh, Lauryn, that's wonderful! It's just beautiful! Come here, baby." Gabrielle pulled her into her arms and rocked her into a big hug, not even noticing that Lauryn was trying to hand back her wayward glasses, "I'm so happy for you!"

"We are too. Well, I think Elliott is coming around now. At first, he wasn't so - enthused. He thought we should take the doctor's advice and wait for a year or so."

"How far along are you?" The question was a natural one, given their history. Still, it bothered Lauryn that it had to be asked at all.

"Well ... safe, I guess. But-" Lauryn paused as her mother looked levelly into her eyes, "You know how that goes. It hasn't held true in the past."

"Well, we don't have to think about that now, honey. Just focus on *this blessing* now." Her mother rested her hand lightly on her stomach while she smiled a brave smile, doing her best to bolster Lauryn's faith.

"Yeah, I know, it's just hard to stay positive, you know?" Lauryn pulled out of her mother's hug gently, suddenly feeling her proximity stifling. "I don't know, Mom. I'm trying to be sure this time will be different. But- I don't know, I guess the past is just weighing on me."

"Well, I think that's natural, honey. But God is faithful. This will be different."

Lauryn looked away again, not able to acknowledge the steady faith that she knew she would see in her mom's eyes. At one time in her life, Lauryn would have related to it, she would have whole-heartedly embraced that steady faith.

Now? Now she faltered in the face of it, she felt numb to it. If she was honest with herself, she almost felt contempt for it.

What was the point in thinking God was with them in this? He obviously hadn't helped them in the past. If he was involved at all, it was sure from a distance. And his plan for "good" in their lives had been resoundingly buried with lots of bad.

"Lauryn, God knows your pain. Please keep your heart soft to him, honey."

"Honestly, Mom, I don't know what to think about God because all I can think of is how he's let us down in the past." Lauryn gulped down the hurt that was filling up her throat and wiped at the tears that had escaped onto her lashes, "I hope he has enough grace to let me feel like that."

"I know he has enough grace for that." Her mom rested her arm across Lauryn's shoulders and whispered into her hair as she pulled her closer again, "Tough times can bring us closer to him, Lauryn. But we need to let him in, no matter how much we want to blame him for the hurt."

"Yeah. We'll see. I am trying."

Gabrielle pulled back again and looked into Lauryn's eyes, a worried expression knitting her arched, dark eyebrows.

"Are you and Elliott doing okay, Lauryn? It's important that you can rely on each other, especially during times like this. You mentioned he wasn't in full support of trying again to have a baby?"

"Oh, he's just always worried about me. He thinks about the physical side of it, he thinks it takes too much out of me; it's like he can't see how important it is for me emotionally to have a baby. It's become a thing for me now - I need to carry a baby to full term just

193

to feel whole again, like any other healthy, normal woman. He just doesn't understand and I'm tired of trying to explain it to him."

"Well, he is trying to understand, I'm sure. He loves you. But he is just a human, he isn't always going to react exactly how you'd want him to."

"I know that, Mom. I'm not saying that he has to be perfect. Let's just drop it, okay? I wasn't really ready to tell you today anyway so can you keep it quiet for a few weeks yet?"

"Okay–" Gabrielle squinted her eyes and looked down suddenly, deliberating about something in her mind and Lauryn read it in her eyes before she asked the question.

"Oh, all right. You can tell Dad, but only him, please. We just want to wait for a while until we know how this will go."

"Of course, honey. I understand. And, we will pray for your little one, every moment he or she crosses our mind, we will pray." Gabrielle reached for Lauryn's hand and tugged her gently towards the front door of the house on Promise Place, "Now, tell me more about your plans for this gorgeous front porch."

CHAPTER 16

2017, September

Rebecca wiped clean the last of the apples and set them next to the large bowl on the counter. For a moment she wondered if she could possibly remember her mother's apple crisp recipe by heart, they had made it so often during her childhood. It was her father's favorite dessert and Rebecca remembered fondly the many times years ago during harvest where she'd add a piece of apple crisp with a funny note taped to the Tupperware and sneak it into his lunches. Her father always commented on them, her funny notes and her delicious apple crisp.

She had many good memories of growing up on a farm with its predictable patterns with parents who loved her, who made time for her, but never seemed to understand her.

Even before drugs and alcohol altered who she was as a person, Rebecca was what they called a "rolling stone," the one that never grew the moss. To her, though, that had always sounded like a pretty pathetic way to live. Like why would anyone want to be covered in moss?

But, of course, the proverb was about never growing roots - and growing roots was considered a positive thing, the proper thing. That was something she was simply unable to do, be proper and grow roots.

Roots felt a lot like rot to her. Growing in the same spot of soil for years on end with the debris of your life shedding around you, as they piled up, the mistakes you made would bury you. How were you supposed to flourish in that environment?

Rebecca likened herself to one of those floating green plants that were sold as aquarium accessories or the ones growing free in the ocean. They were beautiful too. They just weren't held in one place.

She was beginning to feel like this place, living and working in her hometown with her family close and now holding a responsible job, was becoming a system of roots. These roots were intertwining together, with people expecting things from her, people relying on her, people looking to her for answers to life's problems.

Sometimes she felt like an imposter - like how could they really believe she had any answers, given her history? Had she fooled them all into thinking she was a mature adult? That she was somehow a responsible person now, trustworthy with hearts and people's feelings?

More and more, she felt the need to be free. Free to begin again. First, the break-up with Kyle and now this new job in suburban Milwaukee, these were steps on the path to really starting over. Working as a domestic violence advocate through the court system, this new job paid more than she made now, and she didn't have nearly the same amount of responsibility as her current job co-directing the women's shelter. To her, that sounded good. It sounded like she felt - a free, floating ocean plant.

Now that her train of thought had taken her to the depths of the ocean, Rebecca abandoned the challenge of trying to recall the recipe by memory and reached into her cupboard for the small book of recipes that she'd been collecting since she'd moved into her own place a few years ago. Her recipe book was slim with a mix of solo meals and salads and desserts, bars and cookies that she could bring to the women's shelter whenever the baking bug randomly bit her.

Thumbing through the scraps of paper and magazine-clipped recipes, she found her mother's apple crisp recipe written on the back of a coffee-stained envelope from the electric company. It occurred to her then, she didn't have any cinnamon. And, probably not enough butter either.

Maybe she would skip it. She didn't really need to make apple crisp and her dad would never know how close he was to having it if she didn't tell him when they met up later today. Certainly, she could find another activity to pass the time this Saturday morning, something else to keep her hands and mind active, something so she wouldn't have to debate her life decisions with her own worst critic - herself.

She had invited her parents and Elliott and Lauryn over for dinner tonight - the lasagna was already assembled and resting in the refrigerator. They could have Schwan's pecan praline ice cream for dessert instead, she reasoned, there was still some left in the freezer.

They didn't know that tonight's dinner had a purpose, of course. She had been planning for a week already that she would tell them the news tonight. She had accepted another job and she was moving next month. In some ways, Rebecca felt she had already moved, and they just didn't know she was gone. She needed to get away, it was almost like a churning feeling deep inside her soul. It was something she *had* to do.

She knew it wouldn't be easy for them to hear her decision. They would be sad to see her leave, but more than that, they would be worried about her motivations for leaving. It would be important for her to convince them this was what she *needed* to do. It would strengthen her as a person, and it would strengthen her lock on her sobriety.

That's it, she thought as she reached for her keys next to her purse on the counter by the refrigerator and slipped into her flip flops that sat just inside the garage door. She had to make her dad some apple crisp. The look she was sure to see on his face was worth the extra effort of going to the store to buy cinnamon and butter. Maybe it would help reassure him that, even if she was moving away, his little girl was still safe and healthy.

The humid air clung heavy over Lake Belle Grocery's newly paved parking lot that steamy, early-September morning. While some sure signs of fall were evident - Labor Day had come and gone, school had started, photos of autumn-inspired, copper-colored hair styles were abundant on Pinterest - the weather hadn't quite relinquished its hold on summer. Rebecca was glad she hadn't packed away her jean shorts and flip flops.

She reached across the car console to her purse which sat in the passenger side seat and caught a glimpse of herself in the rearview mirror. Combing her short blonde hair behind her ear, she smoothed some gloss over her pale lips and shifted her leather purse onto her shoulder while mentally adding coffee and creamer to her grocery list as she walked across the parking lot.

"Hey, Rebecca-" The voice spoke from behind her, but the low timbre with its underlying tone of laughter was unmistakable. Kyle.

She turned slowly, willing her heart to stop its crazy acrobatics routine. Is that all he had to do to make her heart do this? Say two words? Is that all he had to do? She sighed deeply, hoping to prepare herself in some way to speak to him, but the sickly, singed tar smell of fresh asphalt was her only reward for the deep breath she took.

"Kyle. Hi." She smiled and felt her freshly glossed lips stick to her teeth as she did so. Obviously, her smile was weak if it could be impeded by a little lip gloss. She tried to widen it and convinced herself she could pretend that seeing him was no big deal. She could do this.

Kyle's thick hair which was dark with grayish strands coming through on the sides and it was shorter than the last time she'd seen him. He must have gone back to the hair stylist in the strip mall next to his office, the one who always seemed to cut it a bit too short but whose location was more convenient. He didn't like to think about haircuts or scheduling them, so he frequently just took whichever stylist was open at the time. As soon as the thoughts bolted through her mind, Rebecca's smile stiffened. Why did she think about these things? These thoughts were too personal, too familiar.

"You– you look great, Rebecca." After a brief hesitation, Kyle finished his thought and then politely stepped aside as a silver-haired lady who wore a nylon scarf over her freshly permed hair made her way past them into the grocery store.

"You too, Kyle." Rebecca shifted her purse higher onto her shoulder and ached to grab her cell phone. She *had* to do something that could make it look like she didn't have time to talk to him – like she had *anything at all* going on in her life, unrelated to missing him in it.

"Going grocery shopping?" He moved out of the path once again as two teenage girls ambled by, both of them enthralled by whatever they were reading on their cell phones. Then, as if hearing himself, he laughed, "Well, obviously, right? You're at the grocery store. Me too. We're completely out of food at the cabin."

He laughed again and waved her in front of him, following a respectful distance behind her. What was she to do now, she fidgeted slightly, and she wondered if he was watching her. What was he thinking? Would he feel the need to follow her throughout the store?

Once inside, Rebecca reached for a cart and pulled it off to the side, out of the way of the people going about their Saturday errands. As she turned to face him, she found him quietly watching her. His face, with its distinct features and laugh lines around his mouth, was unreadable but his deep brown eyes were soft– if that was a word that could be used to describe eyes. Maybe instead, it was a feeling she read in those eyes. Soft.

"I've missed you, Rebecca." The words were spoken quietly, intimately and jarringly out of context as he stood next to the produce section with its brightly printed sign, Pineapple $3.99. But she heard the words.

"I've missed you too." She nodded slightly, surprised that she'd said it, but relieved in a way that she'd spoken the truth. Maybe some things about her *had* changed.

His shoulders lifted a little and then lowered with a sigh and he glanced around a bit awkwardly as if realizing where he stood. It was obvious that he wanted this conversation to be held anywhere else but a busy grocery store as he scuffed his foot against the bottom of the cart that he held in front of him. Rebecca focused on his long fingers where they gripped the plastic handle.

"Things are good with you?" He continued, obviously trying to stay noncommittal and friendly.

"Yes. Things are good. How 'bout you? How are the kids?"

"Great. Yeah, the grandkids are in school now, of course. We have the first gymnastics meet next Saturday. Chelsea –" He stopped at the mention of his eldest granddaughter, the one who had taken a special liking to Rebecca, the one who had spent a few afternoons after school with her this past spring when her parents were both out of town travelling with their business.

Roots, she thought, those darn roots. Like moss. Not like free, floating aquatic plants at all. And, that was a dumb proverb anyway, moss didn't even have roots. She'd Googled it. No roots.

"Well–" Kyle's discomfort was painful now and Rebecca wanted to crawl under the stack of peach crates next to her and pretend like she didn't have any connection with him or his beautiful little grand-daughter with the ash-blonde curls and innocent, hazel eyes. "Well, anyway, Chelsea is doing great. She's mastered the balance beam now, you know. Remember how she was practicing? She's nailed it, she showed me last weekend-" Kyle's voice drifted off and he reached for a bag of green grapes, resting it carefully in his cart before looking up at her again.

"That's great, Kyle. Tell her I'm proud of her, I knew she could do it." Rebecca *was* proud of the little girl and she tried to smile but felt it was completely fake, so she finally let the smile drop altogether. This wasn't working. "I'm sorry, Kyle. I have to go. I will see you around, I'm sure. Take care and say hi to the kids from me."

She watched his expression for a moment, the light in his eyes shifted in a weird way, like a shade had been lowered. He nodded a little, tried to smile, but it was not really a smile at all. It was an acknowledgment - I knew you. I loved you. I let you go. That's what the smile said.

Rebecca lifted her hand with a small wave in his direction and pushed her cart forward towards the dairy section, her mind a complete blank on why she had come to this grocery store in the first place. Was it butter she needed, or milk?

Roots, she muttered to herself. Those darn roots.

Lauryn gathered her long hair to the side of her head, smoothed it down the front of her chest and rested her head backwards against the bathroom wall, allowing her exposed neck to touch the cool tile wall behind her. For some reason, it felt really good, that coolness on her neck.

As she sat on the floor and tried to gain back some strength, she noticed again how familiar this bathroom next to their bedroom, and the one on the main level at Promise Place, were becoming to her. From this vantage point, she was painfully familiar with the texture and color variations of the tiles, the nicks in the wood floorboards behind the toilet bowl, the grout that needed to be replaced. Nothing like getting up close and personal to see what household repairs were needed.

Mostly they were drive heaves, a terrible retching that would suddenly overtake her body, and then leave her breathless, her eyes watering and her legs shaky. Afterwards, she was tired and still nauseous. Not like when you have the stomach flu and the agony of vomiting released the disease from your body, often leaving a person feeling a little better. With this, there was no release.

They called it morning sickness, but it trailed her all day long and into the night too. Like now. It was almost 8:30 pm and she had been sick off and on all day. Too sick to even go with Elliott to his mom's place for dinner tonight. Of course, they will all guess the reason, Elliott wouldn't be able to call it the stomach flu or tell them Lauryn was just tired from working too hard.

They had joked about it before he left, how he would tell them, because they had passed the dates on the calendar and added a couple extra weeks, just for good measure. Their baby was safe. Tell the world, she'd told him, scream it from the rooftop for all I care, let's even announce it on social media this week.

We are having a baby!

Lauryn closed the lid on the toilet and pushed herself up from the floor. Feeling a bit unsteady, she walked to the vanity, washed her face and brushed her teeth again. At least her dentist wouldn't have any complaints about plaque build-up at her next dental appointment. This was the sixth time she'd brushed today.

Turning the light off in the bathroom, she ambled over to their bed and crawled on top of the soft, cotton comforter, slowly sinking her head down onto her pillow. Everything had to go in slow motion or else the nausea returned, and she was reminded again that these days of sickness were starting to put a major dent in their workflow at the house.

Elliott had picked up the slack though, as much as he could. He gave direction to the carpenters, electricians and plumbers who were trying to wrap up their work at the house and he kept uploading the progress to their website and YouTube right on schedule. He was beyond amazing, that guy.

She smiled as she pictured him telling his mom and grandparents about their baby tonight at dinner. Or, maybe he had decided to wait until she could be there to announce it with him. That would be great too.

As she laid there, listening to the quiet, empty house, her heavy eyes ached to close, but her mind was still moving through a hundred tasks she had to do. Trouble was, even though the list was lengthy, and all the tasks seemed to have deadlines, she had no energy to do them.

She turned her head slowly catching sight of Cameron Berndt's journal sitting on her bedside table with its inconspicuous leather cover hiding beneath it the story of a man with a life so normal, yet so tortured. They were having a baby too, she recalled from the past entries she'd read. Theirs' wasn't a happy experience.

Lauryn reached out and pulled the journal across the bed towards her, unable to resist. Maybe just for a little while, she really needed to get some sleep. Tonight, she would read for just a little while.

CHAPTER 17

1967, September

All I have to say today, Lord, is please help me stay strong. I must stay strong-

Cameron tossed the pen aside and pushed the notebook away from the edge of his desk in frustration. Really, what were they doing here, what was this marriage about anyway? What was the point?

Could he really be so blind? In what fake, imaginary world did he live? Going about his days being a husband, father and pastor - just believing that, while life was often a challenge, it wasn't supposed to be a simmering tragedy, ready to explode at the slightest upset.

He replayed the past seven to eight months in his mind, the months of this pregnancy, and he tried to separate what he thought were normal pregnancy mood swings apart from something far more serious and heartbreaking. As one month turned over into the next month, and he watched as her figure rounded out as she carried their third baby, he felt Cassie slip further and further away.

It wasn't just the fact that she bemoaned the changes to her energy level and her appearance, it seemed that this pregnancy had snapped her dreams right out from under her. She was unabashedly vocal about how the pregnancy affected her work life and her plans for the future - she wasn't at all happy about the timing of it - but he thought that over the past couple of months she'd finally started to accept the fact that they were a family and often plans were meant to be changed.

Cameron remembered their prayers – holding hands over the kitchen table, next to each other while they sat on the couch, sitting outside on the lawn chairs – they had prayed prayers together many times over the past few months. As man and wife, a team.

He lifted the glass tumbler to his lips, and took a long drink, allowing the bite of the liquor to roll over his tongue slowly. There was a sweet agony in drinking alcohol again, he noticed as he poured a few more ounces into his glass. He did it by turning off the part of himself that cared.

This person who needed the alcohol was just a sliver of him, not the whole, just a wayward sliver. It was a disobedient sliver that the rest of him loathed and yet grudgingly accepted because at least this wayward sliver was experiencing this pain honestly while the rest of him – the part that people saw each day – the rest of him was a fraudulent sham.

This drinking – it was a slope he'd never dreamed he'd find himself on ever again. If you had told him two years ago that he would be here, at this point, midway down a mountain going nowhere fast, he'd have politely given you a piece of his self-righteous mind.

"–Cameron, please open the door. We need to talk about this." Cassie's voice was cracking with emotion, evident even through the heavy sliding door of his office, which was securely locked.

Cameron glanced at his watch, noting dully that he'd been locked in his office now for almost an hour. He realized it seemed childish and he was concerned about what the kids were thinking about the erratic actions of their father, but where else could he go to retreat? He couldn't very well go to one of the bars uptown, could he? The way it was, over the past few months, he'd had to purchase his occasional whiskey bottle in the neighboring town. Couldn't have the congregants seeing their pastor purchasing alcohol at the local liquor store, now could we?

"You said quite enough, Cassie. I don't want to talk right now. I need some time to think." He spoke to the locked door, not really caring if she still stood outside, and took another long swallow of the liquor.

His mind was starting to numb, and he realized that he rather savored this feeling. Somehow, the inner turmoil that was eating him from the inside out felt soothed with each swallow, almost as if the liquor was the anesthetic administered before surgery. It's an irrational thought, he knew it, of course. But maybe if he took enough of the "juice" – *Give me more, Doc* – he wouldn't feel a thing.

This baby. It all had to do with this baby that was coming. Due now in less than two weeks. A cause for celebration. A gift from God.

But not in this house. No sir. In this house, this baby was the daily reminder of all that was wrong with their life. The cause for every argument. The impetus for division between him and his wife. This baby was the cause for their marriage falling apart, right before his eyes.

But, that's not fair, he corrected his own thoughts. He knew better. Of course, this helpless baby growing inside his wife was an innocent bystander in this whole affair. What this baby had done was bring everything to the surface. This baby forced Cassie back to the reality that she was a mother first, and a career woman and potential law student second.

Or, as she constantly reminded him, now she would *never be* a career woman. And, law school? Well, she'd stated flatly, that was obviously meant for other, less "shackled" people, not her.

But this baby's influence was not felt by Cassie alone, this baby also served as a catalyst for Cameron; it brought him back to reality too. He couldn't convince himself differently any longer, no matter how hard he tried to fabricate a positive spin on the circumstances of his marriage, all the things she said and did. The reality was – deep down – his wife didn't love him. Probably never had.

He took another long swallow, finishing his third glass. She had told him as much, that she didn't love him, just an hour ago.

"Cameron, please. Open this door." He raised his head and regarded the door again. He wasn't thinking clearly, the effects of the alcohol were dulling the raw edges. If only they could be on the same page about *anything.* Why couldn't she just be happy with their life together? They were married, right? That meant forever. Right?

Cameron sighed heavily as he hoisted himself out of his leather covered desk chair and walked across the room to unlock the door. Once he opened it, he found Cassie leaning sluggishly against the door frame, one hand on the small of her back while the other rubbed the top of her swollen belly trying to relieve the tightness as the baby shifted position inside her. She looked drawn and tired in her plaid-patterned maternity top with the ridiculous lace sleeves. She looked the way he felt.

"Cameron, I'm sorry. I don't know why I said such a thing." Her red-tinged eyes pleaded with his, but she held herself back from touching him, he noticed. They rarely touched anymore, he realized sadly, as she continued, "You know I love you. I don't want to leave you. It's just- well, it's just that this pregnancy has been hard on me. You know. I've had to accept things for what they are. That's hard for me."

He wanted to call her out on the specific, hurtful words she'd thrown at him an hour earlier during their argument. He itched to ask her, how do you get to the point of telling your husband you want to leave him? How do you say those words unless you mean them? Help me understand in what version of reality are those words not the death sentence for a marriage?

But, when he spoke, all Cameron could do was address the obvious, the children. Having to deal with the precarious state of their marriage was way more than either of them wanted to address directly which would ultimately force a conclusion. They'd become pros at avoiding the conclusion.

"Okay, I guess." He slid a glance around the living room and down the center hallway towards the kitchen, making sure the children weren't within earshot before he continued, "But, you need to be straight with me. Is our life so awful for you, Cassie? Being a mother - having our baby - is it really so bad?"

"No, it's not the children and it's not this baby." Cassie walked past him and pulled the door closed behind her. As she sat down on the leather couch in the corner of his office, she pulled a pillow behind her back and with a puzzled frown crossing her face, she noticed the uncapped whiskey bottle on his desk. But, for now, she didn't address his infraction as she continued with a sigh, "And, it's not you ... or your job. It's me, Cameron. I'm the one that's tripping here. Maybe it's hormones, I don't know."

She looked like she was going to cry again and in his current state where the moment was hazy and distorted by alcohol, he wasn't exactly sure how to act or what to say. This sense of losing his bearings - he'd forgotten how much he disliked this particular sensation.

"Cass, I would do anything for you. I love you." He tried to walk towards her but found his path wasn't perfectly straight. Finally, he slumped next to her on the couch, doing his best to stay in the moment, trying to keep his mind focused but he found his attention was diverted out the windows of the French doors as a small bird landed on a dogwood shrub.

"So, there's something else, Cameron." Cassie looked down at her hands sitting in her lap and twisted her wedding band slowly around her swollen finger, "This isn't the first time I've noticed. You've started drinking again."

He tore his gaze from the window where the bird had flicked it wings and took off in nervous flight. His eyes focused on the empty glass and open whiskey bottle sitting on his desk. As she stated the obvious, the self-loathing inside him started with a whisper, it was buried way below the self-pity and self-righteousness, but it was there.

"Yeah. There's that." What could he say, anyway? He had no excuse for his weakness.

"You promised me that was over." The way she passed judgement on him sliced straight through to the river of guilt, allowing it to freely wash through every pore of his body. He was struggling to stay afloat in all this, he needed his wife to keep from drowning, but it felt like he was completely on his own, left to flounder in the waves alone.

"Yeah, promises are like that. We make them; sometimes, we break them." The alcohol was loosening his tongue and his inner dialogue, that wayward sliver, came out brutally honest. Might as well keep going, he thought as he regarded the woman whom he loved but was no longer sure she felt the same way.

"I'm hurting here, Cass. I'm trying to be strong through this, but it's dragging me down. When you tell me after eight years together that you question your decision to marry me? That's not easy to hear. I love you and I want us to be a happy family. But I don't know how much more of this we can take."

Just then, Cassie turned her head at the sight of little fingers curled around the edge of the sliding door and it opened slowly on its track. Aaron poked his head through the space tentatively, questions filling his wide, angelic eyes.

"Mommy? Daddy? Is it time for popcorn yet? We've been really good, and the big hand finally got to the twelve."

Cassie turned to face Cameron, her mouth had a small smile at the innocent interruption of their son and his mention of their tell-the-time game, but her eyes were shaded as she reached for Cameron's hand and brought it to her lips. As she kissed his hand softly, she whispered just loud enough for him to hear.

"I'll try harder, Cam. Really, I will." Tears were welling up in the corners of her eyes as she tried to smile at him. With a small sigh, she squeezed his hand and shifted her weight upwards as she stood awkwardly, using his knee for leverage on her way up and spoke to their son. "Yes, Aaron. You have been good for a very long time. Let's go make some popcorn."

The Gazette, Happenings Around Town Monday October 9, 1967

Gemma Anne Berndt was born Thursday, October 5, 1967 at 10:25 am. The healthy baby girl weighed 7 lbs 8 oz and measured 20" long. That same day, towards evening, she was greeted by her older brother Aaron and her sister Charlotte at the hospital, where her siblings proclaimed, "She's cute!" and "Even better than having a puppy!"

The happy parents Pastor Cameron Berndt and Cassandra Berndt are both doing well and are excited to bring their new baby home in the coming days. Congratulations to the Berndt family!

CHAPTER 18

2017, September

"–I forwarded you his voicemail two days ago, the same day that we scanned the photos and you finished writing Milton's story. But this other guy seems persistent, I think it might be interesting to talk to him."

The steamy, stifling air of Saturday and Sunday were gone, replaced by a crisp autumn chill that better matched the September date on the calendar that Monday morning as Lauryn and Elliott arrived at Promise Place.

They spent the drive this morning reviewing their To Do list for the week, the most recent social media analytics and the many messages she had to return.

The persistent morning sickness had knocked her off her game so much the past few weeks that Elliott was constantly reminding her of things she left half-done or people she had to follow up with. Like this guy who had reached out earlier this summer as they were writing the history angle on Promise Place.

Lauryn had forgotten all about him and the fact that he said he knew Dr. Berndt. But there were plenty of people who knew the Drs in this small town, and she had gotten more background stories of their lives than she could possibly deal with in her videos, so this message had naturally fallen off her radar. She didn't really need to talk to him but could tell that Elliott thought she should. The trouble with Elliott? He was just too nice.

"Okay, fine, I will call him back. I promise." Lauryn said as she got out of the car, relishing the fact that she didn't feel car sick this morning. Maybe it would be an easy day, she could hope that she wouldn't be on the bathroom floor today, couldn't she?

"Hey, I like the way the walkway turned out, don't you?" Lauryn propped her sunglasses on the top of her head as she surveyed the stamped, walnut-colored concrete walkway that wound around the house and down the newly sodded front lawn to the city sidewalk.

"Yeah, it looks great! Those guys sure knew what they were doing. Did you check out the video I have on it? I shot short sequences on the entire process. I thought you could do a voice over since you weren't here." Elliott spoke as he followed her along the side of the house towards the porte-cochere door.

"Uh, no, I guess I didn't get to that video yet." Lauryn muttered, just one more thing she hadn't gotten done. As she struggled to find the house keys in her purse, Elliott dug into the front pocket of his jeans, reached around her shoulder and dangled his set of keys in front of her face.

"Here, use mine," He teased her with a laugh. "You seem to be having some trouble finding anything in that suitcase you call a purse."

"Yeah, good thing you made an extra set." Lauryn remembered his insistence at making the extra set once she started coming in late or leaving early when the morning sickness became too great.

"Yeah, someone needs to tell people what to do around here." He agreed with a grin, teasing her, because he knew how much she hated to give up control. Lauryn bristled, why did he always choose to needle her about the things that bothered her the most?

"Okay, whatever." Her words came out sharp and bitter and she tried to soften the tone with a smile as she pushed open the door.

Elliott gave her that look she'd seen often lately - like she'd dealt a low blow, but he was going to choose to ignore her bad mood. It was a common circle for them. She'd snap at something he said or did and then she'd be immediately sorry. After all, she'd remind herself, where would she be if he wasn't here to pick up the loose ends on the house renovation, keeping everything on deadline? It wouldn't be good, that's for sure.

As usual, Elliott began setting up the camera for that day's video which was focusing on installing the last of the new lights throughout the house. The electrician had already strung cord and was returning today to hang some antique light fixtures she'd scored at a flea market including a chandelier that she was planning to mount over the kitchen island and some captivating, re-wired vintage wall sconces from the 1920s.

A few lights and some painting in the upstairs rooms were the last tasks on the renovation To Do list for Promise Place. It was crazy to think that later this week, she would take photos and load them onto her mom's real estate office website, and they would officially be done at this house.

The electrician showed up an hour late but was all business when he finally arrived. A few hours later, the lights were all hung, the electrician was gone, and Lauryn and Elliott sat at the kitchen counter, their laptops open, each working in their own zone while they ate their late lunch of oriental salad.

Elliott, distractedly bobbing his head to the beat of the music in his wireless earbuds, was scrolling through messages on his phone. Lauryn assumed he was double checking things for his meeting the next day where he was considering a new business opportunity with his friends Mark and Lina, both IT professionals who happened to be married to one another and were looking to venture out to start their own company. This company would develop custom programs for businesses where various aspects of the company (finance, supply chain, sales etc) would all seamlessly "talk to one another," as Elliott described it. He seemed super excited by it all.

So, it surprised her when he spoke suddenly of something completely random, not in that vein at all.

"Mom is wondering if you want that antique mirror that she has in her living room," He took out an earbud to hear her response before he continued, "She said she doesn't want to move it and she remembered that you said you liked it."

Lauryn looked up from her laptop, somewhat bewildered. The mirror had been a gift from Rebecca's boyfriend Kyle, purchased during a happier time in their relationship, while they were antique shopping together. Rebecca had proudly shown it off to Lauryn earlier this summer, the night she introduced Kyle to them. Even though the relationship hadn't worked out, to just give away such a personal gift seemed oddly callous. Not like Rebecca at all.

"Wow, that hurts." Lauryn said, thinking of how Kyle would feel if he knew she gave it away. When Rebecca told them about their split, it came as a complete surprise. Kyle seemed like such a nice guy, he respected the battle that Rebecca fought with addiction, he accepted the scars she bore and seemed to love her more for it. Now, after such an unexpected break-up, she had this plan to move to Wisconsin? Things just felt off about the whole deal.

"Yeah, tell me about it," Elliott agreed, "She's cold. Poor guy. You'd think moving away would be enough-" His voice dropped off before he finished quietly, "Maybe she doesn't want anything around to remind her of the guy."

"Maybe. But I think you nailed it the other night when you said it's like she's running from something and it's not Kyle."

Elliott had come home from dinner last Saturday and shared the news with her - his mom was paying out on her lease, packing up things in her place and moving to Milwaukee for a new job. The shock of it dimmed the happy news he'd shared earlier in the evening that they were having a baby and that, except for Lauryn being really sick, the pregnancy was progressing normally.

"Have you talked to your mom since Saturday? Told her what you think about this plan of hers?"

"No." Elliott admitted, almost sheepishly. Lauryn could tell he'd thought about it though and she wondered why he hesitated to discuss it with his mom if he felt it was a mistake, "But, really, what do I know? She's the one who's gone through all the counseling and treatment. I'm sure she's dealing with it the best way she knows how."

"Yeah, maybe." Lauryn agreed verbally but didn't really believe it. "It's just too bad. I thought she was really happy with Kyle and now with the baby coming and you're finally back in Minnesota-"

"I know," Elliott interrupted, as if hearing Lauryn recite the list of reasons for Rebecca to stay was a torment that he'd already put himself through too many times, "Interesting timing for her to move, isn't it?"

Elliott set his phone down and as if to avoid talking further about the topic, he moved his mouse on the counter, springing his laptop to life again and scrolled through some emails.

"Elliott," Lauryn drew his name out slowly and watched him closely as he intentionally avoided her eyes, "You can't possibly think it has to do with you being back here. That's not why she's leaving."

After a moment where Lauryn watched a panorama of emotions pass across his face, Elliott pushed the laptop away and sat back against the upholstered leather of the counter stool while stretching his legs out below.

"All I know is," He finally continued, his tone of voice clearly reflecting that he was unconvinced, "This feels familiar. I know you can't really understand, Lauryn, I don't expect you to see it. I just know her."

He was so vulnerable in that moment that Lauryn couldn't help but remember their childhood when Elliott struggled to find security in a world that offered very little of it. Deep addiction wiped out all sense of responsibility, its power subtle and insidious, it didn't care who you were, whether or not you had children who depended on you or what you did for a living.

It wanted all of you. Just look at Pastor Cameron Berndt - even a guy like him struggled with its influence.

"Are you saying-" Lauryn spoke breathlessly, searching for a way to speak the unspeakable, "I mean, are you concerned about her sobriety?"

It felt like sacrilege even voicing the words out loud after witnessing the transformation they'd seen in Rebecca over the past few years. Her transformation hadn't only been physical, it had also been mental and spiritual, and Lauryn had joined Elliott in trusting one hundred percent that it had been real and permanent.

"I'd like to believe she's fine, I pray that she's solid in her faith. But, this type of thing, the decisions she makes-" Elliott bit the inside of his mouth, his eyes squinting slightly as he stared above her shoulder, out the kitchen window. Lauryn could just imagine the heart-rending snap shots of his mother's erratic past that were flicking through his mind.

Slowly, as if he suddenly realized that she still sat there next to him, he turned his green-gold gaze back towards her and she melted inside the hurt she saw reflected there, "I don't know- I just don't like it. This feels too familiar."

CHAPTER 19

1968, June

The Lord is my strength and my shield; my heart trusted in him and I am helped: therefore, my heart greatly rejoiceth; and with my song will I praise him. Psalm 28:7

Your love is unending, I cannot fathom the depth of your love, heavenly Father. I am just so grateful for your patience, for your grace and for your sacrifice on my behalf. In Jesus name, Amen.

"-Just bring this one over to the dessert table, Cam. I will bring Gemma." Cassie held the pineapple cake towards him, as she deftly transferred the rather tattered orange and white striped, obviously third-child, baby bag to her other shoulder and reached for their infant daughter who'd fallen asleep on the front seat of the Bel Air.

"Daddy, I want to swim! Can we go swimming now?" Charlotte pulled at Cameron's trousers as she pushed the tangled mess of sun-bleached curls out of her eyes and shifted her bright pink sand bucket with its brightly colored shovels more securely onto her dimpled forearm.

"No, Charlotte. First, we eat, then we swim." As he reached for the cake, Cameron laughed at the crest-fallen look on his daughter's face and glanced towards the shimmering lake in the distance with its kid's slide and bouncing red and white buoys that roped around the swimming area.

Even though it was a few miles drive out of town, this year's church picnic was being held at the state park's swimming beach instead of the picnic shelters at the city park, which was the usual gathering spot. If his kids' excitement to "swim with dad" was any indication, it had been the perfect choice.

"Daddy, please, can we go swimming now? Are you going to change into your swimsuit too?" Aaron called from the back seat as he shamelessly shifted out of his church shoes and trousers and into his swim trunks, not caring if anyone was walking past and might notice his state of undress.

"Not yet, you two. Like I said, first we eat." Cameron stood in front of the door to provide some cover and laughed at his son's exaggerated dismay through the window. "Tell you what, you take your sister over to the swings and play with the other kids for a while. I will come get you when it's time to eat."

Once the children were taken care of and running off to play, Cameron set the cake carefully on the roof of the car and began to remove all the gear for their Sunday afternoon picnic.

"Can I help you carry something, Pastor?" Cameron turned at the voice and found Bradley Harlowe coming towards him, his youthful appearance altered by the severe injuries he sustained in Vietnam.

Bradley's dark hair was still shaved short in the cut of a serviceman and his once-round face had become gaunt, his smile more reserved. He'd been home now for a few weeks already, but hadn't left the house much, according to his mother Vivienne. Today was the first time he'd been in church since arriving home.

The changes in his appearance, including the white eye patch he wore on his left eye under his sunglasses and the lilting gait where his left leg dragged slightly, were shocking to those who knew him before he enlisted two years ago.

"I might be a little slow at walking, Pastor Cam, and I can't defend to my left, but my arms still work great," Brad joked with a half-tilted smile.

"Brad, perfect timing, my man! Sure thing. Cassie would probably trust you more with this dessert than me anyway." Cameron laughed as he handed the cake pan and some beach towels over to Bradley and then reached into the trunk for the aluminum Coleman cooler.

"It's nice to have you home again, Brad." Cameron commented as they took their time walking over towards the group of people congregating by the charcoal grills at the edge of the tree line, "We were all praying for your recovery and for your safe trip back here."

"Thanks, Pastor Cam. That means a lot. It seems funny to say, but it's like I could really tell you all were praying for me. It's hard to explain, but it's like I just knew it. Even before I got the letters from Mom. I just knew it."

"That was the Holy Spirit. You know, the helper. That's what that feeling was, Brad." Cameron set the cooler down on the ground next to a wooden picnic table and set his hand on Brad's shoulder, noticing that Brad's mom Vivienne and some other ladies were watching and smiling from a distance. Brad was the obvious topic of their conversation, now that he was safely home, injured but still alive, "Listen, if you need anything now that you're getting settled back in, you just let me know, ok?"

Cameron searched Brad's face, fully aware that the young soldier was struggling with adjusting to his life back home. Vivienne had shared with Cameron about his sleepless nights and his bouts with depression as he dealt with the side effects of his recovery and the dark memories of war, "I mean *anything*, Brad. Anytime. Just call me, ok?"

Brad smiled self-consciously and misunderstanding him slightly, he said, "Oh, yeah, that's right. You're basically a doctor. I forgot about that."

"Ha, yeah–" Cameron agreed, "I was close to the finish line, almost added the D-R to my name, but God kind of side-tracked me a little, didn't he?" Cameron was adept at his reply, it was a frequent comment from those who knew his history with medicine.

"Well, I tell you what, they sure could use a guy like you over there. Never enough docs around when you need 'em. I hear they take anyone who can stand the sight of blood. It was one crazy place, that's for sure."

"I can't imagine, Brad. I appreciate your service and the sacrifices you made over there. And, if you ever have any health-related questions or just want to talk, you know where I am." Cameron paused, watching carefully as Brad nodded and smiled shyly, as if he didn't want the conversation to end with small talk, as if he needed to say more.

Cameron knew from experience that some soldiers came back and didn't want to discuss anything about their service in Vietnam;

a few in his church had made that clear to him. What, and how much to share, had to be left up to them and sometimes the clues they gave were easily overlooked. Not quite sure he was reading Brad correctly, Cameron casually reached into the cooler and with his brows raised in an invitation, took out two cans of 7Up and held one out to Brad, who eagerly took it.

"How's your recovery going, Brad?" Cameron sat on the bench of the picnic table, pulled off the tab on the can of soda and waved his hand for Brad to take a seat. "Did the docs do a good job?"

Brad quickly slid into a seat and awkwardly pulled his left leg out of the path of some of women who were milling about setting food onto the tables around them.

"Well, they put the pieces back in their right places, I guess, but it must have been quite a jumble judging by all the scars on my back. My leg is messed up because of the shrapnel; they tell me I'll probably deal with that for the rest of my life. But, I'm just glad they could save it. The guy next to me lost both of his-" Brad stopped talking abruptly and glanced around furtively to see if anyone was listening, then lowered his voice and looked down at his leg, "He lost both his legs, I mean. He came home in a wheelchair."

"I'm sorry to hear that about him and about you, Brad."

"Well, my bum leg is not that big a deal. God has gotten me through worse." Brad paused, took a long swallow of soda and wiped his mouth with the back of his hand before leaning forward towards Cameron and said almost in a whisper, "I really miss the eye, though, Pastor Cam."

He reached up and lightly fingered the white patch under his sunglasses as if to prove to himself that the day his unit was ambushed wasn't all just a horrible nightmare.

"I wish they could have saved that," Brad said simply and dropped his gaze.

"Yeah, I do too." Cameron nodded and sat quietly with him, letting the thoughts of war and men sacrificing body parts sink in for a long moment. Brad had been close to dying over in Vietnam but instead of letting his life slip away, God had given him another day.

Cameron glanced around at the members of his church and their families. A table of women sat visiting nearby while others gathered up their children from the swing sets and slides. A small group of men stood a few feet away discussing the weather and how the Twins were doing this season. From two tables away, Cassie pulled a bib over Gemma's messy blonde curls and opened a small jar of baby food. They were working on peas now. Gemma didn't seem to care much for peas.

It struck him then how sobering it all was, this fine line between life and death. How brittle and tenuous was the line between this life on earth and the life eternal after death.

"Brad," Feeling an overwhelming connection to the young man and the struggles he was having, Cameron continued quietly, "Most people live entire lives without testing their fortitude in the ways you've been tested. God notices how you're dealing with it all - and how your experience has deepened your faith in Him - well, you're an inspiration to everyone around you-"

Just then, three boys ran past, Aaron the last of them, pulling to a sharp stop in front of Cameron and heaving out deep gasps of breath from his run.

"Dad, is it time to eat yet?" Aaron's brow was glistening with perspiration from the warm sun and his voice was high and seemed on the edge of panic.

"Ha, yes. I think it is, bud. Come on, I will help you get your plate." Cameron glanced towards Brad with an apology as Aaron pulled on his arm as if dragging him towards the food table, "Sorry, Brad, a dad's job is never done. You want to join us in line? It looks like quite a feast over there." He pointed towards a table heaped with chicken casseroles, charcoal-grilled hot dogs, green gelatin salads and fruit pies.

"Sure, thing, Pastor Cam." Brad stood up slowly, shifting his weight onto his good leg as he stood. "Thanks for the talk, by the way. It's good to have someone to talk to."

"Sure. Anytime, Brad," Cameron said.

Then, noticing a problem was brewing as Charlotte budged in front of her brother in the food line, Cameron moved quickly into the fray to avoid an embarrassing blow-out between the pastor's children at the church picnic.

1968, July

The afternoon was steamy a few weeks later, that Friday in July. It was the kind of day that left an uncomfortable trickle of perspiration between Cameron's shoulder blades as soon as he left the church's office, which was kept an artificially-cool 70 degrees now that the church had installed one of the new window air conditioners sold by the heating and cooling retailer uptown. He could get used to being perfectly cool and comfortable all summer, he thought as he gingerly avoided sitting against the hot, black leather sections on the black and white houndstooth upholstery in his car.

Most summer days, he walked to the church or rode his bicycle. Today, thankfully, he had driven. Not only would it speed his trip home so he could change into some cooler clothing, but he could also stop at the diner to pick up dinner.

Dinner take-out was an infrequent extravagance for them. Not only because it was expensive, but also because Cassie preferred to cook herself, even when she arrived home late from the office.

About a month ago, once baby Gemma had shown a preference for a baby bottle instead of nursing, Cassie had decided she wanted to return to work. They had gone around and around about it because Cameron preferred that she stay home longer at least through the summer to be with the children. Once she negotiated to work three days a week with the law firm, however, they eventually compromised.

Although he couldn't understand it, Cameron had to admit, Cassie did seem happier once she was back working at the office. It wasn't lost on him, however, that all the turmoil surrounding Gemma's birth late last year was still brewing somewhere under the surface. And the hurtful words she'd said about "needing time away" still played around in his brain.

Each day they seemed to just float through life as they clicked them off the calendar on their way to the end of the year. And, once that year was finished, they'd just begin another one, realizing a couple months later that they still shared the same house, were raising a family together, but all the while, they were each wandering in separate directions, away from each other.

Cassie was living in an obvious, and perpetual state of disappointment, a kind of disillusionment with their life. He was living with a low-voltage frustration – an annoying tiny blue flame that he simply couldn't seem to squelch – that often flamed into anger when she refused to appreciate the life she had.

He was trying his best to keep his old habits – uncontrolled anger and alcohol – in check and he thought he was doing a decent job of that, at least to the outside world it looked that way. But the old habits taunted him at night in his nightmares.

With the pressure building, Cameron found it much easier to *just not think* about the relationship between Cassie and him. If he contemplated their marriage too deeply, he recognized his repeated, almost desperate, prayers to God to salvage their marriage were beginning to feel like fruitless appeals to delay the obvious conclusion. But he had become adept at refusing to see or state the obvious and so he plodded on by focusing his energies on his job and his kids.

Earlier this afternoon, Cameron had called Cassie to tell her that he would take the family out for dinner tonight, maybe to the Fancy

Freeze. The drive-in was the kids' favorite restaurant in town; they would sit in the backseat and watch fascinated as the servers, all dressed in matching red and white striped uniforms, would coast up to the car window on their roller skates and serve hamburgers and strawberry malts topped with whipped cream and a colorful mix of sugar sprinkles.

But now it was early evening and still unbearably hot and the thought of sitting in a stifling car with a tired baby and two young children eating messy hamburgers and ice cream just didn't sound appealing at all. So, making a change of dinner plans as he drove, he decided to just pick something up at the diner uptown and bring it home instead.

Dot's Diner, owned for many years by a lady named Dorothy, who never went by the nickname Dot from what Cameron knew, not only had the best pie in town but it also had the best Friday specials.

Main Street was rather quiet this time of day, most of the businesses having closed at 5:00 pm, except for the Mack's Pool Hall located in the basement of the big brick hotel on the corner.

Cameron pulled his car to a stop in an open space in front of Dot's and pushed open the antique windowed door to be greeted by the restaurant owner who was wiping down the coffee counter and pie case.

"Well, hello, Pastor! How are you?" Dorothy pushed a few stray strands of her frizzy gray hair more firmly into the loose bun she had on the back of her head.

"Excellent today, Dorothy. What do you have for specials?"

"We have chicken pot pies, they went over so well at lunch, Harold made more for tonight, so they are fresh out of the oven. Do you want to have a seat and I will bring you an order?" She reached for a water glass and started to fill it from a water pitcher sitting near the counter.

"No, thank you. I'm bringing home dinner tonight. But that sounds excellent. I think three orders would be enough for the whole family."

"Sure thing! Isn't it nice of you to make dinner tonight? Ha, ha." Dorothy laughed at her joke as she reached into her pocketed apron and retrieved her pad of green slips and a pen.

"Yes, that's what I thought! I promised Cassie I would take the family out tonight but decided we'd do this instead."

While Dorothy spoke through the kitchen window and directed her husband Harold to make up trays to go, Cameron found an empty seat at the counter, near the pie case. While he waited patiently, he listened to WCCO evening news blaring from a radio in the kitchen and glanced with disinterest at a Life Magazine that someone had discarded near the ketchup and mustard bottles.

A few minutes later, Dorothy returned with steamy take-out boxes packed inside a bag. As Cameron stood and reached into his front pocket for his money clip, he nodded towards the pie case with a smile. Surely it was a sin to visit Dot's Diner and leave without a piece of pie, wasn't it?

"By the way, Dorothy, could you box up a piece of your cherry pie and add a piece of the blueberry pie too? You know my favorite's cherry, but I know Cassie enjoys your delicious blueberry pie."

"Sure thing, but maybe you should choose a different kind for her tonight. She already had some of the blueberry pie earlier at lunch." Dorothy laughed, her silvery blue eyes twinkling at the compliment.

"Oh?" Confused, Cameron looked up from the green ticket on the counter and stopped unfolding bills from his money clip. "Cassie was here for lunch?"

"Yes," Dorothy nodded affirmatively as she expertly placed a piece of cherry pie in a take-out box, leaving a space open for another piece. She put one hand on her ample hip and squinted her eyes slightly, as she attempted to recall, "I think she had a turkey sandwich, but I can't remember for sure though, it was quite busy. But I think you're okay to go with the chicken pot pies because I would remember if she had one of those." She bent her head and added a piece of cherry pie to his ticket before she looked up and continued, "But, I distinctly remember her having the blueberry pie because she said they were going to share it and asked that I bring two forks."

"Was she here with some work colleagues then?" Cameron regarded the pie case trying to decide which flavor she would like. He knew she'd ordered lemon meringue pie before, that would likely be a safe bet. He glanced up towards Dorothy and pointed out his choice.

"Well, yes," Dorothy continued as she walked towards the case with the pie spatula in hand, "I would think that's who he was, all dressed up like that with a suit and tie. I've seen him before, but he doesn't ever come in with the whole group of law office ladies. Just with Cassie sometimes. He must be Cassie's boss?"

Cameron found his mind was muddled, and he heard a faint buzzing in his ears, as he considered the fact that his wife was having lunch - and sharing dessert - with another man. Certainly, the man "dressed up like that in a suit and tie" was none other than Devon Hearst.

Working or not, knowing the man as he did, Cameron didn't like the prospect at all. The buzzing became a pounding that emanated from somewhere behind his eyes as he wondered with a deep sense of betrayal, how often did they eat lunch alone together? How many other stolen moments were there between the two of them? Did everyone know this was going on? And, why was the husband always the last to know?

As if in a trance, he watched as Dorothy slid the lemon pie next to the cherry pie in the dessert container and carefully set it on the top of the bag of take out trays. When he reached for the bag, he noticed the tips of his fingers were numb and eerily white from his iron grip on the forgotten money clip he still held in his hand.

The little bell on top of the restaurant door cheerfully chimed his departure as he stepped outside into the smoldering summer evening. Once outside, as he reached for the door handle on his car, he realized that he didn't even remember giving Dorothy the money to pay for the dinner and he had completely lost his appetite.

In fact, he felt decidedly nauseous.

CHAPTER 20

1968, July

As your word says in Romans 12:12, Be joyful in hope, patient in affliction, faithful in prayer.

But, Lord, how can I be joyful when my hopes and my dreams now seem like the distant dreams of a stranger, how can I be patient when my ability and my desire to fight is so close to gone, how can I pray when, honestly, I don't know if you're listening?

Still, each day the sun comes up and I rise to live this life the same as I lived it yesterday. And I realize once again I will bring these tortures to you, Lord, because where else will I go with them?

"You've been awfully quiet tonight, Cam, and you barely ate anything for dinner. Is something going on at church that you want to discuss?"

Later that evening, after they put the kids to bed, Cassie turned her head to address him from across their bedroom while she sat on the upholstered bench in front of her dresser mirror. Cameron, his back propped with some pillows on their bed, and dressed in his boxers and a t-shirt, looked up from the Bible in his lap to watch her pull a hairbrush through her shiny dark locks.

In the ten years he'd known her, how many times had he run his fingers through her hair, he wondered. It was silky, and the color of rich, dark chocolate. In the sunlight, it's shimmering bronze highlights glittered like flames in a fire. Sometimes he found himself transfixed by her hair as it moved in the sun, the blinking of those burnished autumnal colors fascinated him so.

Tonight, he felt like she was a stranger. Someone he didn't even know.

He dragged his eyes from her hair, reluctant to look at her. He had been consciously avoiding her eyes all evening, avoiding the confrontation, avoiding the reality. The kids had provided a safe cover during dinner and bath time. Now that they were all asleep, the cover was gone.

"No, things are good at church." He finally answered her and glanced down again at his Bible. Romans 12:12, *be faithful in prayer.* He repeated the words again in his mind ... *patient in affliction and faithful in prayer ...*

"Oh, okay. Well, that's good. Have you finally convinced Reginald and the others about formalizing a ministry for returning soldiers? I know it's been on your heart for so long to get that going." When she sat forward like that, her eyes shining in the dim lamplight, she looked like she meant it, she looked like she cared about him and the things he cared about. But, looks could be deceiving.

"Well, no, not yet. They are still praying about it." He looked down again at his Bible, but as he read, the words started to swim in front of his eyes in a blurry mess of black and white.

"Cam. Look at me. What's going on with you?"

The burning in his eyes made it difficult to see her and the fullness in his throat made it impossible to talk to her. All he could do was shake his head in a slow motion and even that hurt.

She stood and walked towards him but stopped short of the bed when he looked up and she saw the tears in his eyes. Frozen in place, in the middle of the bedroom, her sleeveless nightgown glowing a filmy, iridescent pink around her silhouette, she swallowed nervously.

"What's going on, Cam?" Her voice was shaky and uncertain. He could hear the tremor.

"You tell me, Cassie. You tell me what's going on." He wiped at the burning tears in his eyes as he uttered the words, but as he spoke, it was as if he wanted to pull the words back in somehow. He felt emasculated, insignificant, ashamed ... truth was, he didn't really want to know what was going on. The implications were too great.

"Wh- what do you mean?" Her eyes widened in shock and Cameron searched them for a glimmer of truth about Devon Hearst. Could she possibly be- ? He couldn't even complete the sentence in his mind.

"Are you going to *make* me ask it, Cassie?" His voice croaked out from somewhere deep inside the hurt, "Are you going to make me say his name?"

"Wh-I don't understand-" Her words stammered from inside her throat. He wondered feverishly, had he gotten it wrong somehow? Or, was she just unable to admit it?

"Okay, I will say it." He continued against his better judgement, "Devon Hearst. Tell me what's going on with Devon Hearst." There, someone had to say it, he thought, as anger seared his heart and his throat as he spoke the man's name.

"I don't-" She stammered again, and her eyes glistened suddenly with tears.

"I know about your lunches. Just the two of you. *Sharing desserts.* And always alone with him. That doesn't sound like work to me. So, you tell *me* what's going on."

"N-nothing, Cam. Nothing is going on. How could you ask me that? How could you even think that?"

"Because I'm not blind and I'm not stupid, Cass. I see how he acts around you and it hasn't gotten any better over the past year, it's gotten even worse. When I'm around him, I have to work hard at not wiping that sickening look clean off his pompous face." Cameron was losing it now and part of him felt good saying it out loud, "I see how you act at home and- with me. You're different, something has radically changed with you. I think it's because of him."

"Well, you can think that, but it doesn't make it true, Cameron." Had he gotten it wrong about Devon, he wondered again, debating his intuition. But still, as she stood in front of him, Cassie's lips tightened in defense of all things related to her *precious job*. Well, he wasn't imagining everything. *Something* was not right about all of this.

"What other explanation do you have then? How else do you explain what's going on with you, Cass? I'm not sure if you've noticed, but I certainly have and it's not PMS and it's not pregnancy hormones. It's like I don't even know you anymore. I don't even know my own wife."

"Stop, Cameron. Just stop. Please." She had tears on her lashes, tears so large he could see them from where he sat on the bed. But, unlike most times when he saw her cry, this time he had no sympathy. None at all. Because having sympathy with her - that would sidetrack them. Right now, the only thing he felt was a burning desire to figure this thing out.

"Please, what? How long are we going to pretend like this isn't happening? How can we fix it if we keep pretending it's not happening?" Cameron raised his voice, as if by doing so, he could force her to see things his way and revert to the way she used to be.

"I don't know, I just don't know-" She put her hands over her eyes and shook her head as if to clear her mind of him altogether.

"That is not an answer. I don't know, I don't know," Cameron repeated her words angrily, unable to stop himself from verbally pushing her relentlessly, "*What* don't you know?"

"Okay, okay then! Fine! *I don't know if I love you.*" Her shrill voice was edged in a panic that he'd never heard before and as her words rushed out, they hit him with a force that left him breathless and dazed.

"Wh- what did you just say?" Even though he asked, he didn't want her to repeat it, God knows he didn't.

His mind retraced the past couple of years within the span of seconds, resting painfully on the fight they had just before Gemma's birth when Cassie said that maybe they should consider some "time away" from each other to get perspective. *This* is what she meant then and what she was finally verbalizing now. She didn't want time to sort out their differences to make their marriage stronger. She wanted to be free from him altogether.

"I don't know! I told you I just don't know and I'm trying to figure things out. I'm really trying here." Her tearful eyes were haunted and bottomless, the darkness of them cloaked in a panic like that in her voice.

"Well, seems to me it's a fairly basic concept, Cass." He found his voice, but certainly wasn't thinking about what he'd say before he said it. He just wanted out of this room, away from all this pain, "Either you love your husband, or you don't. I guess it's pretty clear it's the latter."

He gathered his Bible and pillow and left her standing in the middle of their bedroom, her head in her hands. She didn't try to stop him.

CHAPTER 21

2017, September

The tissue she'd been using to dab under her eyes was trashed, it had become a warm, twisted mess, wet with the tears that she couldn't stop.

A few minutes ago, as she was reading the passages in Cameron Berndt's journal, she laughed sheepishly at herself for the stray tears, blaming them on pregnancy hormones and glad that Elliott was out fishing with his grandpa so he wouldn't happen to witness her as she sat crying to herself, legs propped up on the arm of the oversized chair, in the sun porch of the rental house.

As she kept reading, however, she gave up the pretense of hiding, or stopping, the tears and allowed them to flow with abandon as the words of his journal leaped off the page and permeated straight into her, finding a soft place hidden deep inside.

Whew. So much pain. Lauryn pulled a new tissue from the box that sat on the table next to her chair and dabbed her eyes again, glancing outside the window while she fanned her face with her hands in an attempt to dry her face, but more just to collect her emotions.

It was a warm Sunday in late September, and she was enjoying a quiet afternoon relaxing after a busy week of cleaning the house on

Promise Place and preparing to list it while writing house history segments and editing things together for her YouTube channel. She had tried to contact Bridgette again to see if she had watched any of the videos they had uploaded or if she had any input on the few story segments they had shown so far, but no response.

In the meantime, Lauryn and Elliott had begun talking in earnest about what was coming next for them with their careers, especially given the fact that they had a baby due in a few months.

After spending the entire day yesterday clicking through pictures of various homes in the area as candidates for the next renovation, she felt completely uninspired. Of course, her enthusiasm to dive into a new project was tempered by the prospect of this pregnancy, as was obvious when she frequently diverted from her house search and found herself deep in the rabbit hole of nursery decorating ideas on Pinterest.

Figuring out what to do next was a dilemma. The renovation work she did was arduous, even if she hired crews to do the physical labor side, there were still many demands on her time at the site and on-line and it all required a level of mental energy that often left her completely spent. And that was without a tiny human requiring constant attention. One thing she was certain about was that she wanted to spend as much time as possible with their little human, once he or she was born.

Another part of her angst, was her mother's job offer at Belle Homes, working with her in real estate again. Lauryn confessed to Elliott that she really missed selling real estate and that the ideal situation would be combining home renovation and real estate sales into one career. She just couldn't quite see how that kind of career could tie into the on-line presence she had built thus far with My House.

And, of course, there was Elliott's career plan to consider too. There were some things he had quietly been pursuing for months now, one a new start-up opportunity and the other, joining into an on-going partnership. He was excited about both, but their current location, living outside the Twin Cities metro, wasn't ideal for either.

Her brow knit in concentration as she mulled over these major life decisions, Lauryn took a long drink from the water bottle she had tucked next to her in the chair and then laid her head back into the chair cushion. Closing her eyes briefly, she listened to the fluttering of oak tree leaves and the concert of insect sounds outside as the noisy cicada bugs and the chorus of crickets all chirped raucously, as if trying to drown each other out.

A flicker and an almost indistinct whoosh of wings next to her ear startled her and she turned to see a large monarch butterfly had landed on the window screen just inches from her face. He sat there silently, watching her through the fine mesh from outside the window, daring her to reach over to touch where his legs gripped through the screen. She stared at him, fascinated by his courage to come so close to a human being, someone so much larger than him. He had to be frightened, but still, he stayed there perched precariously on the window screen.

Maybe he sensed the mesh provided protection from her and he was interested in watching her. Or maybe he stayed because the window screen was something steady, a solid perch in the face of the breeze outside that threatened to pull him away and toss him around as it wanted.

Pensively, Lauryn turned her thoughts back to the journal and the man who wrote it. Cameron Berndt was a man searching for a steady perch. He was a man of faith. From what he wrote, he was a man with a strong faith in God. He was a good man. Still, his life was pretty messed up.

Often in her life, Lauryn had asked the age-old question, why do bad things happen to good people? For a Christian, it was a dangerous tunnel to walk down, that question.

Her conclusion? There was no light at the end of the tunnel. No answer that explained away all the pain people suffered through. No answer for Cameron Berndt and his struggles in his marriage. No answer for Rebecca and her struggle with addiction. No answer for her and Elliott and why they had to lose the babies they lost.

God was silent on these matters.

Belief in God was something she always took for granted. She'd never known a life without belief. Of course, she believed in God.

But, did she trust him? Did she trust him to give generously, love deeply and never leave her side?

Lauryn touched her stomach gently, cupping her hand around where she imagined their baby lay and with a laugh, she remembered a video call earlier this week from Madison and Daniel. The four of them were just catching up on life when suddenly Daniel turned his cell phone camera towards Madison's swollen belly as the baby shifted and the whole thing wobbled, causing

Elliott to stare at Lauryn with an incredulous, dazed look on his face.

She could tell what he was thinking, this would be happening to them in a few short months. Elliott had been stunned and Lauryn had been amazed too and a little envious.

Although she was rounding out, she wasn't really showing yet, even though she wanted to. At her last visit, her doctor said that it often took longer for young mothers to "show" since her stomach muscles were still taut, and this was her first pregnancy.

Fourth, she corrected him in her mind, frustrated and hurt by his tactless remark, as she stared at the ceiling tiles above her while he listened to the baby with his stethoscope. It was her *fourth* pregnancy.

Lauryn knew she was testing God, in a weird way, with this pregnancy. Just like Cameron Berndt was testing his faith in God through the struggles in his life. For her, it was like she was holding back from God, waiting him out - watching and waiting to see what He would do in her life. It was her way of testing his love for her.

But as suddenly as she admitted that to herself, another thought fluttered through her mind, just as the butterfly gave up his safe perch and flitted away on the breeze in search of another perch on which to rest.

Maybe God was testing her.

Maybe instead of wondering if God's love towards her was deep enough to reward her heart's desire, maybe the question was, would her faith be strong enough, no matter what happened?

CHAPTER 22

2017, September

Rebecca looked up from her open Bible and glanced out the kitchen window at the sound of his vehicle pulling into her driveway. He had removed the top of the Jeep, obviously enjoying the gorgeous fall afternoon, and as she watched her handsome son step out of his vehicle, he pulled his wind-blown hair back between his fingers and put his cap back on, backwards, like he frequently wore it. If you didn't know any better, you'd think he was still a college student, without a plan, without responsibilities.

Rebecca was proud of Elliott and what he'd become. A man who loved Christ, a husband and a father. He was a rock, despite his mother—

Stop.

She glanced down at the verse she'd highlighted in her Bible in 2 Corinthians, the weight of shame receding as she repeated in her mind, I am a new creature, I am a new creature, I am a new creature.

> Therefore, if anyone is in Christ, the new creation has come: The old has gone, the new is here!

How many times did she need to be reminded that she was forgiven? How many times did she need to repent of the same sins, again and again? Christ died on the cross one time. He said the battle was won. Did she believe him?

"Hey, Mom. How's it goin'?" Elliott said with a smile in his deep voice as he walked up behind her counter stool and gathered her into a loose hug. She felt the heat of the afternoon on him and breathed in the familiar lake smell he carried, a mix of suntan lotion and lake water.

"Good. It's going good. Did you catch anything?" She turned to face him, loving the way his deeply tanned face set off his bright smile and hazel eyes.

"Oh, boy," He laughed sheepishly. "Do I smell like fish? I promise, I cleaned up at Grandpa's, even changed clothes, before I came over!" He laughed again, looking over his cargo shorts and t-shirt. "Yeah, we caught a few perch." He continued as he casually reached into her cupboard for a glass and filled it with ice, "Grandpa's cleaning them and said we need to figure out a date for a fish fry before you leave."

As she watched him fill the glass with water at the sink, she felt a squeamishness in her gut and she thought again, Well, this is it. Are you going to be able to do it? Are you going to be able to say what you need to say?

"Yeah, I want to talk to you about that."

"Okay–" Elliott held onto the word and raised his eyebrows in a question as he sat down near the kitchen counter.

"I know you – and mom and dad – think this decision to move is a mistake." She knew that was true, even though no one had said it directly to her face.

"Well, I–" Elliott started to explain himself, but she interrupted him.

"No, that's okay. I understand. I see how this looks to you. Here I am, I have a good job, a good guy, a good life and I'm *clean*. And, believe me, no one is more amazed than *me* that I am here, and this is happening to me. And, what do I do with all that?"

It wasn't a question, so Elliott didn't even answer. She continued.

"I toss it away. Like it's worthless. Like I'm not worth *it*."

Rebecca sat still and forced herself to keep talking while her son sat still and listened.

"In treatment, they talk about triggers. People and situations that can threaten your sobriety. You spend a lot of time identifying your triggers, because they're different for each person. They give you coping mechanisms to deal with them."

"I thought I knew mine – certain people, some of the old neighborhoods, even certain music, if you can believe it. It's scary to realize how tenuous it all is, just one bad decision, and it's like this new life of mine never even happened."

"I know I'll always balance on that thin line. But now when I'm wobbling – now I think of Christ. I'm not left to wonder if I am strong enough to walk away from trouble on my own. I know through Christ I've been made whole again."

"But it's ironic, that even knowing Him like that, the enemy moved in. I got over-confident, I thought I had it figured out and I just moved ahead with this new life without thinking about what was happening."

Rebecca felt like she was rambling, and she wanted to make sure he got the bottom line before she ran out of courage, so she hurried on as she tried to summarize all this soul-searching into one simple thought.

"Oh, Elliott-" She breathed out nervously and reached across to grip his arm to anchor herself as she searched his eyes for inspiration, "Okay, here's what I want to say and I hope you don't take it the wrong way. I've realized that relationships are like a trigger for me. When I'm in one, I want to run. I want to use again. I want out. I don't trust myself because I think that I'll be hurt, and I know that I'll hurt the other person. It's true with Kyle and your grandparents and Lauryn and with- You."

He just sat there, not moving, he just sat there as she delivered that tough blow. In her mind Rebecca scorched herself, what mother has to tell her son that she can't trust herself not to hurt him?

"Well," Elliott finally spoke quietly as he covered her hand with his, "I guess it is what it is. We're your family. We aren't going anywhere." He paused and then smiled at her, "Mom, I'm not going anywhere."

"I know you aren't, baby." Rebecca felt the burn of the tears in her eyes and she wiped them away nervously, "I know you aren't going anywhere. I think I just need time–"

"Time to do what, Mom?" Elliot spoke up firmly, "Start to love yourself? Time to believe that you deserve to be a mom again?" He paused as she wiped at her eyes, unable to answer him, "Because the way I see it, you *do deserve* to be a mom again. I *need* you to be my mom again. That's not something that should scare you. Being a mom and now a grandma, it's a gift you've been given."

The silence that fell between them was heavy and tender. Finally, with a small smile on his face, Elliott leaned towards her and hugged her, releasing the tension of the moment.

"I understand though, Mom, if you need to figure this out in Wisconsin." He said, "We want you here, but we can let you go, too. I remember how it felt when I had to go to California. I get it."

At the love and acceptance that he so willingly gave, her mind halted its rambling, anxious deliberations and she smiled weakly at him while she wiped away the stray tears.

"Oh, my gosh–" She laughed, "Who *are* you? And how did you turn out so great?"

"Ha, well you're required to think that, you're my mom." He rolled his eyes and laughed along with her.

"That, I am. And you're right. Being a parent is a gift."

"Yeah, I'm starting to see that myself," Elliott agreed and then looked up from under his brows, "Is it a tough gig, being a parent?"

"Ha –Don't ask me," Rebecca said as she patted his arm and stood from where she sat and reached into the refrigerator for a can of soda, "I've had enough trouble being a functioning adult. But you will do great! Plus, Lauryn will be a great mom. You two have so much to look forward to."

"We want you involved, Mom. I hope you're excited too." He said.

"I am. I really am." Rebecca paused as the feeling washed through her and she enjoyed the sensation. It was a kind of peace, a settled feeling of peace.

"Mom," He spoke hesitantly, like he was sorry to bring it up, "I'd like to hang out longer with you tonight, but Lauryn and I were planning on going to a movie, so I'd better get going. It's something she wants to see, some chick flick, I guess. Hey– do you want to come with us?"

"No, you go ahead, thanks though. I need to call someone."

Roots weren't so bad, she mused, the thought playing in her mind. They were necessary for plants to grow, and as some plants' lives ended and new ones began, the roots contributed to even healthier soil. They made the soil good and rich.

"Oh, you need to call someone, huh? You say that like I should ask who it is you need to call," Elliott teased her.

"Well, I think you know who. It's someone who needs to know that I'll be staying here in Minnesota after all."

"What? I'm confused. I thought you asked me over to discuss your reasons for moving. Now you tell me you've decided not to move?"

"Yes, I guess I am. I suppose I will need to look for a new job, but yes, I guess I am telling you I've decided not to move." She laughed as she hugged him and bent his head down to kiss him on his forehead, "You have no idea your gift of persuasion, young man."

"Wow, really? Good to know," Elliott said, but was obviously still stumped by her reversal, "Seriously now, what made you change your mind? Did you talk to Kyle?"

"No, not directly. Yet."

"He's a nice guy, Mom. I think he really wants it to work out with you."

"Yes, he is and yes, I think he does." Nodding in agreement to both of his points, Rebecca paused before continuing, "Plus, there's you and Lauryn, and this new baby and your grandparents. It's just everything, I guess. And, honestly, Elliott, I hadn't fully committed to staying until today. I think just talking to you, it's finally sinking in that I don't want to miss out on all this life happening here. All of this is *my* life, too."

"Of course, it is. We don't want you to miss out on it either." Elliott moved towards the door, and turned with his hand on the handle, "Love you, Mom. I love you so much."

Rebecca nodded, kissed her fingers and waved to him as she watched him leave.

CHAPTER 23

1968, September

As your word says, Trust in the Lord with your whole heart and lean not on your own understanding …

" – we'll conclude our prayer, Lord, with the words we've studied tonight that Paul shared in Philippians, *I can do all this through Him who gives me strength.* Let that be the song of our heart, Heavenly Father, today and tomorrow; each hour of every day. Let us never forget that we are sinners, in need of your Son's sacrifice and your eternal grace. In Jesus's name we pray, Amen."

Cameron breathed in deeply while he sat back on the metal, folding chair in the Bible Study room, knowing full well he was praying the prayer as much for himself as he was for any of the others in the room with him.

The past few weeks he'd felt numb. His body went through the motions of living, but his mind and heart were disconnected somehow. In his mind, he was drowning in an ocean of doubt and anxiety, replaying her words like the needle was stuck at the end of a record. And, the pain in his heart was a constant, physical pressure interrupted at random moments during the day with a sharp twist that would make him want to cry out in pain.

Cameron forced his attention back to the small group of men who sat in a circle with him. He had been doing his best to hide his internal struggle. He had a job to do and people to serve and there were many times when he thanked God for the privilege of serving others because it lightened the load of his own struggles.

This Bible Study varied in number from week to week, and was a mix of returned soldiers, concerned family members and a couple of the church board members. The young soldiers, all with one injury or another, included a few men who were shortlisted to go back to Vietnam over the coming months and many with injuries significant enough that they were released from active duty. All were experiencing traumas of various sorts and many times Cameron felt the urge to stop the Bible study mid-stream and just pray for the specific needs of a particular man or circumstance mentioned.

He had started this Bible Study group over a year ago. The original intention was to provide encouragement to departing soldiers and their families through studying scripture. But as the war raged on, the group had also become a source of strength and encouragement for returning soldiers; those wounded physically, mentally and spiritually.

As he prayed about this group and reflected that they were already starting into a second year, Cameron thanked God for continuing to open doors. As long as the doors opened, he was determined to keep going through them. He found comfort in knowing that he was doing something, however limited, to help these people find Jesus in all the hell that was war.

The vision of the letter he'd received last week flashed in his mind and the invitation outlined in it worked on his spirit. Now, *those* people – the missionaries mentioned in the letter who were in Southeast Asia aiding the wounded– they were really helping, he thought. Those people denied themselves the comfort of home to bring the name of Jesus to the battlefield. Talk about following Jesus through opened doors. Those people were committed.

Cameron brought his wandering mind back to the room as he smiled and shook the hands of the last of the young men as they left the room. It was obvious by the way his board chair Reginald and his friend Ken, who also served on the church board, hung back in the room that they wanted to discuss the observations they had after attending the group for the first time. A few months ago, the board had been asked to pray about whether the church would support extending this type of group to a community-wide effort and judging by the fact that they were here tonight, it appeared at least a couple of the members were ready to give their opinion.

"Thanks for coming, guys," Cameron shook their hands cordially, "Do you see what I mean about the needs of this group? And, why I'd like to include other area churches in an effort like this? Some of these guys are literally on the edge, they need our support, they need Jesus so much and this is one way we can help them find him."

"No doubt about that, Cam," Ken spoke first as he smoothed his trimmed reddish beard along his chin and contemplated what he'd heard, "It's hard to believe what some of them have had to deal with at such a young age. Are they always so willing to share?"

"Well, sometimes I think it has to do with who is in the room." Cameron left unsaid that the presence of two board members, both new to the group, might have kept some of the more heart-wrenching comments under wraps this evening, "But generally speaking, yes, they share willingly. As long as the topics are respectful, I don't have any rules about what's covered. I try to relate as much as possible to the scripture we're studying so they can take it home and pray about it."

Cameron glanced at Reginald who had moved quietly back to his chair, obviously deliberating about something but not readily communicating what he was thinking. He wanted to hear what Reginald thought but his attention was diverted as Ken spoke again.

"Do you ever feel like they need more than you can offer?" Ken asked as he too sat down and Cameron, feeling obligated to join them, sat down alongside Ken.

"Well, I try to support them spiritually, try to give them direction that way, if that's what you mean." Cameron answered, his tone measured with caution.

"What about those that need help psychologically? I can't imagine what being over there has done to them psychologically. Do you think they come here for that kind of help?"

"Maybe they think this will help that way. But you can see by tonight that I don't set it up to be for that purpose. This is about seeking Jesus and applying his example to their lives," Cameron sensed that there was something the men had discussed privately, something they agreed upon but weren't saying, "Are you concerned that I'm confusing spiritual guidance with psychological

255

guidance? If so, I can make a point to clarify our mission each week. I can tell you though, when I counsel people individually, when I see psychological issues, I always refer them to a doctor. I'm aware of the signals."

Reginald, his white, button-down shirt straining against his barrel chest, took a deep breath and stood up from his chair suddenly as if he'd listened long enough and had made his decision on the matter.

"Pastor Cam, it's obvious that you have built a rapport with these young people and their families. And, we appreciate that you have a desire to pray for them and with them. But, we just don't see how coddling these returning soldiers is doing them any good." Reginald swung his head side to side firmly, as if by doing so, Cameron would just agree without any push-back.

"Well, I don't think I'd call it coddling," Cameron spoke unflinching, "I'm just giving them a place where they can share their experiences and together we can try to make sense of it all, through the perspective of God's word."

"No doubt, what they've seen is pure evil, we get that," Reginald rebutted, "But, don't you think you're doing them a disservice by encouraging them to relive it when you meet in these groups? I just don't believe they should be pushed to show their emotions. Sometimes these things are better left alone, so they can deal with it privately, like their fathers dealt with it in past wars."

"So," Cameron was starting to understand that Reginald didn't support the idea of the group at all, not even in their own church. But if that was the case, Cameron wanted to hear him say it to his face, "If I'm hearing you correctly, Reginald, your concern isn't about the community-wide effort I've called for. You have questions about these small group sessions we've been having in our church?"

"Well, honestly, yes," Reginald sputtered, finding no way to deny it, "One on one visits with you might be different, though. We understand that they need prayer and they may need someone to pray with occasionally."

"But, Reginald," Cameron countered, "You saw the way the group responded to each other, they realize they aren't alone in their experiences. They see others who've gone through similar things. That's worthwhile."

"Yes, I know. I just think they can share these experiences with their American Legion club and the like. I'm concerned that it's not the church's place to take a stand on this war. There are too many opinions on it - should we be in it or should we not - I see a recipe for division if we give a public forum for these soldiers to display their grievances and their stories."

"I agree," Cameron replied, unable to let the opportunity to serve Jesus be wasted, "There is the potential for division because there are high emotions on both sides of the debate, and we may sacrifice peace and tranquility in our church during some of these conversations. But I think that sacrifice pales in comparison to the sacrifice of these soldiers. They are the most damaged, the most in need. And there's more of them every day. That's why I'd like to expand it beyond our church members, make it more of a community-wide effort, housed in our church where the message of Jesus's sacrifice and his redemption can fill in the holes of hopelessness left in them by war."

While Ken nodded his head slowly in agreement with Cameron's argument, Reginald crossed his arms and shook his head again, side to side, in doubt.

"Well," Reginald said with a cautionary voice, clearly changing his tactic, "It just seems there is a lot on your plate already, Pastor. We don't want you to be stretched too thin. Leading a church comes with many responsibilities."

"That's true, of course," Cameron agreed, wondering what other thoughts Reginald had on his mind that he hadn't shared, "Is there anything specifically that you're concerned about? Somewhere I'm dropping the ball?"

"Well, I do have some things to discuss with you, yes. Considering the financial burden that building onto the Sunday school rooms has added, we are wondering if maybe you shouldn't put out some goals to encourage people to give more. And then there's the hospital and shut-ins visitation schedule, it seems like that gets rushed somewhat, according to some folks who have felt slighted. And, there have been several requests that you and your wife join the choir, so that people can get to know you on a more personal level -" Reginald paused on that one, but the air was filled with the expectation that he wasn't done with his recitation of pastoral responsibilities.

"Well, that's quite a list." Cameron spoke into the silence, a small smile on his mouth, but a tinge of resentment in his heart.

"Yes, and there are other items too, but like I said, the bottom line is we don't want you to spread too thin. Of course, some of these tasks could be covered by Cassie - if she was so inclined - but of course, we understand that she is busy elsewhere, with her job."

There it was. Another swipe at Cassie. Cameron wondered to himself, what had she ever done to this man that he resented her this way?

"Yes, she is busy with a job and small children, but Cassie has helped me with the hospital and shut-in visits, and she has contributed to various committees and study groups at church, so I think she is doing her part." Cameron tried to keep his voice controlled and cordial, even though the bitterness was eating away inside.

"Yes, I know she has in the past. I bring it up now because of her telling other ladies in church that she won't be managing the Ladies Aid Group for missionaries anymore."

That was something Cassie had neglected to tell him, Cameron thought, which truthfully wasn't surprising since they rarely spoke about anything unless it was related to the children. He struggled to appear as if this didn't come as a surprise and decided that getting back on topic was the best route because this discussion of Cassie's contributions was pointless and irrelevant.

"Nevertheless, I don't see how this relates to the soldier's Bible Study." Cameron entreated, hoping that the cause was not lost.

"I think what we're saying is that a community-wide ministry of this type will take a lot of time out of an already heavy schedule, Cam," Ken spoke up with a conciliatory tone in his voice, "We just want to make sure that you're certain that it's what God is directing you to do."

"Yes, exactly," Reginald agreed with a nod, "And I still want to say that I'm not one hundred percent sure this is the correct way to go about helping these young men. I have some major concerns. But, since it would be a community-wide program, let's bring it to the board and see what others say."

"Okay, thank you," Cameron nodded, glad and grateful to have gotten this much commitment from the men, "But, I can assure you that I have been praying about this for over a year now. And, yes, I am certain it's a door that God has opened for us and that he's waiting for us to walk through it."

"Well, if it's meant to be, then it will be." Ken agreed and stood up from his chair, motioning his desire to end the conversation.

A few minutes later, after Reginald left the church and Cameron was locking the back door of the church, Ken walked alongside him towards their cars.

They went way back, he and Ken, growing up on the same block, playing football together and graduating high school the same year. Even though they lost track of each other for a while during their college years, now that they were both back in their hometown working and raising families, they were close friends again.

But, even so, it had been many months since they'd spent an evening with Ken and Louise and their three kids, Cameron realized faintly. He'd like to invite them over for dinner sometime, but like many other aspects of married life, inviting friends over to visit had gone by the wayside in their marriage.

As he turned towards his car, Ken stopped, a concerned frown on his face as he regarded Cameron.

"Hey, Cam, I've been meaning to ask you something-" Ken left his statement hanging in the air as if he needed some additional prompting to ask it.

"Sure, what is it?"

"Well, it's not easy for me to ask and I only bring it up because Louise and I love you and Cassie," He hesitated, looked down at the gravel under his feet before he looked up again, "We've heard some things - and, please know that we've squelched the talk when it's been brought up - but ... well, is there anything you want to talk about? Anything about you and Cassie? Because I want you to know I'm here if you want to talk about any - problems."

Cameron's mouth went dry and he held his breath as he asked, "Well- what have you heard?"

"It's idle gossip, Cam, I know," Ken's expression was earnest and uncomfortable, as if he really didn't want to continue, "But, according to our neighbor who works at the law office, Cassie has shared some things with a friend at work."

"About what?" At this point, with so many things wrong in their marriage, he couldn't begin to guess which ones she was sharing with her co-workers.

"Well, about troubles in your marriage and some things about you- maybe falling back into old habits," Ken hurried on, "But, like I said, we know it's nothing more than gossip."

Cameron was silent as he stared at Ken, unable to form words because of his deep shame.

There it was - he was finally called out into the open for his sin, and he was called out by his own wife. But, what did he expect would happen? Did he think he would live the way he'd been living, and no one would ever know? Would that somehow have made it okay? Cameron dropped his gaze, unable to look into his friend's concerned eyes any longer.

"How bad is it, Cam?" Ken asked quietly.

"It's not good," Cameron replied, his voice flat and emotionless as the guilt for all his failings replaced any false sense of security, "It hasn't been good for a long time, but I keep praying for our marriage to be repaired and it just seems to get worse, Ken. Cassie isn't happy and it seems that she's lost all desire for me and for our marriage."

"Oh, man-" Ken stopped speaking, as if he didn't know what the proper response should be.

"And, the other - the drinking - well, I'm battling that too," Cameron continued, pushing through his shame, unrelenting in his confession, "I know it's a crutch, and I hate myself for it when I allow myself to slide."

Cameron thought desperately over the situation and where they stood right now. It was time - this was the moment to make it right. He knew it, but the challenge of doing so was so daunting. He looked at his friend in defeat, "Have you mentioned this to anyone in church?"

"No." Ken shook his head adamantly, but with a question in his eyes.

"Because I know that's only right," Cameron answered the question without him asking, "The board should know. I have been praying for so long and I was just trusting that things would work out."

"Cam, the way people talk, this probably won't stay private for very long and you should have people praying for you and Cassie. Maybe that will help Cassie see. We love you and want to support you."

"It's just not that simple, Ken," Cameron replied, "I know we go back a long way, and it's hard sometimes to separate our history as friends from me as your pastor, but this is one of those examples where it's not the same for you and me."

"I don't understand what you mean-"

"Ken," Cameron urged, his voice rising with frustration, "I'm the *pastor* of this church. *I'm* the one that's supposed to be praying for and counseling others with marital problems, not the other way around."

Ken blinked at the hard truth of the statement and a crestfallen look passed over his face as the full impact of what Cameron was facing seemed to hit him.

"I guess I can't know how you're feeling right now, the burden of it all," Ken set his hands upon Cameron's stooped shoulders and gripped them tighter for added emphasis, "I don't know what to say except that I'm here for you, man."

"Thanks for letting me know and I appreciate your friendship, I really do," For some reason, caught in the never-ending roller coaster of emotions, now Cameron felt oddly numb and his words came out stilted, as if he was drained of everything, "I guess in the end, I've known since this all started falling apart that God is the only one who can help. What I really need is someone to pray with me."

So, the two of them stood by their cars in the parking lot of Freedom Church and prayed for both the healing of Cameron Berndt's marriage and the healing of Cameron Berndt's spirit.

Where will this end, Cameron wondered later that night as he watched Cassie close their bedroom door behind her, leaving him alone in the hallway. Thinking back over their argument tonight, he wondered if they would ever be able to heal this.

By the time Cameron arrived home, after his conversation with Ken in the parking lot, the kids were already in bed sleeping.

Her response to his confrontation when he told her about the conversation he had with Ken? A nod of the head, acknowledging that she had confessed to a coworker about their marriage issues and how she felt *trapped in a marriage* to a man who had expected perfection from her but was far from perfect himself, especially ironic because he was a pastor.

When he tried to apologize for his part in that and talk it out with her, she said it was too late. She said she felt peace in her spirit about saying these things now because she had finally admitted that "they just weren't going to make it."

For the past two years, every time they fought and even when they hadn't, Cameron would pray about their marriage, he'd be on his knees, often Cassie would join him. He'd beg God to intervene, he'd plead with God to deliver on the promises he'd made in multiple passages in the Bible including Jeremiah 29 and Matthew 11, about resting in his peace and finding hope in his grace.

Never once over the past two years had the word *divorce* been uttered. Until now. Now, she said it was the only solution. It was best for them both, and for the children, she said.

But that was her perspective, not his. Divorce went against everything he ever believed, everything he stood for. Marriage was something God designed, it was meant to be cherished and nurtured. In their case, something to be salvaged.

"I can't, Cassie. I *won't accept* that as the solution." He'd croaked the words out, his mind racing that she'd gone this far in her mind.

"But, can't you see? We've tried, Cam. This is killing us. I want to be happy. I want you to be happy. We're not happy together."

"But we can't give up. You can't give up on me. I won't give up on you and our family. It's too important; it's not God's will for us to divorce."

"Cam, I know this is hard for you as my husband. I know this will be hard for you as a pastor to accept, but it's what I've decided. I have a say in this too."

Cameron didn't remember the details of the rest of the conversation. His memory was a blurry mess of words as he quoted scripture to try to convince her otherwise, he tried the standard arguments including the impact on their three young children, their history together, the prospect of her being on her own after spending her entire adult life with him, the fact that he loved her and always would. Any number of arguments. All he could remember afterwards was the image of her walking away and closing their bedroom door behind her.

Cameron turned, defeated, and walked towards the spare bedroom, where he had been sleeping for the past few months, the one next to Aaron's bedroom.

Sitting on the edge of the thin, unyielding mattress, as the white wrought-iron bed frame creaked under his weight, Cameron put his elbows on his knees and his head in hands while the sobs racked his entire body.

Broken hearted. That's how he felt. He knew medically what was happening. Right now, inside him an overabundance of stress hormones was raging, and it was causing his heart to contract wildly, making it incredibly difficult to breathe. He knew it wasn't a life-altering medical condition. He knew it would improve with time. But, all of that being true, he also knew his heart was broken and he wondered if it would ever feel the same again.

The light above the bathroom sink blinded his bleary eyes as Cameron washed his hands. He had finally fallen asleep after hours of tossing, only to be awoken as a car roared past the house, its music blaring, at 3:30 in the morning. As he flipped off the light after using the bathroom, he stepped into the hallway of the silent house and wandered back towards the spare bedroom, dreading the next few hours where his mind would surely torture him before finding rest.

Just as he reached the door to the bedroom, out of the corner of his eye, he thought he saw a small figure hunched into a ball on the hallway floor next to the stairway. It took a moment, and a few more steps, before Cameron recognized the blue and white striped flannel pajamas and the little white feet that stuck out from them in the dim moonlight streaming through the window at the end of the hallway.

"Hey, bud, what's going on?" Cameron whispered to his son, as he knelt low towards him on the floor.

"I– I was looking for you, but you weren't there–" Aaron looked up, his face wet with tears as he pointed towards the still-open door of the master bedroom. Oh, that. Given their early bedtimes because the children were so young, Cameron realized that they had done a good job hiding the fact that he had been sleeping in the guest bedroom for months already.

"Oh. Sorry, I wasn't there." Cameron sat down at the edge of the stairway, his legs draping down a few steps, and gently pulled his son towards him, settling him on his lap. Soon, he realized sadly, the boy would be too big to sit on his lap.

"Why aren't you in bed? Bad dream?"

"Yes," Aaron's head bobbed against his chest and his shoulders shook as he sucked in a deep breath, "It was that bully again. From school."

"Oh, he showed up again in your dreams, huh?"

"Mhmm, he was chasing me on my bike, we were going faster and faster down a big hill and he was catching me and laughing at me and I was going to crash and-"

"And, then you woke up, right?" Cameron interrupted him gently, hugged him a little more tightly and whispered quietly in his ear, "You woke up, Aaron. The bully is gone. And, I'm here. And, Jesus is here. You're safe."

"Yeah," He nodded again, a small, tentatively brave smile peeking out, "I'm not scared of him, right?"

"No, you're not scared of him. He's nothing to be scared of."

"Right. He's just gotta grow up, right?" Aaron repeated the phrase that Cameron had rehearsed with him the last time Aaron shared a story of the bully from school.

"Right you are, young man. He's just gotta grow up," Cameron agreed and hugged him closer, breathing in the fresh smell of bath soap and shampooed hair. Oh, how he loved his children. His resolve to fight for his family deepened instinctively. He *needed to do something* to protect his family.

"Come on, bud," Cameron ruffled his hair gently, "You want to camp out with me tonight in the guest room? It will be fun."

"Won't mom be lonely? She's not used to sleeping alone."

The innocent statement of their son knifed straight through Cameron's already-wounded heart.

"Oh, I think she will be okay tonight. She's sound asleep, I don't think she'll notice I'm not there."

"Okay, Dad, thanks," Aaron pushed away from him and stood up in the dark hallway. As they walked towards the spare bedroom at the end of the hallway, Aaron looked up at him and whispered, "Dad, do you think *I'm* grown up?"

"Yes, I do. You are as grown up as a seven-year-old can be, young man." Cameron reached for his small hand in the dark and gathered him into his arms before saying with a quiet laugh, "I love you, son."

"Me too. I love you, Dad." Aaron murmured against his neck, already sounding sleepy.

As they lay side by side under the weighty, calico-colored quilt in the guest room, Cameron's mind played through the many scary scenarios about his position as a pastor, about his marriage and his family. He reached out his hand and touched the soft curls of Aaron's hair and then softly rested his hand on his small shoulder, feeling his body move with each breath.

There was a solution out there somewhere, but it certainly couldn't be divorce.

Chapter 24

1968, October

Heavenly Father, I ask for your words to come forth out of my mouth, not mine-

A mid-month board meeting was an unusual occurrence and was considered an emergency. Given the haste with which Cameron called the meeting, he was mildly surprised the entire board was able to make it and were sitting around the table this rainy, autumn Monday evening.

The only people in the room who knew the topic of conversation were Ken, who had been faithfully praying with Cameron the past few weeks after their conversation in the parking lot and Glenda, who Cameron had confided in earlier that day. As he related the story to her this morning, even after rehearsing it aloud to himself in the car coming to work, he found himself choking up when he met her eyes at the end of telling it. By then, she was crying along with him.

But it was not going to be that way this evening, he vowed to himself. This time, he would maintain his composure as he read his prepared statement about the whole affair. This time, he would have the emotional cover of words on a sheet of paper, distilling the harsh truth to black and white. By reading it aloud, he wouldn't have to look into their eyes to see the reflection of his failure.

Cameron purposefully chose a seat in the middle of the table so he could be surrounded by their presence, somehow feeling that he deserved the painful pressure of their judgement. As they settled in with amicable smiles and greetings to one another, he cleared his throat, just wanting to get this over with as quickly as possible.

With shaking fingers, he pulled the written statement out from inside his Bible and noticed his throat was incredibly parched as he began to speak.

"Hello, everyone. Thank you for making time for this board meeting on such short notice. I'm going to read a statement tonight and I would ask that you prayerfully consider the next steps. I am trying to respect my role here as Pastor while also respecting the privacy of my family so I would prefer not to discuss details publicly. I hope you can respect those wishes."

Cameron intentionally avoided the eyes of the members but couldn't help but see Glenda's folded hands in her lap, the tears in her eyes and her encouraging smile. God is here, Cameron thought, even in the midst of it. He is here.

He smoothed the paper out in front of him and sat up straighter in his chair as he began to read.

"To start, I want to say there is nothing I desire more than to follow our Lord's son, Jesus Christ. I've known this now for many years and it has changed my life forever. The role as Pastor at this church is one that I take whole-heartedly; it is an expression of my passion to follow Jesus that I arrived here at Freedom Church. And, it is a deep honor and privilege that you have given me. It's a role that is precious and sacred in that it's meant to shine the light of truth in the darkness. I understand the gravity of that.

This is why what I'm going to tell you may shock you. Because, despite my passion to follow Christ, I am a fallen man. I am - and continue to be and will always be - a sinner. In my case, despite knowing Christ, I allowed alcohol into my life again, and that sin took root. I allowed alcohol to become my crutch during some struggles and because of my past battle with it, I knew the signs and I knew where it could take me.

Nevertheless, I allowed it to control me over the past year or so. I did not fully turn to God with my struggle; instead, in this particular battle, I turned away from him and allowed this sin to flourish. For this, I am sorry and have begged for His forgiveness. Once again, he has given me grace enough to sustain me and I have again put it out of my life completely. I know He has forgiven me. You, of course, deserve to know this about your Pastor, and I ask for your forgiveness as well.

Also, I want to confess that there is an additional source of conflict in my home. The truth is, Cassie and I have struggled in our marriage for the past few years. The reasons are many and I would prefer to keep those private. But you should know that she has asked me for a divorce. I have not conceded to one, however, and I continue to pray that our marriage will be healed. I ask that you pray not only for our marriage, but also for our children; that God will find it in His grace to heal the wounds, open the eyes and heal the covenant we took before Him.

Thank you for the honor of serving here at Freedom Church and I am deeply sorry for the burden this puts on you. I will continue with my daily work here as your pastor as long as you trust me to serve and I appreciate your prayers. Your servant, Pastor Cam"

The room was deathly quiet, and Cameron's memory leapt back to the meeting many months ago when the board wrestled with the dress code issue and his defense of his wife over the past few years.

When he cheerfully accepted the calling to this church all those years ago, would he have guessed that being a pastor of a small Minnesota congregation could be so fraught with unbearable conflict? But, then, we're all human beings, he reasoned, we're messy, uncomfortable, conflicted human beings and the thought gave him a measure of comfort. No one, not one, is perfect. That's why we so desperately need His son, our Savior.

Cameron folded the statement and slid it slowly across the table towards Glenda, who nodded at him as she added it to her board meeting notebook. Slowly, she wiped the tears from her eyes with a white handkerchief she had tucked into cuff of her pink cardigan's sleeve.

He glanced at the board members, one by one. Each was a precious child of God, given a responsibility to guide this church in their faith. If they decided it was best for him to serve somewhere else, it was beyond his control and he would be grateful for the time he had spent here.

In the end, did it really matter where he served? In what church? In what capacity? He had covered this all in his mind over the past few weeks. As long as he served Jesus, what did it matter?

Cameron's eyes rested on Reginald, the man on whom the rest of the board relied to speak first and speak the boldest. Without even realizing it, Cameron braced himself for the rebuke he was sure was coming and he buffered himself in his mind with the reminder that this wasn't the only place on earth to serve Jesus.

"Well, Pastor," Reginald's voice was solemn, "Speaking for myself, this comes as a surprise. I appreciate that you addressed these issues with such honesty, and I am sorry to hear that you and Mrs. Berndt have been struggling. I'm sure we all agree-" He glanced around at the fellow board members, assuming they would agree before he stated his premise, "I'm sure we all agree that your service here has been fruitful. But you are correct, that we should take this under consideration as a board. It is critical that our leader be of strong moral character. That is biblical and our responsibility. Are we all in agreement on that?"

The various members nodded in agreement, but no one else spoke. From two seats to his left, Ken smiled at Cameron, already having told him that he was fully behind him and having suggested that he would speak in his defense tonight. But Cameron had told him to please not do that publicly yet, let the others absorb the news and come to their own conclusions. Other board members looked confused and seemed to search Cameron for more information, while still others seemed to avoid his eyes altogether. It was unclear to him where the group consensus might lie.

"Okay, then," Reginald continued, "Let's plan to pray and we will discuss this amongst ourselves. Pastor, we will not let time waste on this. When we've reached a decision on the path forward, we will let you know."

"Thank you." Cameron said quietly and was about to stand up and leave the room, feeling like a chastised child, when Glenda spoke up, her voice sure and steady.

"Pastor? Before you leave, would you please close in prayer?"

Cameron hesitated and then eased back to his seat slowly as he contemplated his church secretary through the tears that were suddenly burning in his eyes. He marveled again at Glenda's strength, her sense of loyalty and her grace. With a renewed sense of nearness to his Savior, Cameron rested his folded hands on his Bible and prayed.

CHAPTER 25

2017, October

Elliott rolled over at the sound of his cell phone alarm and swiped off the annoying tone. Thoughts of his meeting scheduled for later this morning had been tumbling around in his head all night, waking him on the hour almost every hour and accosted him immediately now that he was awake. His list of questions was growing longer the closer they got to making the final decision and doubts nagged him incessantly.

For months now, the offer had been out there to join his friend Mark and his wife Lina in a new business venture. Now, they were ready to leave their current gigs where Mark was an IT Director and Lina was VP of Development at a software company. What they found in Elliott was someone who had first-hand experience developing and using ERP (enterprise resource planning) systems not only with his own company but also from his days when he worked for a mobile communications development company.

The three of them agreed on what made the best system – it would seamlessly connect a company's supply chain, financials, operations, reporting, sales and manufacturing. The best systems were also custom, able to adjust to the specific needs of the client. Not some cookie cutter solution offered by the big players.

Elliott had already met with the husband-wife duo on multiple occasions and after each sit-down, he left even more excited about the opportunity. It was an open horizon and they were free to make this consultancy company whatever they wanted.

Lauryn knew both Mark and Lina, of course, and was supportive of the direction the conversation was going. In the end, she'd told him, if he really believed it was right, she was with him all the way.

Later today, he planned to meet with Mark and Lina and tell them he was all-in on the plan because he knew his doubts were just that - doubts, not certitudes. He felt comfortable with the way they thought and worked. He would just remind himself that the day to day details would fall in line, just the way they had at EL Go.

But the office location was something that he wanted to work out with them. They wanted an office in a trendy, renovated old warehouse in downtown Minneapolis. However, he had his eye on a cool, high-tech space on the southern side of the Twin Cities that would be a much better location with easy access to the airport and less traffic. They didn't know his plan, but he'd invited them to meet him there this morning at the building, located within 30 minutes from his house, near River's Bend. It was perfect. Just perfect...

Realizing that he'd almost drifted back to sleep, Elliott roused himself again and glanced with foggy eyes towards Lauryn's spot in bed expecting to find her sound asleep next to him since she usually slept through his alarm.

Instead of finding her sleeping, however, he found her spot empty and when he ran his forearm over the sheet, he found it cool to the touch. She must have had another bad night of sleep, he thought, swinging his legs from under the blankets and set his feet on the floor.

Rubbing his tired eyes to clear his mind, Elliott wandered through the hallway and down the stairway towards the kitchen. Maybe she was up early making something for breakfast, he thought. After the first few months of terrible morning sickness where the smell of eggs made her sick, her appetite for spinach and cheese omelets had returned in recent weeks.

Once he reached the bottom of the stairway, instead of finding Lauryn in the kitchen cooking breakfast, he found her seated on the couch with her back to him, a table lamp shining over her shoulder in the hushed living room. He knew she was probably reading the journal and judging from the blanket she had pulled up around her, he guessed she had been reading for quite a while already.

"Hey, babe. You're up early, couldn't you sleep either?" Elliott spoke into the stillness and noticed then that it was raining, the drops spattering the living room windows in sporadic bursts. Although she turned her head slightly to acknowledge his presence, she didn't speak and as he walked closer, Elliott noticed her blinking away tears as she rubbed at her eyes lightly with the back of her finger.

"Lauryn, honey, what's wrong?" Elliott bent down slightly from behind the couch as he threaded his arms over her shoulders, breathing in the scent of her hair as he kissed the back of her head.

"Nothing, I'm fine." She said quietly as she turned her eyes up to glance at him and patted his arms where he held her, "I'm just reading."

"Yeah, so how's Cameron Berndt doing?" Elliott smiled to himself, thinking she's really into this guy's life, should he be concerned that his wife was so fascinated with a guy from the 1960s?

"Oh, my gosh, everything is piling on the guy, he's having trouble at home and in his church. His life is literally falling apart."

"Wow, that's not good." Elliott walked around the couch, lifted the blanket that rested on her lap and sat down next to his wife, spreading the soft, flannel blanket over the two of them.

"I suppose his faith helps him get through all these things?" He said, still somewhat distracted by thoughts of his upcoming meeting.

She stayed quiet for a long moment and frowned slightly as if considering the answer. Belatedly, Elliott realized Lauryn hadn't answered his innocuous question. The guy was a pastor after all, of course his faith would get him through tough times.

"Yes, but he has had some doubts too." Lauryn finally said slowly.

"What do you mean 'too'?" Elliott sat back slightly to look more closely at her expression, now fully engaged in the conversation, "Do you have doubts about something?"

Lauryn's eyes shaded at his question as if he'd put her on the spot and she looked down at the journal in her hands to avoid his gaze. Normally an open book with her feelings, now Elliott wondered what was going on inside her and he found himself replaying the past few months of the pregnancy and the business partnership he was considering. What doubts did she still have?

"What is it, Lauryn? Do you doubt that this baby will be okay?"

"Well, yeah sometimes, but that's nothing new, right?"

"Okay, 'cause it's going great. We should be happy about how this pregnancy is going." He reached out and patted her round stomach lovingly.

"I am happy about it, Elliott. It's not that-"

"Okay. Then is it about the business with Mark and Lina?"

"No, of course not. I'm excited about that too."

"Well, then what is it? You can tell me."

"It's almost like I don't want to say it out loud. I don't want you to think-"

"Hon, just tell me."

"Okay, so I'm just wondering about God lately. Like all this struggle that we go through to just live our lives here on earth, why does it have to be so hard? Have you ever asked yourself, why would he do that to people who love him?" Lauryn watched him carefully, her eyes wide and uncertain.

"Because he loves them," Elliott answered with a confidence that had been built not only through his life experience, but also through his study of the Bible, "Because he loves us. It's through the struggle that we lean on him, we're refined through adversity. It's hard, I know, but we have to stay strong and trust. It's his will, not ours."

"I know, I know. It's just sometimes so hard to trust him."

"Lauryn, I know how you feel. But we have to stay strong together. You need to talk to me about it and we need to pray about it. Together, ok?"

Quiet again, she nodded, and Elliott took the journal out of her hands. Then, he prayed with his wife about their baby, about their businesses, about their lives.

Lauryn reviewed the invoice once more, scanned the change orders carefully to make sure they were correct, and reached for her checkbook as Reese, the finish carpenter who did the indoor trim and hardwood floor repairs, completed a call on his cell phone and joined her at the kitchen counter.

"So, Lauryn, the place turned out great." Reese glanced around appreciatively, his brown eyes appraising the details in a way that only a finish carpenter can.

"Thanks in large part to you, Reese. You did such great work, sometimes I have to look really hard to find your repairs. It's a gift you have, sir." Smiling broadly, Lauryn ripped the check out of her checkbook and handed it to him with a flourish.

"Thanks, it's been a pleasure working with you," Reese folded the check and put it in his front shirt pocket as he walked towards the back door.

He glanced towards her rounded stomach with his eyebrows raised, "I suppose with the baby coming, you won't be looking for a finish carpenter again for quite a while."

"Oh, I don't know about that," Lauryn laughed at his obvious appeal for more work, "We'll see. But, if my next project is anywhere around here, you know who I will be calling. Just make sure you work me into your busy schedule again."

"You bet I will. And say hey to Elliott. Tell him he's an alright guy but I won't miss that camera of his."

"Ha, yeah, right. You know you loved it. He made you a YouTube sensation, but I'll tell him you said that, Reese. See ya." Lauryn waved as he stepped out the door and she closed and locked it behind him.

Well, that's the last of the workmen, she thought with satisfaction. All done and all paid. And, according to her mother, the publicity generated by her social media and YouTube following had been instrumental in sparking an offer on the house already, not even two weeks after it was listed. Everything was lining up to look like they would make a decent profit.

Lauryn scratched at her stomach where her black and white striped top pulled tight against the baby bump. It was the most unnerving feeling, this fluttering inside. Not movement actually, nothing like undulating movement of Madison's belly with their baby due in a few weeks, but still, fluttering. Just enough for her to know there was life inside her.

As she often did, and because she had some time to kill before her next appointment, Lauryn walked into the wide center hallway and glanced down it's imposing stretch of wood panels, appraising all the work they had done. It was quite an accomplishment, the renovation of this stunning home, and she was quite proud of the end result.

This week they would be uploading the last of the history segments with old photos showing the Berndt families, their medical staff and patients alongside photos of the newly renovated rooms. It would be presented as a complete picture showcasing the complex and interesting history housed within the walls of 316 Promise Place.

But even though she was proud of the story-telling work of the renovation, Lauryn knew that the world would be missing a significant piece of history that had also lived in this house.

Letting her mind wander over the story of Cameron Berndt, Lauryn walked through the main level and the second floor, ending her tour at the bottom of the stairs where she sat down on the third step and surveyed the wide living room.

She pictured Cameron's family, the children Aaron and Charlotte running through the wide hall as they played and them staring up at the Christmas tree in the living room with shimmering lights and gifts all around. She looked to her right and out the front door to the covered screen porch where Cassie had announced back in 1967 that she was pregnant with their daughter Gemma. So much life in these rooms. But where had all those people gone? Where were they now?

She hadn't finished the third journal this morning, although there were only a few pages left. It was as if she didn't want it to end, this journey into someone else's life. It was her connection to someone who struggled like she did. She found inspiration in his strength and like Elliott said this morning, we are refined through adversity. Cameron Berndt was surely a refined man.

She sat there, lost deep in thought for quite a while, until she heard a rap at the antique front door and looked up through the pretty beveled glass window to see her next appointment – a coffee date with Graves. After a few visits together over the summer, sometimes discussing the house, sometimes discussing life in general, this would probably be the last time they got together, and it made her a little sad.

"Hello, Graves!" Lauryn called through the door as she pulled it open, "Are you ready for our coffee date?"

"You better believe it!" From under his hat he pushed his heavy rimmed glasses up further on his nose, "Norwegian blood plasma, that's what I call it. Coffee instead of blood in the veins, y'know." He leaned his cane against the door jamb and pulled his roomy gray trousers up higher on his slim waist as he stepped aside to allow her past him.

"Is that right?" Lauryn laughed as she gathered her purse and her phone from where she left it near the front door, "Well, I'm a mix of Italian, Swedish and German so I guess I wouldn't know. But I still like coffee."

"Of course, if you'd rather drink something else since you have the little one, I think they serve tea and lemonade as well." He suggested cordially as they began their slow, three-block walk towards the cafe on Main Street in River's Bend.

"No, that's alright, coffee sounds great. I allow myself one cup per day and I haven't had one yet this morning so I'm looking forward to it."

"And, Elliott? Will he be meeting us there?" They stepped into the crosswalk after the light changed, carefully avoiding the puddles left from the rain showers earlier in the morning. Graves and Elliott had become friends because they both shared an interest in collector cars. Although they were decades apart in age, earlier in the summer, they had even exchanged phone numbers and had attended two local car shows together.

"Ah, no, not today. He has a meeting this morning. He's close to a decision on the business."

"Oh, excellent! Well, I hope he finds partners as good as you kids are. It's been wonderful getting to know you two."

"We feel the same, Graves. You've been a wonderful neighbor."

Lauryn reached out and loosely half-hugged him as they passed the brick-faced hardware store and dry-cleaning business with the big green awning.

This stretch of the block was so pretty, Lauryn thought again as she looked ahead to River's Café with its outdoor seating and outdoor planters filled with orange pumpkins and corn shocks. The owners of the café told her that they had purchased Dot's Diner many years ago and not long after, they changed the menu and the name. Graves said he preferred the café over the new coffee shop down the block where Lauryn and Elliott frequently visited. Graves liked the fact that at River's Cafe they refilled your cup as many times as you wanted.

A short while later, after ordering coffee and pastries, they sat at a table near the window discussing the relative notoriety of Promise Place now that it was featured on her YouTube channel and in social media. It had become the buzz of the town and Lauryn was happy to share the details of the renovation with people who stopped her as she worked in the yard or elsewhere around town.

Graves asked her if she had another project in mind, and she answered that she did not. As usual, when the topic of conversation touched on their future, Lauryn felt a nagging desire to make their temporary rental a more permanent home and to make their spare bedroom into a nursery. Her mother called it the "nesting instinct" and told Elliott not to be alarmed by it, "Just let her do what she needs to do, it's completely natural."

As she sat listening to Graves discuss another house on the block that was recently listed for sale, she wandered in her mind. Yes, she thought, it's settled, I'll go with the soft, dove gray and mint green color palette for the nursery. She could just picture the crib in the corner and the vintage bureau she'd recently purchased next to it-

"-have you heard from her recently?" Graves swallowed the last of his cup and turned it over on the ceramic saucer so that the cafe server wouldn't come refill it again. Today seemed to be a slow day at the cafe, she had refilled their cups three times already.

"Ah," Lauryn took the chance that while she'd been daydreaming about nurseries, he'd turned the conversation to Bridgette Townlin, "No, I haven't connected with her yet. Is it common for her to be out of touch for so long?"

"Well, when she had the place for sale, she'd check in more often. But, since you bought it, I guess she doesn't need to."

"Yeah, still, I sent her a few emails and I've left some voicemails on her cell phone. I hope she gets them soon because I have some questions I'd like to follow up on."

"About her grandfather?"

"Yes, her grandfather the pastor."

"I wish I could tell you more, but I never knew the man. But you said that you were focused more on the elder two Drs. Berndt's, right? Were we able to give you enough information for your story about their time in the house?"

"Yes, the story is focused on the doctors and you've been a great help getting me connected to people with some of that history. I might be a little biased, but I think it's very interesting."

"I'm sure it is! You know, even though I have started to use a cell phone, I'm not much into computers, I've never felt the need to learn. But I've been thinking, maybe I will go to the library and have Penny Reynolds help me watch those videos Elliott recorded on his camera." He pushed his glasses up further on his nose, "Now, how does that work? Do you think she could find them on the computer there?" Lauryn smiled as she nodded and took the last swallow of her coffee.

It was misting lightly as they stepped out of the cafe onto the sidewalk and Lauryn wished she'd thought to bring an umbrella. As she cinched the waist of her jacket tighter against the cool October breeze, she abandoned any hope that her hair would survive the drizzle and reached into her pocket, happy to find an extra ponytail in it.

As she pulled her hair through the ponytail, she glanced over at Graves who was setting his gray safari hat over his thinning hair. She would sure miss her coffee dates with her new friend. He was a timeless classic and such an enjoyable guy, always telling her funny tidbits about his life. Like now.

This humorous one featured his neighbor's dog, a springer spaniel with lush black and white fur, he said. The dog's name was Snickers. Can you imagine that, he asked with a good-natured laugh, who would come up with such a funny name like that for a dog?

Lauryn's smile bubbled into laughter as she started to tell him she didn't think it was funny at all. It was, after all, her childhood nickname too-

And then it happened. In a split second, but like they say, it seemed like time stood still. Graves's eyes opened wide in shock and his mouth dropped open as he instinctively reached for her arm.

The next moment - an awful vibration, like the pavement was being ripped out and shredded underneath her, the smell of burnt rubber and the ear-splitting sound of metal crunching and glass shattering. She felt a whoosh of air and her eyes opened wide in horror as she realized something was wrong, something was very wrong with those two cars. Why were they careening out of control, one impossibly wound into the other, sliding as if on ice across the sidewalk?

Then a flash of pain at her neck, unlike anything she'd ever known or could ever imagine.

She felt her legs give way as if they were cut out from under her and she greeted the sidewalk like it was a soft, fluffy bed even though when she hit it, the sand–paper sidewalk felt scruffy against her cheek.

The fluttering in her stomach stopped.

The baby...

Then, nothing. Black.

CHAPTER 26

1968, October

Come to me all who labor and are heavy laden, and I will give you rest.
Matthew 11:28

That evening, after the board meeting, as Cameron entered the house through the back door and set his car keys on the side table, he noticed the television with its volume low was blinking a silvery blue and pink color across the living room walls and floor. Their new RCA color television had been last year's Christmas gift from his parents and the entire household was captivated by the vibrant colors leaping out at them from their favorite programs.

The kids must be in bed already, Cameron thought to himself, given the house rules. Because the television was such a distraction for the children, it was decided that they would turn it off each night at 7:00 pm to allow for bath and bedtime. The routine was set; after the children were in bed sleeping, Cameron and Cassie would go their separate ways - he to his office to read and her to the couch to watch her favorite programs.

Tonight, she was sitting on the easy chair next to the couch, her knees curled tightly under her, the portable phone with its long cord was pulled over to her chair. Sitting in her lap was a sheet of paper which Cameron surmised must be the copy of his board meeting statement that he'd left for her on the table this morning.

She looked up when he joined her in the living room, wiped anxiously at her eyes and ended her telephone call with a hasty goodbye. He raised his eyebrows and wondered briefly who she was talking to that she was crying and realized it could be any number of people – her parents, her sister, one of her friends – whoever it was, they were hearing only her side of the story. Another reminder that he had little control over how this thing was unravelling.

Ignoring the obvious question of who was on the other end of the distressing telephone call and her thoughts after reading his statement, instead Cameron sat down on the couch and tried to keep the resentment out of his voice.

"Kids in bed?" He asked noncommittally. The children were one of the few safe topics right now. They were one concern that they shared equally. But the truth was Cameron wanted to avoid discussing the board meeting for as long as possible. His short drive home hadn't given him enough time to work out a plan in his head.

"Yes, but you know how it goes," She said, "They like to have you read them a story so I'm not sure they're asleep."

Avoiding his eyes, Cassie moved her legs out from under her, set the phone on the coffee table and pulled a cigarette from an open pack that sat next to a half-full ashtray. As Cameron watched and waited while she lit it and settled back in her chair, his mind worked through the various approaches he could take to this conversation. Above all, he wanted her to see that they must work this out somehow. It wasn't too late.

Holding the cigarette off to the side of her face, its smoke swirling in between them, Cassie smoothed her long hair behind one of her ears and squinted her eyes towards him as if she was straining to figure something out. Finally, with a glance down at the paper that still sat in her lap, she tilted her head to the side quizzically and shook it slightly, as if confused.

"Cameron, I'm not sure what you think will be achieved by making me the bad guy in this, except to hurt our children."

"I don't know what you mean. I only stated the facts in that statement."

"Yes. The facts as *you* see them."

"No, the facts *are* the facts. And, I'll tell you, it was one of the most difficult things I've ever done, writing that and sitting there tonight while I read it to them." He paused and took a breath, trying to control his emotions before he continued, "But, the facts remain the same - I've messed up with the drinking and you've asked for a divorce. I want to keep this family together and I don't want a divorce. Those are the facts."

"But, of course there's more to it than that, Cameron. You know there is." With her exaggerated sigh and obvious disdain for his limited view of the many *trials* she faced in their marriage, his temperature began to rise and his impulse to lash out was unrestrained.

"Well, what did you want me to tell them?" He lashed out, "You want me to relay every sordid detail? How we fight all the time? How I haven't slept in my own bed for months? How my wife hasn't touched me in so long that I can't even remember the last time? How she's told me that she doesn't even love me anymore? What? Is that what you wanted me to tell them?"

"Oh, Cameron, stop. Don't do that. It doesn't help anything to get so worked up all the time. This is why I can never talk to you about this."

"Well, I guess I get upset because it's my marriage – the very survival of my family – that we're talking about here."

"I just thought the whole thing made it sound like you were blameless. And knowing them like I do, I'm sure they were all quick to believe that and totally blame me."

"No one blamed anyone, Cassie. I've done nothing but defend you to everyone on the board and at church. Why would I cut you down when you're my wife – I want this marriage saved – and I love you?"

Cassie shook her head again and stood up abruptly, taking a ragged drag on her cigarette as she walked over to look out the living room bay window. After a moment, she turned towards him again, with her hand on her hip. "Well, what did they say?"

"Nothing tonight. They said they have to talk about it. I don't know, could go either way, I guess."

At the uncertain – yet clearly defeated – tone of his voice, she began pacing between the bay window and the staircase, her brow knitted into a frown as if she was trying to decipher a puzzle.

"I don't know what to do. This is just putting me in an impossible position, Cam."

"You?" He barked the word out, incredulous, "You think you're in an impossible position? I might lose my job!" Her self-absorption was beyond belief.

"I know, I know. But I can't help how I'm feeling." She grabbed the ashtray and sat down on the window seat of the bay window, nervously flicking the long ash off her glowing cigarette before swiping at the tears that were on her lashes.

"I am just feeling so trapped, Cameron," She continued, "I don't know what I want exactly, but I know *this* isn't it. This - our life here, like this - it isn't right." She paused and breathed in deeply, as if to bolster her confidence, before she spoke, "Maybe you should move out so we can work towards the next phase? If we do this gradually, it will be less traumatic for the kids."

"Not having me here will be traumatic for the kids. Can you hear what you're saying?"

"Yes, I know what I'm saying. But it must happen. They will just have to learn to accept it like other children have. Their parents still love them like always, they just don't live in the same house."

"But, Cassie, I don't want to leave. I won't leave my family." Cameron said stubbornly, not willing to even give an inch towards her plan.

"The bottom line is, I can't live like this," Her words came out forcefully as she enunciated every syllable, "I know I've let you down and this is hard for you, but I can't pretend to be your wife when I don't feel it anymore. I won't pretend for our family or friends and I certainly won't pretend for the church."

"*You can't pretend–*" Cameron's voice was rising in concert with the rage going on inside of him as he felt his whole life crashing down around him. "*Do you know how that makes me feel?*"

"Well, I don't know how else I can tell you– I need out! Maybe I should leave this house – it's your family's house, it's not mine anyway. I could move back to Edina near my parents, mom can help with the kids, I can work at dad's practice, get my law degree. That way it would still be close enough for you to see them–"

"See them– you mean you– you would take the kids?" The voice coming from him was completely foreign, it sounded shrill and panicked.

"Well, of course–"

"No. Absolutely not. No way! You can't take my kids away from me!"

"I'm not taking them away from you, Cam! It would be close enough for you to see them as often as you want!"

"No, Cassie. Please think about what you're saying! No. I won't let you do this!" He was shouting now, and he had lost complete control of his temper. Again.

"Cam, please!" Cassie raised her voice louder and then whispered harshly, "Don't yell at me, you will wake the children!"

Cameron turned roughly away, and strode towards the back door, as a mind-numbing rage coursed through his entire body. He had his car keys in his hand before he noticed the striped white and blue pajamas of his son as Aaron peeked around the door of the kitchen. He must have snuck down the back stairway that opened into the kitchen instead of announcing himself on the main stairway that opened into the living room, Cameron thought. And, he'd heard the whole thing by the look in his terrified eyes.

"Come here, bud. Come here." Cameron softened his voice, knelt on the floor and drew Aaron into a hug, trying to stop the freight train of anger from barreling over his innocent little boy, "Shhh, don't cry. How long you been out here?"

"A little while -I was w- waiting for you to read my library book. Are y- you mad at Mommy and moving away?"

"No. Your mom and I were just having a grown-up talk. We were upset, not mad."

He pulled back to look into Aaron's tear-filled eyes and unable to stand the guilt he felt for his role in creating them, he ruffled his hair and kissed the top of his head before whispering in his ear.

"It's okay, Aaron. Daddy's gotta go out for a little while. Why don't you go sit with Mommy and she can read your library book tonight, okay?"

As Cameron stood, Aaron started to step away but suddenly turned back and grabbed Cameron around his legs in a desperate hug.

"Daddy, you're coming back, right?" He pleaded earnestly as he tried to gulp back another cry.

"Yeah, bud, don't worry about your daddy. I will always come back." Cameron ruffled his hair again and turned him towards the living room with a gentle push. As he left the warmth of his house behind him, Cameron found himself rubbing his fingers together, trying to memorize the feeling of his son's soft curls.

It was a Wednesday afternoon, just over a week later when Reginald called Cameron at the church office and asked to meet with him. In the call, he said the board met the previous evening and had made their decision.

Because Glenda was at a dental appointment, the outer office was empty when Reginald filled his doorway less than an hour later.

Since his phone call, Cameron had been debating in his mind the rationale for meeting with Reginald alone versus in front of the entire board. It could be taken either way, perhaps they were keeping him on and felt the infractions were so minor that the entire board was not necessary. Or, they were letting him go and the entire board was considered overkill to witness the painfully embarrassing sacrifice of their pastor.

"Hello, Pastor Cam. I see Glenda isn't here today?" Reginald glanced back towards Glenda's neat desk, now vacant.

"Ah, no. She had requested this morning off for an appointment. Please, come in and sit down, Reginald."

Once he had settled himself in the chair across the desk from Cameron, Reginald sighed deeply, held his breath for a moment and then exhaled slowly. This didn't look good, Cameron realized with numb foreboding. This didn't look good at all.

"Well, as I said over the telephone, Pastor Cam, the board met last evening and discussed the situation and your position here at Freedom Church. Individually, we all spent time praying and then discussing as a group, we came to the decision. I will tell you that it was not unanimous, but there was a majority decision."

As he spoke, Cameron felt a strange, displaced sensation take over his mind, like he was floating somewhere in the corner of the room, somewhere up there, next to the highest bookshelf.

"At our meeting, some other matters came to light - I understand that it's become known in the community and in the church about your marriage troubles, including some rumors of an unsavory sort about Mrs. Berndt. Pastor, I won't add insult to injury by repeating what I've heard, but these rumors are concerning. And now, with the additional admission of your stumble with alcohol, we just don't think that you're in a position to serve as our moral leader. It was a difficult decision for all of us. But we had to ask ourselves, how can you counsel others and lead this church when your own house is in such disorder?" Reginald moved in his chair uncomfortably, studying the tops of his shoes which looked like they'd just gotten a new shine this week.

As Cameron sat there, shell-shocked and unable to say a word, he stared dazed at the pens and notepad on his desk sitting next to his open Bible. Reginald cleared his throat and looked up again with a downturned mouth and a forlorn look in his eyes, "Pastor Cam, perhaps with time, things will work out for your family, and we all pray that they do. But, for now, we have decided to ask for your resignation."

CHAPTER 27

2017, October

"No! No, no, no-" Elliott's voice emanated from somewhere deep inside and sounded ominously lower and louder than his normal voice, like something primal. His eyes moved in a dazed pattern across the faces of Lina and Mark in the conference room while they stared back at him with open-mouthed shock at his eruption. They had just finished their meeting and were joking about something inconsequential, when he took the phone call. Only moments before they were discussing- now, he couldn't remember what they'd been discussing. His mind was completely blank.

He pulled his cell phone away from his ear and looked in horror at Graves' name on the display as his brain struggled to comprehend. Lauryn was planning to be at Promise Place to pay a vendor and then have coffee with Graves this morning, while he'd been sitting here at this meeting, talking about this stupid business deal. And he realized - his mind in a tortured hot mess - that he couldn't remember if she'd even crossed his mind since this meeting started.

A car accident - Elliott was sure that's what he'd said - Lauryn on the sidewalk, unable to speak, unable to move. Lauryn taken away, unconscious, in an ambulance. Could this really be happening – was this a nightmare?

Graves was still speaking, Elliott could hear his voice still speaking, but it sounded tinny, like a toy, through the speaker. What had he just said?

Elliott brought the phone back to his ear and suddenly found himself running through the hallway of the building, pushing his way through the lobby and then through the glass front door, nearly rolling over a startled woman who was on the other side.

"–they took her to Riverside Hospital, Elliott. It's the one on the south side of River's Bend. That's all I know. Go there." He had reached the Jeep now. A short pause on the phone as Elliott fumbled over shaking fingers to get his car keys inserted into the ignition, "Elliott, be careful driving. Please."

The waiting area at Riverside Hospital's ICU was stark and uninviting, light gray floors, darker gray walls and black chairs, the only color coming from the oversized floral photographic prints that covered the walls. There weren't many chairs and they weren't comfortable. Visitors weren't meant to spend much time there because patients weren't meant to spend much time in the intensive care unit. It was not a happy place to be, waiting for the doctor, waiting for the nurses, waiting for someone to tell you what the heck was going on behind those walls, down those halls.

His wife, his best friend, his life. And, his baby. Somewhere in this hospital, on a table, hooked up to machines, getting prodded, cut into, patched up again by a set of strangers, people who didn't know her, people who didn't realize how special, how precious, she was. And, he was just sitting here on this stupid chair, staring out this stupid window. Doing nothing. Useless.

He closed his eyes again, as he repeated the feverish words to God in his mind - he hoped they passed as prayers, but he wasn't stopping to really form rationale, logical sentences in them.

Instinct had taken over. All he could do was ramble incoherently to God.

Gabrielle reached across and covered his hand with her cool one and she squeezed it slightly as she tried to smile reassuringly. He hadn't realized that he was clicking his cell phone on and then off again in a half-crazed, repetitive motion that was a visual of the way he felt inside. Wound tight, ready to spring, ready to lose it.

"I just wish they'd come tell us what's going on." Elliott repeated the statement, his eyes boring into hers. It was probably the tenth time he'd said it in the past half hour. And, while his hand was quieted by the presence of Gabrielle's resting on his, his knee started bouncing reflexively below it.

"I know, Elliott." Gabrielle spoke gently, trying to calm him with her voice and her gaze, "I know. All we can do is wait and pray. Todd's talking to his friend in the sheriff's department so we will know more soon. Is your friend Graves okay?"

"Yes, I think so. He called saying that he's somewhere at this hospital. He's pretty banged up, they set his broken arm and told him to wait to talk to the police. He- well, he feels so bad that Lauryn caught the brunt of it-"

At that moment, Todd walked back through the waiting room doorway and sat down alongside Elliott.

"I texted Daniel," He said, "And I called your grandparents and they're calling your mom, Elliott. Everyone is praying for Lauryn and the baby."

"Thanks, Todd," Elliott said. "Did you hear more about what actually happened?"

"It sounds like one of the drivers had a seizure of some sort, lost control and ran head-on into a pickup going the other direction. The cops figure both cars were going too fast for the slick street and somehow they ended up on the sidewalk, took out some tables and the front wall of the cafe. It was the awning that fell on Lauryn from behind, obviously she didn't see it coming. They said the 911 caller - I think it was your friend Graves - he said she was unconscious right away. She didn't speak-"

Todd stopped talking then, swallowing hard as tears filled his throat and he reached for Gabrielle's hand that still rested on Elliott's.

"Have you heard from the doctor yet? How is our baby?" Todd asked his wife, his eyes full of tears.

"No, nothing yet. She will be okay, Todd. She will be okay." Gabrielle replied as she gripped his hand and nodded her head as if by telling them that, it would make it so.

Another forty-five minutes passed as they waited. By then, Elliott's grandparents Jared and Rose had arrived along with his mother Rebecca. Suddenly, the door opened and a woman and a man, both dressed in scrubs walked over to the family and Elliott rose instinctively to greet them, trying to read their expressions. But it was no use, they just looked tired.

The woman, somewhere in her fifties with kind, gray eyes and dark lashes, gestured for him to sit down again as she pulled up a chair for herself and the man next to her did the same.

"I'm Dr. Sanderson and this is Dr. O'Neill. I'm sorry you've been left waiting for so long, but we had a lot we needed to do right away to stabilize Lauryn." The woman paused, making sure she had everyone's attention, "First off, Lauryn is stable, she's still unconscious but she is stable. She took a terrible blow to her neck and head, there were lacerations on her skull, and she sustained a significant concussion and we see some swelling in her skull that we are controlling. Her brain activity is normal, however, so that's a good sign. She has some significant lacerations on her back, but her spine was not injured and given the situation, that is quite remarkable. She has some broken ribs-"

Elliott watched her mouth the words but found that he was fading in and out of focus. Lauryn was okay, she was going to be okay, oh my gosh, she was going to be okay. What about-

"-you are Lauryn's husband, Mr. Grant?" Dr. O'Neill, the guy who looked quite a bit younger than Dr. Sanderson, spoke up quietly and Elliott nodded, holding his breath for the news, "I'm an OB-GYN on staff here at Riverside. We are monitoring the baby, there is a heartbeat but very little movement. We feel hopeful, however, so let's just stay positive while we watch how things go.

We're doing the best we can for Lauryn right now and her body is doing its best to care for the baby."

Elliott sat back in his chair, letting the air out of his lungs that he hadn't even realized he'd been holding since the doctors starting speaking. He rubbed his thighs anxiously as the family asked further questions, all unimportant he thought, not at all what he was wondering.

"Can I see her?" He finally interrupted without realizing he spoke until he heard his voice and they all looked at him as the doctors both rose from their seats to leave.

"No, not quite yet," Dr. Sanderson spoke, her voice kind, like her eyes. "It may be another hour or so before that's possible. We still have a lot to do, but we will be back to let you know when you can see her. Just ask the nurse at the desk if you have any questions. We will talk later." She smiled with a quiet reassurance, then they both turned in unison and Elliott watched as they walked away, on a mission to take care of his wife and his baby.

CHAPTER 28

2017, October

The accident made the 6 o'clock news on local television stations. The driver who had the seizure, a man in his early forties, was in critical condition but expected to survive. The other driver, a young man in his teens on his way to an eye appointment that morning, was shaken up but not seriously injured. And, even though the cars barreled through the front wall of the cafe, luckily, no one inside was injured. The only bystanders who were injured were two people as they walked on the sidewalk outside the cafe. One of these bystanders was treated for a broken arm and released.

And, the other bystander-

Elliott looked up from his hands as the television repeated what they knew about her condition. A young pregnant woman, condition unknown, is hospitalized. We'll stay on this story and update you tonight at 10. Stay tuned.

Elliott reached over to touch her hand in the lone spot of skin that wasn't covered in tape, alongside the hospital drip. It was quiet in her room now. The family had vacated a few minutes ago, all of them agreeing that Elliott needed some space and they would be downstairs in the cafeteria.

Her blonde hair was pulled to the side in a loose braid that someone had laid down the left side of her neck and she was crowned in a white, gauze band that covered her head and forehead. Underneath the white band, Lauryn's eyelids were closed, and her long eyelashes rested peacefully against her ashy-white cheeks.

Ugly bluish-green bruises were blooming under the bright red chafing below her right cheekbone. The bruises continued a nasty trail alongside her neck, onto her shoulder and disappeared under the light green and white polka-dotted hospital gown she wore. Tubes lay everywhere, inserted into her arms and into her skull, fluids going in, fluids coming out. Everything about her looked scary.

He closed his eyes and listened to the machines that were keeping watch over the two people he loved the most in the world. A steady drum whooshed out of the baby monitor alongside him, indicating that his baby's heart was still beating inside there somewhere. The rhythm of the baby's heartbeat was accompanied by the uniform wheeze of the air they were pumping into Lauryn through her nose and the quiet beep of her heart rate through her vitals monitor.

The deep cuts on her neck and back were stitched up and the four broken ribs, which thankfully hadn't damaged her lungs, would heal over time, but the concussion was another matter. They were keeping her sedated and would do so until they felt the swelling in her brain was controlled. They couldn't say how long that might take, it could be hours, or it could be days. They couldn't say what long term effects she may have once she woke again.

The baby was quiet, but the heart rate was strong. He or she was completely dependent on the mother who laid ghostly still in the hospital bed beside Elliott. It was unnerving for him to contemplate, but even as she lay here so close to him, she wandered somewhere else in her mind, somewhere a million miles away.

In the meantime, all he could do was wait for her to open her eyes.

2017, October – 4 Long Days Later

"Ouch." The voice was small in the stillness of the room, almost like a child and Elliott sat up straight in his chair, realizing then that his left leg was completely numb and that he'd fallen asleep next to her hospital bed. The recollection washed over him that the doctors thought she would wake soon and the thrill of it kept him here for the past two days straight. Four excruciating days had gone by without talking to her – it had been years since he'd gone that long without hearing her voice. He missed it. Man, he missed her voice.

As he shifted closer towards her bed, his mouth went dry with excitement as he reached for her fingers.

"Elliott," She whispered now through soft upturned lips, as if her first word took all of her steam and she'd rather communicate with her eyes, "It hurts–"

"Lauryn, it's okay." Elliott urged over his full throat and through tears that he couldn't stop, "You're okay."

She nodded her head slightly, her eyes clouding over again before she shut them quietly. He watched her lips move as if to form a word and then they just quivered for a moment before he heard her whisper.

"Our baby?" Her eyes were still closed, as if in resignation to hear the awful news. She didn't know, he thought in a panic, *she didn't know*.

"No, no Lauryn," He gripped her fingers tighter as if trying to bring her back to him, "Don't worry, the baby is good."

She smiled a ghost of a smile. It was hard to tell, but he was sure she heard him and smiled before she fell back asleep again. His heart was completely full in his chest and it felt like it was going to burst. She was back. His life was back.

Slowly, he bent closer and raised her hand to his lips. As he kissed her cold fingertips and brushed them lightly against his cheek, he let the tears of joy that were spilling over her fingers be his prayer of thanks.

CHAPTER 29

1968, November

So, here I am, Lord. I turn once again to you because I simply cannot turn off the questions that torment me.

I ask myself, how did I get here? What happened? At which point should I have turned right instead of left? Was there a point in my life that I could have changed the story?

Because this right here? As hard as I try to see it differently, this feels like The End.

It had been three weeks since he was asked to sign the letter of resignation. Three paltry weeks – really, a short span of time considering the span of an entire lifetime. But, after living through the past three weeks, Cameron now felt as if every ounce of his soul's energy had been sapped out of him, leaving only his mounting failures. He couldn't even contemplate the next day without a sense of anxiety and panic.

After the initial shock of the board's decision sunk in, his natural reaction was one of bitterness and regret and added to that, a healthy dose of indignation and injured pride. He fought every instinct towards resentment when he interacted with congregants and as he delivered the last two messages from the pulpit. Overall, and with the help of God, he thought he'd done an adequate job of keeping things professional, given the circumstances.

Outside the church, in the wider community, and amongst fellow clergy including Al Newsome, his departure was the type of news that burned a white-hot streak through the collective conversation like gasoline on dry, ditch grass. There were sympathetic words and encouraging prayers, but the hard reality was that the averted eyes and whispers behind his back were less likely about his forced resignation and more likely about the fact that he no longer lived at his own house.

Did you know? tsk tsk The pastor and his wife are separated...

Almost two weeks ago, as they both tried to function under the microscope, Cassie had laid down the ultimatum - leave the house to give her space to figure out her feelings or she would take the children with her to start a new life near her parents and further away from him. He agreed to move out, of course. He believed her threats.

As gut-wrenching as these burdens were, Cameron resolutely avoided liquor stores and refused to succumb to the demons whispering the taunts in his head ... *What does it matter now? You're not a pastor anymore...*

But even stone-cold sober, completely clear of alcohol, he feared he wasn't thinking straight. He'd lost everything, his job, his family, his calling, what else did he have to lose?

He'd begun to think of worst-case scenarios, waking up in the middle of the night in the hotel bed with panic attacks that started somewhere near his stomach, sped up his heart rate, shallowed his breathing and ended up in his tortured mind, the fatalistic fantasies racing around inside his head for hours at a time.

It had been the morning after one of those tortured nights that he had placed the call to them, almost on a whim, not really thinking it all the way through. Certainly, he hadn't expected to hear back from the Southeast Asia Medical Missions team so quickly. But his prior academic degree and residency was attractive to them and the desperate need for medical personnel was so great on the battlefield that even those without full credentials were given the opportunity to train on the job in 12-week intervals.

Their letters were quick to paint a realistic picture, however. Whatever you're expecting about this service, imagine something immeasurably worse and then take that times ten, they said, then you would be getting close to the demands you will face. Although this mission was not on the front lines of military action, it was not for the faint of heart, mind or spirit.

To Cameron, this was just the type of mission program he needed to remove him from his own torture here; it would take his mind off his failures and give his wife the space to see what she was determined to throw away. Even if it was for a relatively short period of time - they wanted him to join them immediately after the holidays and he would be back April 1 - at least he wouldn't be nearby to intrude on her time as she thought through their future.

Hoping the kids would be at the house this morning when he arrived to pack some more clothes, instead when he opened the back door, he was greeted by an eerie silence. Cassie's note was taped to the refrigerator and told him that she had taken the children to her sister's house for the day so they could play with their cousins, because they needed some joy in their lives. As he crunched the note into a small ball in his hand, Cameron wished he could find some joy in his life. He sure wasn't finding any sleeping alone at the hotel.

Sighing deeply, Cameron walked to his office and dialed the number he knew well, his parents' home in San Diego. Leaving his small family without a father, Cameron was concerned that they have a back-up in case of an emergency. And, although he rarely asked for their help, he knew that his parents loved their grandchildren unconditionally. Cameron was sure they would spare no expense or effort to support them in his absence.

His father answered after the second ring and at the deep timbre of his voice, Cameron suddenly felt like the little boy who sat in the corner of this office all those years ago, watching his father conduct his life with such reliability - unfaltering under pressures and demands - always stalwart. Inside, Cameron still felt like that insecure little boy, unsure of what was to become of his life, needing his father to provide security and strength. Some things never change.

"Hi, Dad. It's Cameron. I have a favor to ask of you..."

January, 1969

After attending to some last-minute errands before he left the country early the next morning, Cameron sat in his driveway in the warmth of his car while he watched his home with its cheery light blinking through the paned windows. Inside that home lived the people most precious to him and he recognized the pain his decision would impart to them. Well, three of them at least.

That frigid January evening came on the heels of a Christmas holiday that Cameron would much rather forget. Two separate celebrations, one at Cassie's parents' home to which he wasn't even invited and the second, a solitary affair here at the house. Because his mother was recovering from hip surgery, his parents were unable to come to Minnesota, so that left Cameron and the kids celebrating the day just the four of them, without Cassie. She chose to stay the night at a friend's house out of town. All of it was explained to their young, wide-eyed children with lame excuses and flimsy stories.

But it was a sham. Everyone, including their children, seemed to recognize that the veil of little white lies camouflaged a family unit that was hollowed out completely, nothing but emptiness underneath.

Through it all, Cameron forced himself to view this as just a momentary setback, like a sluggish, tough third quarter, in the long game of their marriage. The game wasn't over, it was all about saving this thing they called their family.

It had been the compromise these past few weeks, after Cameron had been forced to move out of their home and then prepared to leave on the medical mission. He insisted that he wanted to spend as much time as possible with the children, so while she was at work during the day, he was at the house caring for his family. He thoroughly enjoyed every moment of it and when Cassie arrived at the house at 5:30 each evening, he'd have dinner prepared for them, they would eat it together as a family and then he'd leave for the hotel after the kids were in bed.

Baby Gemma, now a busy little toddler, was a handful and just keeping her out of harm's way around the house was a welcome distraction. Meanwhile, Charlotte was constantly wanting to doctor her dolls and stuffed animals with the play doctor kit that she'd received for Christmas.

One afternoon, while Gemma was taking a nap, Charlotte ordered Cameron to "be the daddy" for her shaggy, blue and white teddy bear because she wanted to be the doctor who fixed the bear's broken leg. After struggling to tape a wooden stick to the its fuzzy leg, she finally turned to Cameron and pleaded with him to show her how to do it. Days later, when he was putting some clothes away in her bureau, Cameron found the bear, laying on her bed with a pillow under its head and its leg still firmly set in its splint. It brought him to tears, that bear. But, then, a lot of things brought him to tears lately.

This whole situation was hardest on Aaron, who of course was old enough to know that his idyllic family life – with two parents raising him together – was slowly unwinding. Even though his mouth smiled with appreciation when he opened his gifts this Christmas, his eyes didn't light.

He was honest with his children that he was soon leaving for a long trip and that he would really miss them. He knew that short term, it would be hard on them, but that as they grew up, whatever they remembered about this period of their lives, he prayed that he could explain it to them.

But, realistically, he knew it would be difficult to explain it to anyone else because he hadn't even figured it out for himself. A huge part of him felt like he was completely abandoning his children, as if by getting on that plane tomorrow, in some way, he was flying away from his responsibilities.

But a bigger part of him felt like by flying away, by leaving, he was committing even more, *he was committing everything* – every earthly joy he held dear – to God and to his family.

The knock on the car window startled him and his breath caught painfully when he looked through the frosted glass to his left and saw Cassie standing in one of his old coats, the hood pulled up against the cold, her long shiny hair fanning down the front of her chest. She was still the most beautiful woman he'd ever met.

Cameron reached for the door handle and she moved to the side as he opened his door.

"The kids and I have been watching out the window for almost ten minutes, wondering if you were coming inside. I told them to stay put and I'd come check on you," She pushed some hair out of her eyes and shoved her hand deep into the front pocket again as she shivered in the cold, "Are you okay?"

"Yeah, just thinking, that's all." He wanted to reach out and draw her to his side, snuggle next to her, acknowledge that she was the love of his life and always would be. But she was already a few paces ahead of him, climbing the concrete steps towards the back door.

"Daddy! We wondered if you'd frozen into a snowman!" Charlotte exclaimed and ran to greet Cameron as he shifted out of his winter coat and hung it on the hook by the back door.

"Really? You think that's possible? Could I freeze into a snowman?" Cameron forced a laugh and told himself he simply had to do it. He had to keep this night happy for the sake of his kids.

"Aaron said no, but I think maybe yes."

"Ha, ha! And, what does Gemma think about it?" It was one of his familiar jokes with Charlotte right now. Her childish frustration was so endearing as he asked what Gemma thought about everything from the cereal choice for morning breakfast to what color socks she should wear.

"Awe, Daddy," Charlotte wrinkled her forehead into a frown, "You know she can't talk."

"Yet. She can't talk *yet*." Cameron scooped up his younger daughter who was half crawling, half toddling towards him across the kitchen floor, "But, before too long, you won't be able to get a word in, Charlotte. She may talk even more than you do." He kissed Gemma's soft cheek and buried his cold face into her warm neck drawing her into a laugh that shook her entire little frame and her feet strained against the footie pajamas she was wearing.

"Oh, I don't think so, Daddy. She is little. I will always be the big sister to Gemma, so I will always talk more than her."

"Ha, ha, I suppose that's how it works, huh?" Cameron joked with her as he winked at Aaron who stood a few feet away.

Already Cameron was feeling a hollow sense of dread seeping through him, how would he be able to leave them in the morning? What was he thinking when he set this plan in motion?

He reached his hand out to Aaron, wanting to connect physically with each of his children, as if touching them would sear them into his soul. Once he'd taken hold of Aaron's hand, Cameron looked towards Cassie, hoping she planned to stay with them tonight, but not sure anymore what he could expect. Instead of a direct question, he offered brightly, "Who is ready for some popcorn and television for our special night?"

"I am!" Charlotte squealed and turned in circles, "Mommy made the popcorn already and she said we could have root beer too!"

Cameron captured Cassie's gaze, sure that his eager desire to have her stay with them was written all over his face, "She did, huh?"

He smiled at her, trying to pretend that this was just an ordinary, happy family night.

"I did." Cassie replied and set out four plastic cups on the counter. Well, that could only mean that she planned to stay with them tonight. Cameron's spirit lifted immediately.

"Oh, good, I'm glad." Cassie returned his tentative smile with one of her own and for the briefest of moments, Cameron imagined he saw a flicker of the look she used to give him - one of affection, admiration, love. But then she broke the look as she turned away again and leaned into the refrigerator to retrieve the root beer.

After watching television for an extra half hour since it was a special night, they began their nightly bedtime routine. When he put Gemma to bed, after turning on the small, moon-shaped ceramic night light, Cameron stood at her faded yellow crib and rubbed her back gently with the palm of his hand, while he asked God to watch over her and keep her safe. She would likely be running around like crazy, and probably climbing all over the furniture, by the time he got home in April. He really hoped she wouldn't forget him over the next few months.

Going through their bedtime rituals with Aaron and Charlotte - reading their books and nightly Bible verses and saying their prayers - was even more difficult than Cameron had anticipated. When it was finally time to say goodnight - and goodbye - both children clung to him and cried. It was excruciating.

Cassie stood in the doorway of each child's room while he said goodnight, silently watching. I wonder what she's thinking, Cameron pondered. Is she envisioning a life for her children without their father in the same home? Is she picturing the many goodbyes that would need to be said if this family broke in two?

As he pulled Aaron's door shut behind him, Cameron followed Cassie down the stairs to the living room. He wanted to reach out and touch her shoulder, gather her to him in a big hug, feel a connection with her again. He wanted to forget all that had happened and all that he now had to do. Cameron wanted this so badly, he felt dizzy just thinking about it.

When she sat down on the couch without a word and reached for her cigarettes, he sat down next to her and slowly reached for her hand. She froze. He could tell he startled her at his touch, and he tried to ignore the nervous look in her eyes.

"Cassie, I need to talk to you about this. I need to say some things before I go." He held her hand in his and rubbed the soft skin on the inside of her wrist with his thumb. He loved her so much, and he brooded for the millionth time, where did it all go so wrong?

He had so many things he wanted to say, but suddenly his mind went void and all he could do was sit there, feeling her warm skin under his thumb and stare into her deep blue eyes. Swimming in the memories of their life together, he thought of the day he found the courage to ask her on a date and the sweet butterflies in his gut when she agreed. And, the night he asked her to marry him and the euphoric feeling he had when she said yes. And, the morning she told him she was pregnant with Aaron, their first baby. That was a feeling he couldn't really describe.

All of it – this life they'd built together – it now felt crammed into *this* moment where he sat here with her, staring into an abyss, desperately searching for a way to salvage this life together.

It was so simple for him, sometimes the clarity brought him to his knees. He just wanted to kiss his wife, he wanted them to be normal again. Was that so wrong?

"Cam, please, don't." Her words cut through his stream of consciousness like a cold knife.

"Don't what? I haven't said anything." He protested.

"You know. Don't do - that." She pulled her hand away, desperately reaching for her cigarettes again.

"Oh." He clasped his hands together in his lap tightly, he'd broken one of the ground rules. No touching.

But even though her words were harsh, her face was not. In fact, her eyes and her body language tonight seemed to be full of indecision, timidity, almost fear. He was completely confused by all the mixed signals. Could it be that his leaving tomorrow was becoming a self-inflicted wake-up call for her?

"Will you be staying here tonight?" She asked hesitantly as she lit a cigarette.

"No, I have everything over at the hotel," He glanced up again, and couldn't keep the hopeful note out of his voice, "Unless you'd rather I stay here?"

"It's up to you. You can stay here if you want."

"Okay." He nodded and then took a deep breath as he focused on all the details he needed to cover with her before he left, "So, I know I've told you where I will be and you have the contact information, but there really isn't good telephone communication. I will write letters to the children as often as I can, could you help them write to me? I really want them to know that I love them and will miss them."

"Of course, Cam." Cassie replied as she nodded.

"I want them to know that I see this as a mission for God. It's important to remind them that just because I'm not a pastor anymore doesn't mean I'm not serving God. Okay?"

"Yes." She nodded again.

"I mean it, it's very important that they understand this isn't about anything they've done or that I don't love them. Okay?"

"Yes, Cam, I understand."

"And, you have our savings account to use along with your paycheck, but if you need anything - financially or any emergency with the kids - please call my father. He said he can be on a plane within hours."

"All right, but we will be fine." Cassie tried to reassure him as she snuffed out her cigarette in the ashtray on the table next to her.

"Right. And, about us-" He allowed the statement to hang in the air a long moment, as she turned back to face him nervously. He wondered what she was thinking, but at the same time, he really didn't want to hear her thoughts spoken aloud, "Cassie, I need to know that you will pray about our marriage while I'm gone."

"Cameron-" Her eyes frowned as she winced.

"No," Cameron interrupted her, "Please don't say anything right now that kills the small sliver of hope that I have on this. The way I see it, this is our break. This is your break from me, like you requested – to figure things out for yourself through prayer. You know where I stand and that will never change for me."

She nodded a final time and tears suddenly misted her beautiful blue eyes. And then, as if the no touching rule had never been spoken aloud in the house, Cameron reached out for his wife and pulled her towards him, wrapping his arms around her slim shoulders and kissed the top of her head as she laid it on his chest.

"Cassie, please wait for me," He whispered urgently, "Don't make any decisions until I'm back. Please tell me you will wait for me."

By now, her tears had turned to sobs and he couldn't really hear her answer yes to his question, but he felt her nod against his chest and that, along with the warmth of her resting in his arms, was enough for him for now.

It had started to snow outside, and they sat on the couch for over an hour quietly watching the shimmering snowflakes build into heavy puffs on the tree branches until they both fell asleep.

The sound of the hot water heater hissing behind the couch woke Cameron almost two hours later. Feeling a bit disoriented, he sat up a little straighter and found that Cassie had fallen asleep next to him with her body burrowed tightly against him on one side and a plush pillow on the other. Moving aside so she could have the entire couch, he stood up and covered her with a colorful quilt, a wedding gift from her grandma.

He turned quietly and wandered around his home, drinking in the sights and sounds of the familiar surroundings. Such a comfortable home, generations of children had been born and raised in this home and now his children were added to the long list. He wanted them to experience the same happy, carefree childhood that he had been given and the other children before him. The thought of his own children being the generation that missed that brought a renewed heartache to him.

His brief tour of the first floor brought him to his office where he slid the door closed and sat in his leather chair at his desk, looking out the windows of the French doors at the silvery moonlit snow now blanketing the wrought-iron chairs on the small patio outside.

He would miss this office. Something about the impressive floor to ceiling bookshelves and the cozy fireplace in the corner made him feel safe in this room. Cassie had once told him the marble floors were too cold and when they had installed the wall to wall carpeting in the living and dining rooms, she'd suggested continuing it into this room too, but he'd refused.

This, after all, was his grandfather's and his father's doctor's office, where they had received many patients over the years. It was designed to be cozy, but still a working office, as evidenced by the open shelving in one corner where various medical supplies had once been stored.

Growing up, Cameron had taken for granted the history of his family in this town. Only now as an adult, was it starting to sink in how much this history, and this house, had become a part of him; how much it had impacted the person he was now.

Starting to feel slightly tired, restless and a bit anxious about the weather and his early morning flight tomorrow, Cameron stepped over to the bookcase near the corner and knelt in front of a lower door. After applying the correct amount of pressure on the upper right-hand corner, the door flipped open, revealing a locked wooden drawer. Feeling by memory up inside the front face of the cabinet, Cameron's fingers found the small skeleton key.

All those years growing up in this house and exploring every square inch of it, Cameron had never discovered this hidden drawer. The attic with its rooms hidden behind brick walls, the dumbwaiter and the back stairway to the kitchen had been enough to fuel his imagination. Besides, his father's office had always been off-limits. Certainly not a place to explore when his father was away.

The day his father passed over the house keys to Cameron was the day he showed him the secret drawer. His father had kept his financial statements and important papers inside it. Cameron kept his journals there.

Although he had some earlier journals from happier years of his life that he kept in his closet, he realized sadly, that only recently had he felt the need to hide his inner thoughts in this secret drawer. The journals written during these most recent years had taken a darker turn. Sometimes as he re-read passages, he worried that the voice of the writer didn't even sound like him. This was a man without any fight left inside him, someone beaten by this world, someone without hope. Without faith in himself or God.

Was that him? Could that be him?

He sat in the chair again and pulled the most recent journal towards him. It was almost full, with only a few open pages at the end. But it didn't matter, he wasn't planning on bringing it with him. He didn't think he'd have much time to journal on this medical mission and he was sure he would want to forget most of what he saw there anyway.

As was his habit, before he put pen to paper, he began to pray. He didn't know how he would get through any of this without his faith in his Savior even though the evidence of his Savior was pretty thin right now and the weight of his decisions and mistakes mired him down with an almost unbearable pain.

With tears blurring his eyes and his hand shaking under the weight of the pen, Cameron began to write his brief passage, praying for hope even against the weight of his shame.

I write this final entry the night before I fly out to Laos, continuing on to my final destination, Vietnam. It is with an incredible pain that I leave my wife and three children, but I see no other alternative to this.

I go to this war zone partly because I feel led by God; I know the need is great and I have something to give.

But it is also with deep despair that I admit that part of my reason for going is because I need to feel useful again, I need to mean something to someone again. Cassie's desire to end our marriage and my forced resignation as a pastor has made me question who I am as a man and as a father. In a selfish way, I have chosen this mission to be a servant of Christ, serving as a medic, where I hope I can be useful because I've sure been a pitiful pastor, father and husband.

So - bottom line - here I am, Lord. I turn once again to you because where else can I turn? I am at the end of myself and my ability to cope. I simply cannot turn off the questions that torment me.

I ask myself, how did I get here? What happened? At which point should I have turned right instead of left? Was there a point in my life that I could have changed the story?

Because this right here? As hard as I try to see it differently, this feels like The End.

With those simple words and with a despair that darkened every corner of his soul, he clicked his pen, closed his journal and threw the lot of them into the drawer. God knew the rest of the words anyway and he certainly didn't need to see them scrawled into a journal.

After locking the drawer, Cameron closed the inner cabinet and hid the key up behind the fascia board. Then, breathing a heavy sigh as he stood up from where he knelt, he walked across his office and slid the door open as quietly as possible.

As he walked towards where Cassie laid sleeping on the couch, he decided that it would be best for him to stay at the hotel tonight, he'd already said his goodbyes. So, instead of a dramatic farewell with his wife, he bent low and, after a long last kiss on her soft hair where he smelled the familiar lemony scent, Cameron brushed her soft cheek with the back of his fingers and said goodbye to his wife silently, inside his heart.

The winter night air bit his cheeks and the leather car seat crunched stiff and unyielding as he slid into his car and turned over the cold engine. It was a frigid, harsh wake-up call - *this was really happening.* He was leaving for a mission that would be unforgiving in its demands, throwing him into completely unknown, foreign circumstances that he would have no control over.

As he turned out of his driveway onto the snow-covered, icy street, he glanced one last time at his childhood home at 316 Promise Place and mentally braced himself for what was to come.

CHAPTER 30

2017, December

Lauryn blinked her eyes open, confused. What was up with her arm? She attempted to sit up and frowned as she tried to bring life back to the tingling appendage that had fallen asleep under the weight of her head as she stretched out on her side.

She reached for her cell phone which sat within arm's reach on the coffee table in front of the couch - in her little encampment - alongside her water bottle, her Bible, Cameron Berndt's journal and the television remote control.

Checking her phone for the time, she saw it was 4:35 PM. It was unusual for her to take such a heavy nap at this time of day, but they told her frequent drowsiness was just another side effect of the brain injury she'd sustained and the medication they had her on.

She'd been home now for almost two weeks and was noticing improvements each day, which really encouraged her. Although she couldn't remember much about the actual event of the accident, she vividly recalled the horrific pain and then the floating feeling followed by the numbness. It was like her brain had fallen asleep. And, gradually, like her numb arm that had fallen asleep and was now coming back to life, so was her brain coming back to life. It just took longer.

During those first awful days in the hospital, once she'd gained consciousness again, the pain in her head and neck were debilitating and she could do nothing more than blink or nod in response to questions and then thankfully, fall back asleep.

Ten days into her stay there, the pain in her head was still acute but the pain in her chest, neck and back finally began to recede. It was then that the anxiety and feverish nightmares began as she worried about the impact this was having on the baby.

And through all of it, she prayed that she would have enough faith to tackle another day and trust God that it would all work out.

Now, her continued recovery from the accident was just a portion of what she dealt with every day.

Noticing that she needed to refill her water bottle, Lauryn set her phone aside and hefted herself up from the couch. As her vision blurred, however, she reached out unsteadily and returned to the comfort of her resting spot again. Wow, I should know better than to stand up so fast like that, she admonished herself.

"Whoa there, baby, settle down now," She spoke out loud and watched as her large belly tightened and loosened in rather alarming succession and her back pain deepened.

Preterm contractions. They had started a week after the accident. It was like the baby woke up suddenly and decided maybe her womb wasn't the safest place to be and he or she had wanted to come out ever since. A healthy, fiber-rich diet, lots of water and strict bed rest were the doctor's orders. Oh, and no stress.

Lauryn really couldn't blame the little human. She wouldn't want to be inside there either. First, this baby endured those days where mom was out cold, unconscious, her brain in zombie-mode. Then, the big wake-up and the memories of the accident terrorizing her sleep, living out some kind of PTSD without ever leaving the hospital bed. And, now mom lying flat on her back, not able to walk more than twenty-five steps without her body shifting into contractions, doing all it could to go into labor. The poor little human.

"I pity you, little baby, your momma is sure a mess." Lauryn murmured and smiled as she rubbed her stomach, envisioning her womb quieting down.

Lauryn closed her eyes and waited for the contractions to subside, confident that they would. It was really a test of faith, all this they were going through, she thought as she glanced again at the journal sitting in front of her. Everyone telling them, keep the faith, just have faith, it will all work out.

She had been thinking a lot about faith as she laid here all day, just she and the baby. What was faith in God, really? How do you know if you have it or if you just think you do? Is there a measurement for faith? Like, do some people have it abundantly, consistently and others sporadically? And, why is that?

The thoughts about faith in God made her think of Cameron Berndt. Not really knowing what motivated her to do so, she'd read the last passages in his journal multiple times over the past few weeks as she recovered from the accident. She questioned, was reading his journal a catharsis for her? Like, by watching someone else struggle through pain and the resulting questions for God, that somehow her own pain could be alleviated, and her own questions answered?

A thought nagged at her, like an irritating hangnail. But it wasn't a thought, it was a verse that nagged at her, not something she'd read in Cameron's journal, but something else. Something she'd read in the Bible about a farmer sowing seeds. She thought the passage was in the book of Luke, but she couldn't be sure. What was it again?

Lauryn bent forward awkwardly from her position on the couch, careful not to squash the baby, and retrieved her Bible from the coffee table. She had just read this passage recently after Elliott had texted her saying it was an inspirational picture of walking by faith with Christ - why couldn't she remember it? She smiled wryly as she realized it was just another example of the jumbled state her brain was in since that morning she'd gone out for coffee and ended up being taken out by two cars on a sidewalk.

She found the verse Luke 8:4-8 and 11-15 and instantly she remembered the conviction she'd felt reading the parable Jesus told of the farmer who scattered some seed. Some fell along the path and the birds ate it up, some fell on rocky ground and the plants withered because they had no moisture, some fell among thorns and were choked out when the thorns overtook them. Still others fell on good soil and they yielded a crop far greater than originally sown.

Lauryn read further as Jesus explained the meaning of the parable in Luke 8, verses 11-15:

"This is the meaning of the parable: The seed is the word of God. Those along the path are the ones who hear, and then the devil comes and takes away the word from their hearts, so that they may not believe and be saved. Those on the rocky ground are the ones who receive the word with joy when they hear it, but they have no root. They believe for a while, but in the time of testing they fall away. The seed that fell among thorns stands for those who hear, but as they go on their way they are choked by life's worries, riches and pleasures and they do not mature. But the seed on good soil stands for those with a noble and good heart, who hear the word, retain it and by persevering produce a crop."

The instant she read the passage, Lauryn knew what seed represented her at this moment in her life and, if she was honest, it was where she sat most of her life. Amongst the rocks. On fire one moment, trusting God with her life and cold the next, as soon as it looked like he wasn't going to deliver her wants and desires.

When she doubted God, the tough questions always came back to –Just why was she on this earth anyway? For herself and her needs? Or was she meant to have a noble and good heart, hear the word, retain it and by persevering produce a crop?

Over the past few months, she had done some intense soul-searching and had realized that she had some major flaws in her view of God. She was coming to the deeper understanding that this walk on earth was meant for him, not for her. Yes, he loved her, deeply he loved her. But also, yes, it was *all for him.*

Each tough circumstance, seen through his will, could look entirely different. And, she didn't need to know why, sometimes she had to accept that she might never know why things happened. Each day, as she prayed and read the Bible - even though it was hard sometimes - she found more encouragement to accept this.

Her cell phone buzzed, interrupting her prayer, and she eagerly opened the Snapchat from Daniel with a smile. In it, he held their adorably chubby, baby son Quinn on his lap and was holding up two of Quinn's tiny fingers as the baby cooed into the camera, "Yay! Will meet my auntie and uncle in two weeks!!!" was scrolled across the screen and then disappeared.

Lauryn laughed at the message, and quickly replied with her own picture of her encampment on the couch, with her large belly and her feet propped up. "Can't wait!!" she replied on the picture.

Daniel and Madison were planning on coming back to Minnesota for Christmas and although her parents had gone to Kansas City soon after Quinn's birth to see their grandson, because of the accident and the resulting preterm labor, Lauryn and Elliott had not. Now, the prospect of meeting her new nephew along with all the holiday fun of Christmas gave her something to look forward to. It also gave her more dates to fill in on the calendar, and soon, another month closer to this baby finally being born.

A few minutes later, as she waddled to the kitchen to fill her water bottle, she noticed it was already dark outside. This time of day was tough for her as the hours of daylight dwindled to night. The days passed so slowly, always in the same, monotonous pattern. She would spend them scanning the internet for potential house projects, working on her website and replying to messages on social media, but usually by 3pm, she had a monstrous headache and was bored out of her mind.

She'd just returned to her encampment and had started watching a program on HGTV when her phone buzzed a second time; this time it was a telephone call. She didn't recognize the number and thought it might be a telemarketer. Against her better judgement, she swiped open the call.

"Lauryn, is that you?" The signal was weak with a strange echo on the line and the voice sounded scratchy. But, if she wasn't mistaken, she thought it might be Bridgette.

"Yes. Is this Bridgette?" Lauryn sat up straighter on the couch with anticipation and pulled a pillow behind the small of her back so she could focus on the conversation instead of the back pain.

"Yes, it is! How're you doing, Lauryn? I hope you're okay!" Obviously, Bridgette had heard about the accident, but could she have possibly heard about it while still in Bhutan?

"Oh, I'm fine, I'm good." Lauryn reassured her as she turned up her cell phone volume. She didn't want to miss any of this conversation, she had so much she wanted to ask her.

"That's good to hear, I saw some stuff on your YouTube channel and I was worried. But, I'm so glad to hear you're all right." The noise of city traffic in the background of her call grew louder and Lauryn wasn't sure she heard everything correctly, "– so we're back and headed to the hotel now and I will have internet there. Can we Skype later?"

"Yes! Of course, I will be here, I'm not going anywhere." Lauryn laughed to herself at the irony as she hefted her ankles back onto the ottoman and wriggled her toes, hoping Bridgette would call back right away, "Talk to you soon!"

"–we have been all over." Bridgette's face looked thinner and the roots of her highlight were well grown, leaving her ends ash-blonde and her roots a darker shade of brown, as she sat down and spoke into the camera on Skype, "I didn't expect to stay in Bhutan for so long but I met someone there, an English ex-pat who's from Hong Kong. Thomas was dispatched with the same humanitarian agency, working on the region's healthcare system. I–" She laughed at someone else – Thomas from the look on her face – who must have walked by off-camera, "Well, we just fell in love and decided to stay for a while longer. We almost feel like it will become our home someday, but now that we're back in Hong Kong, I'm quickly adapting to the conveniences of city life like hot water from a tap and the internet."

After updating Lauryn briefly on her travels into the remotest regions of Bhutan, Bridgette wanted to know more about the accident and how the pregnancy and resulting bedrest was going for Lauryn. After assuring her that all was well and that Graves had recovered remarkably well for a man in his nineties, Lauryn noticed Bridgette stifling a yawn and her heart beat faster with the thought that she might hang up before she could get answers to her burning questions about her grandfather Cameron.

Taking over the direction of their conversation, Lauryn brought her up to speed on the details of the renovation and the sale of Promise Place and finally, she told her about her find that had been hidden in the office for over fifty years.

"Bridgette, I know you just got back, you're probably exhausted, and I should let you go, but I found something during the renovation that I've been dying to ask you about-"

"Oh, yeah," Bridgette interrupted with renewed enthusiasm, "I saw your messages wondering about my grandfather. Do you mean Grandpa Devon?"

Devon. Lauryn's heart dropped. What could she mean, Grandpa Devon?

"Well, no. I mean your grandfather Cameron. Cameron Berndt."

Bridgette's expression remained flat as if she didn't even know him, while Lauryn's heart raced. She said Grandfather Devon. Could it be Devon Hearst? It must be Devon Hearst, the other man in Cassie's life, the man she worked for, the "other man" Cameron mentioned in his journal.

"Oh," She spoke slowly as if trying to recall the man named Cameron - the same one that had captivated Lauryn's imagination for weeks now, "I didn't know him. I only knew Grandpa Devon. My grandmother Cassandra married Grandpa Devon when my mother was still a little girl."

She paused again and Lauryn held her breath, waiting for the answer that was finally coming, "Grandpa Cameron died in Vietnam. My mom said she didn't remember her biological father well because he left for Vietnam when she was so little, but Grandma Cassandra always told her that he was a good man." Bridgette's eyes looked vacant suddenly, as if the mention of her deceased mother Charlotte brought her some pain, "Mom always told me that she had her dad's eyes and that's where I got mine."

The conversation paused on the comment, both of them lost in their trajectory of thoughts, both going completely different directions. Lauryn struggled with the emotions she was feeling – a mix of sadness, sorrow, grief and an overwhelming sense of lost opportunity.

A man so full of promise, with such plans for his family, gone so young. And, so sad. Because surely if Cassie eventually married Devon Hearst then she never did make up with her husband Cameron before he died. Perhaps Cameron had been right, perhaps Cassie had fallen out of love with him.

"Bridgette, I don't know how to tell you this because I feel like I've stepped way over the line of privacy, but I found something that belonged to your grandfather Cameron. It's his journal, actually three journals."

"Oh, really? Did you find them with those pictures you found in the attic?" Bridgette seemed to become more engaged as they spoke.

"No, I found the journals hidden behind a wall between the pantry and the office. They were in a secret cabinet in the bookshelves."

"Wow, that's so cool! And they're my Grandpa Cameron's, huh? What year did he write them?"

"From 1966 to 1969, he wrote them up to the point when he left for Vietnam." Lauryn took a breath and met her eyes squarely, "So, you're not upset that I read them?"

"Are you kidding? Who wouldn't read them? I know I sure would have if I was in your position." She smiled at Lauryn conspiratorially, "Was his life really juicy?"

For some reason, it bothered Lauryn that Bridgette was so flippant about it. This man was a giant and she acted like his life was so trivial. But, of course, she would learn once she was able to read his words, only then would Bridgette realize the true spirit from which she came.

"He was an incredible man, Bridgette. He loved your mother Charlotte and his family so much. He loved his role as a pastor and the people in his life. And, he loved God more than anything. It's hard to think-" Lauryn swallowed hard and continued, "Well, I just can't reconcile that these are probably the last journals that he ever wrote."

"Wow, it sounds like I need to read them if they've touched you so deeply."

"They are precious. I don't feel right even sending them in the mail in case they would get lost."

"Oh, keep them safe with you. I will be back in the states in a few weeks so I will let you know where to UPS them-" Bridgette looked over the top of her computer screen and nodded in answer to a question Thomas asked from outside the field of view.

Again, Lauryn felt the tone of the conversation drawing to a close and she panicked a little, knowing she still had so many more questions to ask.

"Whatever happened to your uncle Aaron and your aunt Gemma?" She hurried on, before Bridgette could tell her that she had to leave and end the call.

At the eagerness in her question and the familiarity that Lauryn spoke of her family, Bridgette's eyes opened wider and she smiled patiently.

"My uncle Aaron moved to California at some point after college, I think. He's never been married and is a captain with a shipping company, he captains a route to Asia. My mom told me that their sister Gemma died while riding her bike when she was ten years old. She was hit by a car outside their home. It was super traumatic for them all, Mom said Grandma Cassandra was never the same after that."

"Oh, that's awful. I'm so sorry, Bridgette. Your family has gone through such sadness." Lauryn croaked out the words, feeling as if the people that Bridgette spoke of were her own family.

"Yeah, when I think about it, that's true. It seems like the family kind of fell apart gradually. My mom and her brother, Uncle Aaron, always kept in touch as adults, but we weren't super close to my grandparents when I was growing up. They moved to Florida where Grandpa Devon's family was from and we didn't see them much. Grandpa was always fun, he laughed a lot, but I always thought my grandma seemed unhappy, like she was breakable or something. Definitely not your stereo-typical grandmother. It was hard to get to know her."

"Hmm," Lauryn hesitated to mention that she had some insight into her grandmother's personality because it really wasn't any of her business. But it felt disingenuous not to say something, knowing what she knew, so she ventured cautiously, hoping that Bridgette wouldn't be offended, "Bridgette, I have to tell you, your Grandpa Cameron's journals are very personal. He talks about problems with his church and ... problems in his family life."

"Oh," Her eyes took on a knowing look, not really offended but still somewhat defensive, "You mean that my Grandpa Devon was having an affair with my grandma while she was still married to my Grandpa Cameron? My mother told me that was a rumor that she heard while she was growing up, but Grandma and Grandpa never confirmed it. By then, they were married, and they stayed married for many years up until they died, within a year of each other. Grandpa Devon was the only father my mom ever really knew."

Lauryn swallowed hard at the fact, stated so coldly. Cameron Berndt's daughter – raised by the man that he couldn't stand. Such a picture of life, with all of its twists and turns, almost none of it fair. It made her sad, but still, if Devon Hearst was good to his children, then really, would Cameron Berndt have wanted it any other way?

"That's good to know. It's so sad to hear about Gemma, but I think your Grandfather Cameron would be glad to know his other two children were well taken care of and lived a happy life."

"Yes, they were, they had a good life. But I'm sure they were sad when he left and never came home. Things like that leave a mark." She paused and Lauryn saw her eyes glistening in the light of the bedside table next to her, "I wish I could ask my mom what she remembers about him."

"I'm sorry, Bridgette," Lauryn's heart filled with regret when she saw the pain cross Bridgette's face, "I've made things worse by bringing this up. That was never my intention."

"No, it's okay, Lauryn. Really, it's okay. It just makes me realize how we really don't know people, even those who are closest to us. And it's crazy how it's possible to never know the story of people whose blood runs through our veins."

"True. Very true," Lauryn sighed into the silence, letting the impact of her statement settle between them. "There is one way to know more about your grandfather though, Bridgette. You could ask your uncle, he was older, he's likely to remember his father well. And once you've read these journals, you could let him read his father's words."

"You're right. Of course, you're right. Thanks, Lauryn."

CHAPTER 31

2018, February

It was just one of those days, a busy Saturday morning, one thing leading to another, never enough time and now she had to meet with this guy - something about a project she had worked on previously. Elliott said he was sure that he'd mentioned it to her weeks ago, but she was sure he had not. Couldn't he just tell the guy that she was on hiatus for a while? But, no, of course not. He couldn't do that.

The problem with Elliott? He was just too nice.

At the sound of the doorbell, Lauryn glanced up from the kitchen counter where she was drying the last of the breakfast dishes and waved at the elderly black man in a dark green parka who stood outside on their porch, peering through the glass of their front door.

"Come on in, you must be Clive." She greeted him as she opened the door, the frigid cold February air blasting in along with him.

His smile was wide and bright under his salty gray and black mustache and as he pulled down his parka hood, Lauryn noticed the tattoos on his neck, in full display because he kept his grayish hair shaved short.

"Yes, that I am, Ms. Grant. It's a pleasure to finally meet you!" He laughed a robust chuckle that matched his baritone voice and his presence seemed to fill the entire room as he set the cane he used against the wall and started to shrug off his big coat.

"Well, yes–" Lauryn paused with a question in her voice, what was he talking about "finally meet you?" She threw a glance towards the stairway, what was taking Elliott so long up there? He was the one who had connected with this guy, she had no background whatsoever on him or what he wanted to talk about.

"Elliott? You coming down here soon, hon?" Lauryn called up the stairway but no response. He must be in the bathroom. Great.

"Well, yes," Lauryn turned back to their guest with a roll of her eyes, "Come on in, Clive. I'm sure my husband will be down shortly." She waved for him to sit down as she took the coat that he handed her. "Would you like some coffee?"

"That would be great, thanks! It sure is cold out there today."

"Where did you drive from? I hope the roads were okay." Lauryn spoke to him from the kitchen as she poured two cups of coffee then brought them out to the living room and set one next to Clive's knee on the coffee table in front of him.

"Oh, I just drove from my office in Minneapolis. Roads weren't bad at all. I am headed to Mankato today, so I told Elliott stopping here this morning worked great for me. I am so excited to finally meet with you!"

Again, Clive's bright smile erased the deep wrinkles in his forehead and deepened the ones around his mouth and his deep brown, almost black eyes lit with an electric intensity. Something about the man fascinated Lauryn and she instantly liked him.

"Okay, that's good. What did you want to meet with us about? Elliott said something about a previous project we worked on?" Lauryn inquired as she took a sip of steaming coffee.

"Oh, really? He didn't tell you?" Clive laughed heartily and glanced towards the stairway while Lauryn frowned. What was she missing here?

"No-" She said slowly as she set her cup down on a coaster and tried to smile her way through her confusion, "Please enlighten me."

"Okay, then. I will start at the beginning." Clive sat forward on the couch and rested his elbows on his knees while he took a slow sip from his cup, seeming to enjoy the fact that she was in the dark about all of this, "I follow you on YouTube, I too enjoy old homes and follow a few different people who do home renovations, but I like you the best." He smiled and let out a hearty laugh as he set the cup down on the coaster in front of him before continuing.

"I reached out to you a few times when I saw you were working on the house at Promise Place. You know, that old house over in River's Bend. I mentioned in my messages that I had a connection to the house - well, actually to the Berndt family. I knew someone who lived there, knew him well in fact. But even though I sent a couple messages through your website, I never heard back. So eventually, I got busy and I guess I just forgot about it. Then, I saw something the other day come across YouTube about your next project and it reminded me that we had never connected. So, I sent another message and that's how I heard from your husband. When I told him my story, he arranged for this meeting."

Lauryn watched as he took another swallow of coffee and filtered back through her mind about which messages he was talking about. There were always so many messages, so many things to do.

"Clive, I'm sorry that I didn't respond earlier," Lauryn explained, sincerity in her voice, "We were so busy with the house and we received so many contacts from people who had a connection to the two Dr. August Berndt's who lived there. Was your connection to the first or second Dr. Berndt?"

"Neither of them," Clive replied, "I knew Doc Cam, that's what we - our unit in Nam - called him."

Lauryn took in a sharp breath and the unexpected comment shocked her speechless. But, if Clive noticed her surprise, he didn't show it as his deep baritone continued to fill the room.

"But Doc Cam told us he wasn't a doctor - he was a pastor. We took to hanging out together because we were both from Minnesota and we had some things in common. He said he was trained almost up to the point of being a doctor but never finished his residency. He was just over there helping out the other docs. But I have to say, he was a good doc, better than some of the credentialed ones, that's for sure. The thing was with Doc Cam, he did more than help us with our physical health though. He helped us with our spiritual health too. That was his gift, you see."

Lauryn was dazed, her throat tight and her body stiff with excitement as he spoke. Already, he'd given her such welcome information about Cameron Berndt, but there had to be more. What other answers could Clive give her? With anticipation, she prompted him to continue.

"Please, tell me more." She spoke, trying not to sound too eager.

"So, Doc Cam and I became super close when I was injured, and he was doctoring my legs. They were shot up pretty bad and I couldn't move for over a month while I waited for the evac." He pulled up the legs of his trousers then, revealing the prosthetic limbs that emerged from his wet leather shoes. Lauryn's eyes travelled from his limbs to his face. He met her gaze unwavering and when he spoke, his voice had a note of strength and no self-pity. It was the voice of a person who had been dealt a bad hand but still played the game because he couldn't help but love it.

"He was something, I tell you. Always, steady - you know? Just one of those people, even during the hell of it all, he was just steady. I would ask him, how did he do it? Stay so steady, like that. He would always turn it around to Jesus Christ. Every conversation we had, I swear, he would turn it around to Jesus Christ. He was something, Doc Cam. I still remember his face like it was yesterday."

He smiled then and wiped at his eyes where tears had pooled as he pictured his friend during a time that must have seemed like hell on earth to them both. Lauryn reached across the couch and handed him a box of tissues. She smiled as he laughed, seemingly embarrassed at his show of emotions. She wasn't embarrassed, she was impressed. She let him sit there thinking for a moment.

"So-" He took a breath and continued, "I had a faith in the Almighty, you see. I did, truly. At least I thought I did. Until I was over there. That's when I was tested, you see? I saw it all clearly that night, the night they bombed our base. Usually there was a warning, some word would get to us and we would move camp, but not that night. We were sitting ducks that night."

"The hospital was a tent. Nothing more than a fortified tent. After the first set of bombs, everything was burning, people were burning, it was somethin' awful. I remember thinking, I'm going to die in this lake of fire, 'cause I have no legs, you see. I was saying my prayers, thinking 'this is it' when I feel someone reach around under my arms like this-" He positioned his large hands under his arms, just below his shoulders, as if wanting her to feel exactly what he was feeling that night.

"And next thing I know, Doc Cam is pulling me and my heavy ass outta that tent like I weigh no more than a little girl. He dragged me and all the while he was praying with me - I don't know how far he drug me, just a long way - until we was safe and he left me there, next to those trees with those other guys. And, then he went back." His eyes were filled with tears again and he looked away, heaving deep breaths but refusing to bury the emotion. This time, he let the tears flow freely from his eyes as he wiped at them with the tissue. He sucked in some air, trying to compose himself as he shook his head in disbelief.

"He went back, you see? Again, and again, I bet five or six more times. The last time he came back, he just sat down hard on the ground next to me and he was still praying. That's when I saw it - the shrapnel hole in his gut. Doc Cam died of a shrapnel hole in his gut. Now, there were explosions happening the whole time, I don't know when he caught it. But I know he hauled some of us guys while he had it, that's for sure. Yep, Doc Cam, died like that."

There was a soft cry, the sound of a child, in the room. It was a moment before Lauryn realized that it was her own voice that made the injured sound and Clive sat across the coffee table from her, watching as she wiped her face free of the tears his story had unleashed.

"He's the reason I do what I do now," Clive nodded affirmatively, "I take care of vets, 'cause he told me that's what he wanted to do. Before he even came over to 'Nam, he said that's what he wanted to do. It's like that resonated with me for a long time. So, I've found peace doin' it too. I run a ministry program for vets, we meet in church basements around the city. You know, I *do it* for Jesus Christ, because now I know for whom I serve, but I like to say it's inspired by Doc Cam."

The passages in the journal – the ones where he spoke of a ministry designed to help vets find Christ – were brought to life again by someone else living out the dreams that Cameron Berndt had once dreamt. Life, with all its twists and turns. Yet, somehow, a consistent thread persisted – God always seems to be there.

She supposed it would only be proper to say something to break the silence in which they sat, but Lauryn was completely unable to speak as she sat there, wiping her eyes and staring over his shoulder out the window behind him. Her mind was complete mush as the weight of these men's lives set heavy on her.

As if to break the silence, Clive moved towards his parka which Lauryn had draped over the chair next to him.

"Oh, I almost forgot," He spoke quietly, almost tenderly to her, "I brought you something, it's one of my prized possessions. But I want you to have it, maybe you can get it to his family somehow."

As he turned back towards her, Clive handed Lauryn a small Bible, worn and rather beaten, the faded black cover had been folded incorrectly at one time and it was missing a corner.

"He had this on him all the time. When I packed up, I took it with me."

She reached for the Bible and touched the cover in much the same way as she had his journals. Flipping the Bible open, a black and white photograph floated out from it and landed at her feet on the rug between them.

"Who's this?" As she reached for it, she saw the photo was of a group of soldiers standing around an army Jeep, in various states of uniform, some in white t-shirts casually leaning on one another, others in full uniform, a couple of them still in their helmets.

"Oh, that's where that is, I've been looking for that picture!" Clive laughed heartily as he pointed a thick finger, "That's me and some of the guys in our unit. And, that's Doc Cam."

The young, blonde-haired man he pointed to stood at the end of the line of men, dressed plainly in a button-down cotton shirt and trousers, his hands placed casually in his front pockets and a smile on his striking face as he glanced downwards at a guy kneeling to his left. That's Doc Cam.

Lauryn peered closer at the man with the strong jaw, high cheekbones and deep-set eyes. Did he look happy? Not really. How could he be happy given the circumstances in which he found himself at that moment?

But, did he look content? Did he look like he was meant to be there? Did he look like he was faithfully doing what God wanted him to do?

Yes. He did.

Sudden motion at the stairway behind them took Clive's eyes away from her and his face erupted into another one of those full-face transformations as he stood up to greet Elliott who was now standing at the bottom of the stairs.

The baby Elliott held in his arms was freshly bathed. Lauryn could see the fine, dark curls damp from a bath, and she could smell the sweet, clean scent of baby shampoo from where she stood next to Clive. She watched as a little arm poked out from the blanket and the body went rigid in revolt against Elliott's attempt to keep the arm under wrap.

As if on a timer, Lauryn felt her body respond to the little one's gurgle and soft cry as Elliott looked up at Lauryn in resignation, knowing that he'd done as much as he could do to keep the peace. It was breakfast time.

"Well, my, my-" Clive's voice boomed with the obvious joy of someone who loves children as Elliott joined them in the living room, his handsome face animated with a father's pride as he held the baby, "Who is this little beauty?" Clive asked with a grin.

Elliott handed Lauryn the little human, now all arms and legs and rigid body motions, as the baby kicked the blanket to the floor, the cries becoming more urgent.

"This is our daughter." Lauryn said over the commotion, her heart completely full, so full it was overflowing, as she pulled their baby girl towards her and cradled her against her shoulder to calm her before she fed her.

"We've named her Cameron."

The End

AUTHOR BIO

J. Marie is the author of the inspirational debut novel FIND YOUR WAY HOME (March 2018 Amazon), THE FORGOTTEN HOUSE (October 2018 Amazon) and A PROMISED PLACE (November 2019 Amazon).

After raising three children while also working in consumer products marketing and general management for over twenty years, she left the corporate world to better focus on managing various family businesses.

It was then, even though her days were filled with the telephone calls, spreadsheets and financial statements, suddenly voices of characters and compelling stories of their lives became too much to ignore. So, she wrote it all down and hasn't stopped writing ever since.

In addition to writing, in her spare time, she enjoys volunteering with various organizations, and spending time with her husband and their family on their farm near Canby, MN.

Book Club Discussion Questions

1. Although this book travels between various periods in time, the author wished to connect the characters Lauryn and Cameron to one another. Can you identify ways that was accomplished?

2. Name some of the characters in the book that you felt had the biggest impact – both positive and negative – on Cameron. How did he interact with these characters?

3. What overarching themes did you identify in this book? Can you give examples of how the characters exemplified, lived out, these themes in their lives?

4. Faith is integral to which characters in the novel? How is it demonstrated? Find examples of how it impacts their daily lives.

5. Have you personally struggled with faith questions like Lauryn and Cameron? Were any of their thoughts and reactions similar to yours? How did you learn address your faith questions?

6. If, while reading the majority of the book, you had to choose a one-word descriptor for the relationship between Cameron and his wife Cassie, what would it be?

7. What would be your one-word descriptor for Lauryn and Elliott's relationship?

8. What surprised you about the novel?

9. Take a moment to reflect on the title A Promised Place. Why do you think the author chose that as the title?

CPSIA information can be obtained
at www.ICGtesting.com
Printed in the USA
LVHW021306111119
636960LV00002B/441/P

9 781698 822020